HONOR, FATE, AND FAITH

A Novel by
Dennis Ricotta

Edited by
Susan Kennedy

WESTBOW
PRESS®
A DIVISION OF THOMAS NELSON
& ZONDERVAN

WestBow Press books may be ordered through booksellers or by contacting:

WestBow Press
A Division of Thomas Nelson & Zondervan
1663 Liberty Drive
Bloomington, IN 47403
www.westbowpress.com
1 (866) 928-1240

Because of the dynamic nature of the Internet, any web addresses or links contained in this book may have changed since publication and may no longer be valid. The views expressed in this work are solely those of the author and do not necessarily reflect the views of the publisher, and the publisher hereby disclaims any responsibility for them.

Any people depicted in stock imagery provided by Thinkstock are models, and such images are being used for illustrative purposes only.
Certain stock imagery © Thinkstock.

ISBN: 978-1-5127-3131-6 (sc)
ISBN: 978-1-5127-3132-3 (hc)
ISBN: 978-1-5127-3130-9 (e)

Library of Congress Control Number: 2016902442

Print information available on the last page.

WestBow Press rev. date: 03/10/2016

Dedication

I want to dedicate this book to my father,
who has since passed on to be with the Lord.
His humility showed me where real strength lies.
His respect for all men gave me a heart to try to serve.
And his love for me gave me comfort when I went astray.

Having faith in one another is a sign of love.
Having faith in God and His Son seals it.

ACKNOWLEDGMENTS

First, I am so thankful for my wife, Janice, as she waited patiently for me to finish a thought while our dinner was getting cold and, in her words, "saw only the back of my head" as she passed by my office. Thank you for your encouragement, my love.

I am so grateful to have a granddaughter with such talent in photography and Photoshop as Faith Ricotta. Her work on creating the cover for this book and the "wanted" poster is brilliant. Her artistic talent is growing by leaps and bounds. I will see you on the next book. Thank you so much, sweetheart.

I wish to thank Ms. Bonnie Burro for opening her photography lab to Faith. It was an immense help to Faith in getting this project done.

I also wish to give special thanks to film director and author, Jack Duane Dabner, for urging me to put my story into novel form. My thoughts and words would have never come to fruition without your encouragement.

And, thank you does not cover all I wish to say to an editor extraordinaire, Susan Kennedy. I am indebted to her for giving needed life and meaning to my written thoughts. Susan did a great job of filling in the many holes that I should have caught, putting sequences where they belong and in general fixing, fixing, fixing. Susan also wrote chapters 9, 10, and much of chapter 11, which added so much to this story. As busy as she is, Susan took time not only to do fixes but also to educate me in the errors of my ways. Great job, Susan, I hope I make it easier for you on our next project.

Author's Note

After forty-seven years in the Motion Picture Industry, I have found that one of the most profound aspects of any movie, play, or television production is the imagination of the writers. I have worked as a Music Editor and Foreign Post Production Supervisor on comedies, mysteries, and dramas, and I must say, as much as I love music and the creative brilliance of composers and musicians, I found that story-telling is a creative art form that truly intrigues me. So by the grace of God, I thought I would give it a try.

My experience in creative writing is that of a music editor. It was my job to describe and break down scenes for a composer to make it easier for him to catch the high and low points of a particular character or action in a scene. If you find hints of "script writing" in this story, you will now understand the reason. My story editor, Susan Kennedy, however, did an excellent job of tidying most of that up. Also, it has been a humbling experience to discover that I might (and I do say "might") have found a talent I didn't know I had.

CHAPTER 1

The wind was blowing dry in the dusk of evening on the Caldwell farm just outside the town of Crockett, Texas. It was late July 1861 as Mason Caldwell studied the faces of his wife, Lydia; his oldest son, Mark, eighteen; John, sixteen; and his youngest and only daughter, Jennie, fifteen. Glancing over to his children but still focused on his wife, he said, "A bitter war has been raging between the North and South for months now, and as much as I don't like fighting, a man must do what it takes if he believes in something. I've been wrestling with the problem of should I go or not. But my dear Lydia, I feel I must help in this fight so you and our young'uns won't have to later."

Turning to Mark and putting his hand on the boy's shoulder, Mason said, "You will need to run this farm, Mark. Mr. Neiter's going to be here from time to time to help you."

Mr. Neiter was a slightly rotund man of about fifty with a cheerful face and shock of hair that had once been blonde but was now faded. He had been standing off to one side but now approached to face Mark. "I'm just down the road, you know, and I'll be comin' by to oversee the plantin'. And Mark, don't be shy to git me when you or your mom needs help." Mason smiled warmly at Mr. Neiter. They had been friends for many years and had always been there for each other.

Mason continued, "So do like he says as if it was me speaking. Okay?"

Mark answered in the proud tone of young manhood, certain he could handle this responsibility and eager to show his dad. "Okay, Pa." Then he broke down just a little and, throwing his arms around Mason, continued in a quivering voice, "But I'll miss you, Pa."

Mason returned the hug with, "I'll miss you too, Son."

As he released Mark, he reached into a bag on the ground next to him and pulled out a knife and a rifle. Handing them to Mark, he said, "You're to be the man around here while I'm gone. You can keep these. They're yours from now on." Mark accepted them with much pride and hugged his dad again.

Mason next turned his attention to Jennie, who couldn't hold back, big tears rolling down her face. "I've a gift for you, my pretty one." Kneeling down, he reached into the bag and withdrew an elegant box. Inside was a vanity set composed of a hand mirror with matching hairbrush and comb of tortoiseshell. Sobbing, Jennie took the box, hugging it with one hand and wrapping the other arm around her dad saying, "I love you, Daddy."

Mason quietly and lovingly answered, "I love you too, my pretty little one."

Mason walked to the steps of the porch and sat on the lower step. He motioned for John to come closer.

While Mark resembled his father, tall and lean with dark hair and blue eyes, John took after his mother, who had been born in Ireland. In 1834, her father had inherited a modest farm in Maine and moved his family to America to flee the abject poverty that most Irish tenant farmers endured prior to the great potato famine that a few years later laid waste to that homeland.

Like Lydia, John had soft brown hair that glinted with red in the sunlight and eyes more green than blue. Living in his own world, his wandering mind conjured up imaginary friends and situations, building one daydream after another. His total innocence was what most endeared him to Mason. Reaching under the porch, Mason produced a large box. Handing it to John he said, "You didn't think I'd forget you? This is the only thing I could get you that I thought you would care for."

John just looked at his dad, making no attempt to open the box. Smiling, Mason opened the box and pulled out a guitar. John, not understanding any of this, said to his dad, so softly he could hardly be heard, "I just don't want you to go, Pa. You can give the guitar back if'n you don't go. I want you to stay, Pa."

Fighting back his own emotions, Mason looked into John's eyes and softly answered, "No, my son, but if God so wills, I'll be coming back. This guitar is something you've been wanting ever since you saw it at the general store."

Mason stood and, trying to put both himself and John at ease, drew the boy close in a bear hug. Releasing him, Mason handed him the guitar saying, "When I get back you can pick me some of my favorite tunes."

John had always had the musical talent in the Caldwell family, and Mason figured the boy could turn to what he loved to ease any heartache or frustration. Music might be the outlet to make him feel better.

Next, he walked over to Lydia, took her in his arms, caressed the soft reddish-brown tresses and looked intently into her green eyes. Gathering her strength and fighting back the tears, she said, "I love you Mason Caldwell, and will forever. My love goes with you, my prayers go before you."

"A man won't find a woman like you nowhere," he replied. "Blessed man I am to be the one."

Mason mounted his horse. A tall man who stood over six feet, he sat erect in his saddle with proud bearing. As he rode toward the main road, Lydia walked quickly at his side, trying to keep up and too petite to reach his hand and hold it as he rode. Turning back to the children, his eyes met theirs. No words needed to be spoken for the love that passed between them.

Coming from the cold coast of Maine, Mason had bought this 120-acre farm just outside the town of Crockett, wanting to start a life where he felt his family would grow to love together. It had been a bold move, and now he felt he must fight to keep his dream alive.

CHAPTER 2

Months passed. The Texas summer turned to fall; then the winter winds blew. Christmas approached, but it would not be the same joyous occasion this year without Mason. The boys went to a stand of evergreens and cut a tree, while Lydia unpacked the treasured crèche that had been in her family for years. Made of fine Irish porcelain, the tiny figures made a beautiful tableau showing the birth of that precious babe who came to save us all.

Lydia loved Christmas. Although the primary focus was on the birth of the Savior, she also recalled the history of the Christmas tree, which brought so much delight to young children before they could fully understand the significance of the holy birth. She remembered reading that the Christmas tree first came about in Germany during the seventeenth century. Tradition, she'd been taught, was that Martin Luther walked home one night in awe at the stars twinkling among the pine trees. Tradition further said he was the first to light a Christmas tree, decorating it with candles to emulate the beauty of those bright stars he had seen through the trees during his walk. The Caldwells had put up a tree each year since they first married, but this year they would all sorely miss Mason being there to place the star at the very top.

Then almost before they knew, it was spring again. Mark and John labored long to plant a variety of crops, mostly vegetables. Many others around them only planted one crop or pastured cattle, and families needed more than just meat and corn.

Soon after they had moved to this farm, Lydia and Mason had planted a small vegetable garden about thirty feet from their kitchen to provide fresh food for their table. Over the years, Lydia had planted flowers closer to the house. Then one year, Mason and the boys built a long arbor to shade the path between the house and garden. On this, Lydia planted jasmine and honeysuckle, and all along the path she planted roses, bulbs, and other flowers until she had created her own garden of delight. Here she sought solace from her worries about Mason until he should return to her.

The area around Crockett was known for its abundance of pecan trees. David Crockett, for whom the town was named, had stopped in the area on his way to San Antonio. Legend held that upon discovering the sweet, delicious nut meats, he vowed to return and take some pecan trees back to Tennessee. Alas, that vow was thwarted by Crockett's death at the Alamo. Mark had long wished to plant a sizable stand of pecan trees on part of his father's acreage. A number of these trees planted the previous year were thriving, and the boys had just added another acre of saplings.

Spring ripened into summer, and one by one, the crops matured. Mark had worked hard to bring in the harvest—with help from Mr. Neiter, whom he now called Uncle Lucas. Mason would have been very proud of the man Mark had become.

Lydia wrote to Mason every day. They didn't hear back from him very often, as his company moved from battlefield to battlefield. It was a miracle that he got his mail at all most times. Combat does not allow a soldier to be in charge of what he does or when he wants to do it. Mason did get a letter off as often as possible and, rather than tell the truth of what he saw and felt, he wrote hopefully, expressing more the feeling that soon it would be over so that he could return home safe and sound. It was better, he thought, to put his Lydia at ease, than to describe the horrors of what he was seeing all around him.

When Mason had been gone almost two years, one such letter reached the Caldwell house. This time Mason explained one of the more heart-breaking events of this war. Lydia started to read to the children.

"My dearest Lydia,

"Little did I imagine when I went through training back in the Crockett camp what I was letting myself in for. This war's been going on for some time now, and because of my age they seem to think I'm smarter than the rest of these recruits, so they made me a captain already. Here I am in my 40's, and the oldest soldier in my company is only 18. They have given me responsibility over a passel of young men. Lydia, they're still just kids—only a few years older than our own. It seems they are going to send us back to the front lines again real soon now. We're going to a place called Chickamauga Creek."

Lydia's face became drawn as the words "back to the front lines" sank in. She restrained herself, however, and gathering her strength for the sake of the children, smiled and told them, "The rest is between Pa and me, but he sends his love and a reminder for you all to behave." As the children left the room, she turned back to the letter and with tears in her eyes continued reading.

"Something that happened in this war hurts more than I could explain. It brings our children to my mind and pierces right to my heart. One of my young men caught a bullet and nothing could be done for him. As he lay dying, he said to me, 'You know, Captain Caldwell, I don't mind dyin'. It ain't a problem, sir. I know where I'm goin' when I die. You see, what I need is to let my family know I love them. We had a bad argument before I came to serve the South.

A family misunderstandin' I guess. Sir, will you find them and let them know that I love them? I can't die with them not knowin' they bin in my heart since I came to war.'

"So help me, Lydia, this war hurts in such a way that it can't be explained. I will find this boy's family. I promise."

Lydia reached deep into her soul to understand his hurt and offered a quick prayer for Mason's peace.

Now on her knees, Lydia read further, "You know I miss you, but I have to say it. I know I'm fighting for what I believe in, and I feel it's my duty as a man raising a family to make a better place for our children to grow up. Still, the ache in my heart for you sometimes makes me want to run back home. I hope you understand, but I got to do what I got to do."

Mason knew his wife's soft heart would be aching and tried to lighten up some. On the last page, she read, "You look out, girl. When I get back, I'm going to chase you through the corn fields, just you wait."

This brought a wan smile to the teary-eyed Lydia. As she finished the letter, she crumpled it to her heart and headed off to bed where again she dropped to her knees, buried her face in the mattress, and fell into deep prayer as she softly called on the Lord. *Heavenly Father we've been walking with you as far back as I can remember. You know I don't ask much from you, but I need for you to hear my heart. I want my man back, I need him back. I'm heavy with fear, and I know you don't like us to be a-fearin' anything. Any peace you got to put in my heart and mind, I'll be takin' it all. I know one thing for sure, I will na' let the Devil take it from me.*

When she and Mason were courting, Mason had carved a small cross from a piece of wood, drilled a hole in the top of it, and hung it on a small chain. Lydia had worn that cross every day since they married. It had never failed to give her comfort when hard times had come in the past, and now as she lay in the empty bed, she needed that comfort more than ever. She held tightly to the cross along with Mason's letter and finally drifted off into a restless sleep.

CHAPTER 3

With Mr. Neiter's help, the family had kept the farm together, and Mark had borne his responsibility well. He enjoyed farming and raising animals. This part of the country could sometimes be merciless when it came to the weather, but that had never been a deterrent to Mark. He loved the farm, and it showed in his work. Mark would go to school in the morning after feeding the stock and come home in the early afternoon to finish the other chores. A bath in the middle would have helped, but who had the time?

Their house consisted of a front room, a kitchen, and three bedrooms with the boys sharing one. Just next to the back porch was an area under trees where they did laundry. Mason and Lydia had talked about adding on, but the war had intervened. Right now, Jennie couldn't worry about that as she had enough to do helping Lydia with the laundry (although she tried to avoid the muddy clothes her brothers brought in).

Jennie did her best to help Lydia and didn't complain much. She was becoming a young lady and knew that she had to uphold her end of the many chores that needed to be done.

Jennie took after her mother, and though still only seventeen, she was already a little taller, a trait inherited from her father no doubt. She had the reddest hair of them all, and her eyes were green such as only the Irish seem to have. Freckles sprinkled her ivory skin, and she had a mischievous smile that told you right off she was not someone to take lightly.

She could saddle her own horse without any help, and she rode straight and tall. She held her own with her two brothers, who had learned this the hard way. More than once the boys tried to give their sister a bad time or tease but usually got the short end of the stick. One night they slipped into her bedroom after she was asleep and put a toad in her bed. Jennie woke up with a shriek and a start and almost fell out of bed. But boy did she get even.

Once she short-sheeted them. Another time, she loosened their saddle cinches, and yet another time she switched their shoes and tied the laces into knots. Finally, just to let them know that she wasn't one to be dealt with lightly, she added hot sauce to their plum pudding. That pretty much slowed her brothers down.

Then there was John. What can be said? He got his chores done, after a fashion. He had taken rapidly to his guitar, being a natural with music. Lydia watched as a warm relationship developed between John and Mr. Neiter, as Mr. Neiter was a happy-go-lucky person himself. One day as John played a tune, Lydia explained to Mr. Neiter the reason Mason gave John the guitar.

"When we came to this town we stopped off at a hotel to get some information. While we were there, a man was playing the piano in the dining room, and John went over to listen to him. The man slid over and let John sit next to him. John could pick out the tune as the man played along and surprised us all. The man commented to us about his unusual talent and said he was a natural. So this guitar is the first opportunity we've had to turn him to music. You see, Mr. Neiter, I play a little piano and miss it very much. Life doesn't take time off for the wants of life, it just keeps movin' us in the needs of life."

Mr. Neiter, looking over at John, replied to Lydia, "When I was a young man, I thought I would never settle down. It would take a fine woman to do that. My Anna has put up with a lot of bull—er—malarkey, and I'm glad she was patient with me. My wanderin' sure is over." Laughingly Mr. Neiter continued, "I'm too old anyway."

John's happy-go-lucky lifestyle was refreshing to Mr. Neiter. He would have had a son of his own about John's age had he and Anna not lost the boy to an epidemic of diphtheria that ravaged the county a decade earlier. Neither of them ever quite got over this heartbreak. His love for the

Lord and Anna had been his comfort. He knew that the one thing he needed to do was remain strong for her sake.

Lucas Neiter could see that Mason and Lydia had raised their children with much love. It was evident in the way Mark, John, and Jennie showed their respect for others. It was plain to see that this family knew the love of God.

CHAPTER 4

It was now late December 1863. Nearly all of the harvest had been brought in. Once again, the family was preparing to mark the Christmas season without Mason.

It didn't get really cold in this part of Texas, but there were seasons. Although Mason had been gone more than two years, things on the farm had continued to go well for the Caldwells. The corn and vegetable crops covered several acres and had brought good prices at local markets. They had prayed daily that they could get each crop in between the rains. Mark had most things under control, still turning to Mr. Neiter from time to time. Meanwhile, Lydia and Jennie had put up enough of their crops to get the family through the winter.

John did his best to help and take orders from Mark. It was not an easy task for John, but at least he was trying. And Jennie? Well what can you say? As she matured into a little lady, she cherished her father's precious gift and hoped the days would be short until her dad's return.

Lydia as usual was in constant prayer. Her time was spent taking care of the needs of her family. Each evening, she gathered her children around her as she led them in prayer for the safety of their beloved husband and father. Her heart ached constantly, but she stayed strong in the Lord for herself and her children.

One cold, sunny day, Lydia was on the front porch surveying the land that Mark had cultivated so expertly. There were a few steers now, and she smiled as a feeling of pride in her son rose in her chest. As she looked down the road leading into the farm, she saw the dust of someone riding fast and hard. It was Mr. Neiter coming down the road at a gallop.

That certainly isn't like him, especially at his age, she thought. He came to an abrupt stop in front of her, and as he dismounted, his face told it all, sadness was written all over it. Mason was coming home, but his condition was very serious. The only thing the telegram said was that he had been shot at Chickamauga. This would be a time of testing, finding courage, faith, and strength when it would be most needed.

Right after Christmas, Mason did indeed return home. Lydia, running out to the road to meet him, was not ready for what she saw. Mason was lying in the back of a wagon driven by two dusty soldiers, barely able to move.

He had no use of his left leg, which was tightly wrapped in splinted bandages, and there was hardly any movement in his left arm. Mason looked at Lydia as he lay there and said to her bitterly, "I wish they'da just let me die. For you to see me like this isn't right for a woman with so much life in her. To be tied down to a cripple isn't fair to you or my children. A burden at best is all I am."

Lydia, fighting tears, tenderly told him, "I got you back, that's what's fair. I got you back."

Unable to contain herself any longer she climbed up on the wagon beside him and, lying down next to him, held him, loving him as she always had. Mr. Neiter, who had been working with Mark on the farm, had held the children back. Now he let them go, and they ran to the wagon as it proceeded toward the farmhouse.

Mark greeted his dad with the new-found strength of a maturing young man, trying not to show any emotion. Jennie was not so strong. She found it hard to look on her pa and could not fight the tears. John too was speechless, and being the emotional person he was, felt only hatred for whomever did this to his pa. Mason reached out to him wondering if his fun-loving son would continue to bring the joy to him he always had done in the past. He prayed it would be so.

The next morning the family sat around the breakfast table. Mason half-sat, half-reclined on a makeshift bench they had quickly put together and brought close to the table. He said to Mark, "Mr. Neiter told me you've been doing a fine job, Son. I'm proud to say you're a man now, a real man."

Mark, trying to look his pa in the eyes, stated in a young man's way, "I like the farm, Pa, and a group of us in town started a marketplace to sell the crops and animals we raised. I did real good this year, sold my bull for stud and used the money to buy some more calves. I got some fence mendin' to do though and…."

As Mark continued, Mason's thoughts suddenly flashed back to that fateful day in September. He could hear himself shouting orders to his troops.

"Now men, now! Let's move forward!" Mason was moving his men forward as a bullet tore into his back. He remembered being in the hospital and the doctor telling him, "No more work for you, Captain, you're goin' home. You can't use your left side anymore. Let's hope it gets better down the road, you're lucky to be alive."

A burst of laughter from the group snapped Mason out of his daydream. He grabbed his crutches and struggled to get up, stopping Mark's discourse. He waved Mark and John off as they tried to help him. Finally, dragging his leg and obviously in pain, he struggled out and settled on the front porch. His bewildered family, not sure how to react, were left feeling empty and lost. Lydia reached out to her children. With all of them holding hands, Lydia started to pray:

"Lord. We thank you for bringing Mason back to us. We don't understand why this had to happen, and we know the trials that lie ahead for us will be won with your help. We know you are with us. You told us so, and we hold you to your promise. Don't be letting us down when the times get too hard to bear."

Tears started to flow as she continued, "Mason never forgot you in all that he did. Now don't you forget him, you hear?"

John, moved by his deep love for his pa, grabbed his guitar and headed out the door. John was too fast for Lydia to stop him, and in just a moment he was beside his pa. Mark just called out, "Pa!"

Mason was startled, his tortured face revealing that he still had not accepted what had happened to him. John continued, "Would it bother you, Pa, if I picked for you? How about *Aura Lea*? I can pick it now. You always liked that tune, and I can play if for you if'n you like, Pa."

Mason hesitated, and with much effort to sound warm, answered, "You never bother me, Son, and I'd be pleased for sure if you play it for me."

John picked the tune, as Mason looked off into the sunlit fields, then closing his eyes in silent prayer wondering about the future.

Chapter 5

Although Mason needed rest, he was too restless and feeling too useless to just sit around. So a few days after the New Year, the boys helped Mason into the back of the wagon for a short look around the farm. It would do Mark good to get his father's approval on the improvements he had made with some help from John and the expert guidance of Mr. Neiter. Mason was silent for the most part, commenting when his mind was not going back to the war.

Once more, Mason's thoughts returned to Chickamauga, the dense underbrush and towering trees that all but shut out the daylight. Again he could hear himself shouting orders to his troops.

"Now, men, now! Let's move forward!" Mason was moving his men forward when he thought he caught something out of the corner of his eye as he turned toward them. Just then, a bullet tore into his back.

Abruptly called back to the present, Mason turned to his son. Mark looked sheepishly at Mason as he said, "Well, Pa, it's held together with spit and bailin' wire but ...."

Mason interrupted, "Not at all, Son, fine job. I'm right proud of you and John."

John quickly interjected, "Well, Pa, you best just give Mark all the credit. I think I was just a little too ornery most of the time."

"Well, John, your honesty is good, but I'm sure you pounded a nail or two."

For a quiet moment they smiled at each other. Turning his attention to Mark, Mason continued, "A farmer you are, Mark. You seem to have a knack for this life. You gonna stay with it?"

Mark proudly answered, "You bet, Pa. We'll build a fine place here. We'll have some good crops, a few more steers for breeding and meat and some cows for our milk and butter."

Mason was pleased that Mark loved the farm, but turning to John, he knew John had a different love for his life. "How about you, Son? Do you think farming's a good life, something you might want to do?"

Reluctantly, not wanting to hurt his dad's feelings, John answered, "Sure. It's fine, Pa."

Mason knew better but elected not to discuss it at this time. He had been holding onto a faint hope that John might have a change of heart and become enthusiastic about farming someday. Still, he couldn't shake the qualms that he would lose his son to the world and perhaps soon at that.

Dark clouds had appeared on the horizon, signaling rain, and the boys knew their pa was in no condition to get sick. Mark turned the wagon around and headed for home arriving just as the rain started to fall and just in time for a fine lunch prepared with love by Lydia and Jennie.

As time passed, the boys continued to do the chores necessary to make the farm a prosperous home and enterprise. Mason's condition seemed to be improving but ever so slowly. Much too slowly to suit him. Also, he still had nightmares.

One night as rain poured outside and Mason lay in bed, his thoughts again returned to the dense underbrush of that thickly wooded battlefield.

"Now, men, now! Let's move forward!" Mason shouted. Something caught his attention out of the corner of his eye. Was that a flash of light? Just then, a bullet tore into his back.

Mason sat up in the bed with a start, grabbing his back with his good arm. He felt like a useless man, and the frustration twisted his face. The rain was adding to his misery as the dampness seemed to melt into his bones.

CHAPTER 6

The months passed, and time did little to heal Mason's mind. Again and again, his memory flashed back to that day in the Georgia woods. As the shock of his injury wore off, he grew gradually aware that something hadn't been right as he and his men had started up the hill during the battle. As his dreams continued, each one revealed a little more of the buried memory. What was it that nagged and made him turn back, time and again, to that day in the battlefield?

He was content for at least one blessing. His family had tactfully avoided talk about his infirmity. Then one day, Mr. Neiter knocked at the door. Lydia answering, opened the door to see Mr. Neiter standing there with tears in his eyes and his face drawn. "She's dead, Lydia, my Anna's dead. I don't know what happened."

Lydia gently took his arm and sat him down. Mason, who was sitting at the kitchen table, reached out and took his hand telling him to take a breath and tell them what happened. Mr. Neiter continued, "She was fine last night but didn't wake up this morning. I don't understand. I...."

At this, Mr. Neiter broke down sobbing. He was a simple man who loved the life he had made for himself and his beloved. The thought of being alone without his helpmate didn't register in his mind. It was a foreign thing, something not real.

At the funeral, this normally jovial and fun-loving man was inconsolable. Mason invited his close friend to move onto the Caldwell farm. Lucas responded with gratitude but was reluctant to accept at that time. His loneliness said yes, but he was a man of integrity who would need time to think things through.

John saw the sadness in this man he had grown to love so much. Like his siblings, Mark and Jennie, John had recently begun to address Mr. Neiter as Uncle Lucas. John was starting to see the reality of life and was now somewhat wary of the world around him. He was still not quite a man, however, and still harbored something of a make-believe outlook on life. Unfortunately, John was also developing deep hatred for the person who had so gravely injured his pa.

Some weeks later, John made a visit to the Neiter farm, where he found Uncle Lucas still deeply depressed after losing his wife. Lucas brightened, however, upon

John's arrival, and they both found joy in seeing each other. His burden lightened, Lucas said to John, "I was hopin' you might come by this week."

John, having slipped easily off his horse, stood in front of Lucas, who was sitting in a chair on the porch, and said, "I ain't quite done with that fancy rope tyin' knot you been teachin' me. I want to show Pa so he'll be knowin' I can tie down a good load when I go to town to pick up supplies."

Lucas, aware that John was not there for that reason, looked at him and quietly asked, "When your pa was gone, what was the one thing I was tellin' you never to do? You remember?"

John looked at him and slyly replied, "You told me a bunch of things but sure as shootin' I don't quite know what you're talkin' about now."

Uncle Lucas, without the usual sparkle in his eyes, responded, "I told you to never beat around the bush, say what needs sayin'. Now don't beat around the sage brush; say what you're thinkin' and say it honestly."

John replied boldly, "Well you know how much I like you, Uncle Lucas,..." Here John paused because he really wanted to say "loved" him, but he continued, "and I don't like to see you feelin' so sad, so you got to stop mopin' around. Your farm will be goin' down, and you look like you ain't been eatin' right and ...."

Lucas was now becoming a bit annoyed and interrupted, "Well, I also taught you not to butt into other people's business unless asked."

Still John insisted, "The fact that we're friends makes it my business so ...."

Lucas, now standing and verging on anger, said to John, "Well, this ain't your business, so if you would go home and leave me alone, I would appreciate it."

John, now raising his voice, answered, "Sure, send me off. Be alone. We want you to come to live with us, but you been too stubborn to listen to reason. I'll go—you bet."

John leapt to his horse and started off. Just then he turned and shouted back to Lucas adding, "Don't you know we love you? Don't you know you're part of our family? Why do you think we call you 'Uncle'?"

John rode off as fast as his horse would go. Lucas watched until John was out of sight. As he turned to go into the house, tears stained his ruddy cheeks. Once inside, he reached for his wife's favorite possession—a silver tray that he had bought her the first time he had any money to spend on her. He turned it over and gazed at the date engraved on the back along with the words *To my Anna, with all my love*.

CHAPTER 7

Mark and his brother were out of school, John having graduated the year before. Jennie still had about a year to go. Mark was working the farm and loving every minute. Jennie, now seventeen, was almost as pretty as Lydia—though she still carried freckles on her cheeks. She had begun to take an interest in boys and was very aware of becoming a woman. John was restless and struggled with a decision to stay on the farm or head out—or just let come what may.

One day in late October when the most of the harvest was in and there was less to take up their time, Mason, Mark, and John rode into town. It was unusual for Mason to go, as he still couldn't get used to his friends seeing him crippled, but on this occasion he needed to do business at the bank. He wanted to set up his account to include Mark, as he knew how mature Mark had become and that he would stay with the farm. That way, he wouldn't have to come as often himself, and he would of course leave Lucas on the account.

Mark had also told Mason he had seen some new farm equipment and wanted his father's opinion as to whether they should get it. The money would come from some of the animals and crops Mark had raised plus money due Mason from the army. All the way to town, John related imaginative stories to Mason in an effort to cheer him up. Mason smiled and tried to be attentive, as he knew what John was doing, but his mind strayed elsewhere.

Mason was moving his men forward through the underbrush. As he turned, Mason thought he saw a man pointing his rifle in his direction. "What's with this halfwit? Why is he already aiming when he's still this far back?"

As the buckboard entered the town, people waved to the trio, and Mason's attention returned to the present. They were not strangers to the people of Crockett, but Mason's pride still stung, even after all these months. He half-smiled back at the people thinking of course they were just feeling sorry for him.

When they entered the bank, Mason wondered how the people in there would see him. Mason didn't want their pity. Nonetheless, he cringed as Gerald Henley, the banker, told him yet again he was sorry for Mason's condition. Mason was grateful that the banker went right on with business. Henley knew better than to let a man dwell on his problems, something one learns in doing business with the public.

Leaving the bank, Mason, Mark, and John were greeted by some of Mason's old friends, and almost against Mason's wishes, they dragged him into the saloon. The boys were happy to see people around their pa thinking it would help lift his spirits. Once inside, John went directly into the corner of the saloon to entertain with his guitar. Mark headed for the corral. John figured a Christian song wouldn't go over very well in a saloon, but he had a surprise up his sleeve, however, a ditty he had written himself on one of those days when his own mood had been lighter. He figured it wasn't all that bad, and his pa wouldn't mind so he started:

> *Remember Lily who lived in town.*
> *She always wanted a wedding gown.*
> *But there was no one as bold as she,*
> *She could whip a man one, two, three.*
>
> *Someone would say, be mine this day*
> *But after a while would just run away.*
> *It wasn't hard to see what went wrong*
> *It didn't take long 'fore her words got strong.*
>
> *She could strap on a gun and scare away*
> *The meanest of men that got in her way.*
> *What was it she thought that men had sought?*
> *Her wedding gown seemed a far off thought.*

Men rushed in to see her golden hair
But found instead a big mama bear.
Tough as nails and not much fun
She had a look that could melt a gun.

Was there a man who could tame this gal?
Yes there was, and his name is Sal.
Six foot five and built like a barn,
He just wouldn't stand for all her yarn.

He told her once and that was enough.
You, dear Lilly, you ain't so tough.
I'll love you, Lil, and you never could say
My big tough Sal will run away.

He tamed our Lilly with his big ole heart.
He had her figured right from the start.
She was laughing and happy as they left town,
She looked so happy in her wedding gown.

After the applause and some laughs from the men, John took a bow and, looking over, saw his father smiling at him. Mason's fatherly pride in his son was obvious, and to see that smile coming from his pa gave John real joy.

The day proceeded with much fun as Mason downed a few and relaxed. He didn't talk much about his army days but instead about the farm and all they were going to do to improve it. His friends were good enough not to ask too many questions about his army experiences, so most of the conversation was light. Looking up at the clock, John noticed it was close to three o'clock. Not wanting to leave too late so they could be home before dark, John cornered Mason, "There's a chill in the air, and if'n we don't leave now, you'll be cold on the way home."

Mason laughingly answered, "With all that whiskey I doubt I'll be chilled. I could probably get a rattler drunk if he bit me."

Everyone laughed, and John was delighted to see his pa in a good humor. With that, they left the saloon.

Mark was still down at the corral looking over some horses and farm equipment. Mark could spend a week looking over what he saw as the future. John assisted his father to a chair outside the saloon to wait for Mark. Mason, not as drunk as he put on, told John, "Maybe people can care for a half a man."

That hit John with a sting. He realized Mason had a long way to go in the healing of his heart. "Pa, you ought not talk like …."

At this, they were interrupted by a commotion up the street. John went to investigate. A small crowd had gathered watching the town bullies, Jeb Bolin and his brother Jesse, pushing around a half-Asian, half-Caucasian boy about the same age as John. It wasn't clear whether no one cared or if they were just afraid of Jeb and Jesse, but no one seemed willing to help the young man. John was never one watch injustice, however, and he jumped into the fray stating boldly, "Pretty tough, two on one I think …."

That's as far as John got before he caught the back of Jesse's hand and went spinning, only to be cuffed good by Jeb. John went down in heap. As he started to get up, the Bolin brothers left their first victim and wasted no time in starting their punch fest on John.

Mason was helpless as he tried to get up from his chair and could only watch helplessly as John took a whipping. This really frustrated him. His frustration didn't last too long, however.

Suddenly Jeb jerked up and pain twisted his face as he cried out. Jesse turned just in time to see a foot. It landed right on his nose breaking it and causing a mess. Jeb, now half-recovered, reached for the young man who was the brothers' first target. The boy blocked Jeb's arm and quickly hit Jeb on each side of his neck using his opened hand rather like a meat cleaver. The onlookers had never seen such tactics. Then, without missing a beat, the boy spun around to Jesse, who had just stood up, and planted a kick into his ribs.

Both men now taken care of, the young hero went over to John who was groaning in pain. Reaching out his hand, he helped John up. Bewildered, John asked, "You can fight like that and you let them bully and beat on you?"

The young man answered, "They were pushing me around as usual because they just don't like people who aren't as white as they are. There is a time to fight and a time to keep peace. Maybe someday I can explain this to you. I thank you for your concern, and I hope you are not hurt badly on my account."

"I'll live." John paused, grabbing his jaw to see if it was still in one piece. Then he added, "I hope."

The crowd of onlookers had dispersed, happy they hadn't joined the Bolin brothers in dispensing such ignorance and hatred.

John and the other young man walked over to an anxiously waiting Mason as John continued, "Where did you learn to fight like that?"

The young man smiled but replied humbly, "My father was a master of martial arts in China and passed it on to me. It is used when really necessary, and then only."

John was immediately drawn to this young man and felt he had found a friend. It was evident to the young man too, who continued, "It is rare when one is willing to fight for someone else."

John's reply was simple, "What are friends for?"

The two boys smiled at each other. When they reached Mason, he examined John's face and cussed himself under his breath for not being a whole man so he could help his son. Looking at the young man he said, "We're in debt to you, young man. You did what I wish I was able to do to those Bolin brothers. I think the sheriff should getting involved."

"No, he knows that this has happened before and doesn't care. I can take care of these two if necessary."

Mason could only reply, "I'm sure of that."

Clearly, there was no love lost between Mason and the sheriff. Mason, controlling his embarrassment, asked, "John will you introduce me."

John looked surprised and laughed as he realized he didn't know his new friend's name. The young man stepped up, offering a hand, and said, "I am Matthew Chen Lo. My mother and I came here from San Francisco a few months ago. It was a long journey, but my mother has family around here."

Mason replied, "I knew I'd never seen you before. Well, welcome to Crockett, Texas. Can't say it was much of a welcoming committee though."

Mason's voice was sincere. Matthew then told Mason and John he must go back home to help his mother. "My mother isn't very strong, and she still hasn't recovered from our journey. I pray daily that she will get stronger. You see she was a missionary to my father's country and gave us an understanding of the Christian life. As frail as she was, she worked hard. She converted my father, and they married. My father ..." Matthew paused for a moment then continued, "I'm sorry; I didn't mean to carry on about me. Let us hope that our next meeting will be, shall we say, less violent."

Matthew said no more about his father, but both John and Mason sensed he missed him. With that, they bid each other farewell. John glanced over to the Bolin brothers who had made a painful trek toward the saloon and were lounging just outside its door. John with a concerned tone told Mason, "I hope they don't try to get even with Matthew."

Mason laughingly stated, "As I said, I don't think Matthew would be too concerned if they did. He seems more than able to take care himself—and others too if need be."

Mason's mood had changed, and he solemnly asked, "Why all the fighting? Why do people want to hurt each other?"

Just then Mark appeared, having missed the whole thing. Settling themselves in the buckboard, John began to relate the story blow by blow as they headed home. Dusk was setting in, and Mason, being triggered by the day's events, started to remember again that fateful day on the battlefield.

This time, Mason saw the whole field of battle. The man with the rifle was behind him and not moving forward as ordered—just pointing his rifle. Mason didn't recognize the man as from his company.

For the first time since returning home, Mason opened up to Mark and John and started to relate the incident to his sons. He felt he had seen the face in his vision before, and turning to John as if his memory were coming to life, said anxiously, "I wonder who shot me. We assumed it was a Yankee, but how could he have been behind me?"

Looking in amazement at his pa, who looked as if a new light had dawned, John queried, "But, Pa, of course it was a Yankee. Who else? Not one of your own ...."

John's voice trailed off as he wondered why that thought even came into his head. Half-smiling , he continued, "Pa, Rebs don't shoot Rebs."

Mason didn't answer; he only continued deep in thought.

When they reached the farm, Lydia came out to meet them as they rode up to the house. In the previous year, the boys had added some comfortable benches to Lydia's arbor and flower garden where one could sit in the shade and enjoy God's glory. Here she sat as dusk settled into darkness, but the men could see the concerned expression on Lydia's face at their being so late. Looking at John's face, which was now showing dark bruises, she tried to control her voice, "My God, John. Your face, who did this? What happened, are you all right?"

John interrupted, "I'm fine, Ma, just a bunch sore. I'll tell you all about it."

Mason and John looked toward the barn and saw a man's figure coming toward them. Lucas reached out to help Mason down. As he did so, he looked over to John, who was mixed with emotion as he thought he had lost a very good and loving friend forever. Lucas smiled at him, and John smiled back. Inside the house over coffee and pie, John again related to the family, which now seemed to include Uncle Lucas, the story of how he came to have these aches and pains.

As the family members retired to their rooms, Lucas left to go outside. John followed him out, and as they crossed the yard, John called after him,

"Mr. Neiter" ("Uncle Lucas" didn't seem appropriate at this moment), "I—ah—want to apologize to you for the way I spoke to you. You're right, I had no right ...."

Mr. Neiter turned to him and with a warm voice replied, "Doesn't mean you don't care for me as you said."

John jumped in with enthusiasm, "Oh no, I do really care. We all care, Uncle Lucas."

There was warmth in John's voice as Lucas replied, also with much warmth, "Well then, you did have a right. Love is an important thing. Loneliness is a terrible thing. I kept thinking what you said about you all lovin' me. I have no children of my own, but being 'uncle' suits me just fine and well, I want to return that love, and if you folks will have me I'll ...."

John grabbed the old man with such fervor the two almost fell to the ground. Both could hardly contain their joy.

From then on, every time someone went into town, John asked to tag along, wondering if Matthew would be there. It had been some weeks since the Bolin brothers had brought the two of them together. Since that time, however, they had met occasionally and had become good friends.

CHAPTER 8

April 9, 1865, was a day no one would forget. Mason, John, and Mark had ridden into town. Mason was doing his banking while the boys picked up supplies. Afterward they met at the saloon to catch up with friends when a booming voice came from the telegraph office steps so loud one could hear it in the next county.

"Watcha s'pose is goin' on?" Mark wondered.

Never one to leave a question hanging, John quickly raced outside and over to a group standing in front of the telegraph office.

"What's happenin'? What's all the excitement?" he asked of no one in particular.

As people began to crowd together in front of the telegraph office, Mr. Nolan announced, "The war is over—**the war is over!**"

With that, John ran back to the saloon just as his pa and Mark were coming out, followed by the rest of the customers.

"Let me read the telegram," shouted Nolan. "Shortly after noon on April 9, 1865, General Robert E. Lee surrendered to Ulysses S. Grant, general-in-chief of all United States forces, at the home of Wilmer McClean in the village of Appomattox Court House, Virginia. The two generals met with Lee saying, 'It would be useless and therefore cruel, to provoke the further effusion of blood, I have arranged to meet with General Grant with a view to surrender'."[1]

As the townsfolk gathered around, they looked at each other with mixed emotions. Some began dancing and shouting. Others were not so exuberant. All were happy that there would be no more bloodshed, but after all, the South had lost.

To avoid being jostled and risking a fall, Mason had climbed into the wagon still tied to the hitching post. As his friends approached him, one of them said, "Well, Mason, you hearin' that? You fought and gave more than many in this war. You must have a heavy heart 'bout us losin' to those Yankees."

Mason looked somber as he answered, "I saw much bloodshed and suffering on both sides, Harold. Brother against brother, friend against friend. This is what I think. This must become a time for healing, a time for this great nation—that both sides fought for—to come together again. We can become great again if we do come together. We once—both North and South—fought together to defeat a foreign land that wanted to oppress us. We must come together and not forget that God gave us this country, this nation, as a gift. We owe it to him as well as to ourselves to heal and become one under him."

Just few days later, on April 15, Mark came riding at breakneck speed up to the house. Jumping off his horse, he rushed up onto the porch where Mason was sitting. He could barely get the words out as he exclaimed, "Pa, I just came from town, and another telegram came in announcin' that President Lincoln has been assassinated. He was shot last night and died today."

Mason was now worried because he knew that Lincoln had been planning to help the South rebuild. Where would this lead, what would happen now? Only time would tell.

CHAPTER 9

In only a short time, John and Matthew had become close friends, and they spent hours together whenever they could. Matthew shared with John the self-defense and combat techniques he had learned from his father, and John reciprocated by instructing Matthew on firearms and, to some extent, farming. The time came, however, when they developed a mutual wanderlust and burning desire to explore the world around them.

Matthew's mother, Catherine, had moved in with her older sister, Alice, and brother-in-law, Paul, on a small spread just on the edge of town. Paul and Alice had moved to town some ten years earlier to explore a new kind of life. In time, Matthew had brought Catherine to meet the Caldwells. As Catherine told them of her experiences as a missionary in China, the two families bonded over their mutual love of the Lord and service to him.

One evening when Matthew and Catherine had joined the Caldwells for dinner, Matthew and John seized the opportunity to discuss with their families their urge to explore. There were questions and protests from the elders, but the young men spoke with such fervor that they persuaded their parents they were mature enough to make the trip. Thus it came to pass that in May 1865, the two boys headed out to see some of what there was in the southern part of their great state of Texas.

Leaving Crockett early one morning, they rode due south until they arrived in Houston, which had briefly been the capital of Texas. Because Houston bordered Galveston Bay and the Gulf of Mexico, it had become a major port for the shipment of cotton. Matthew, who had spent a few years in San Francisco, was accustomed to the pace of a big city. John, on the other hand, had lived in Crockett most of his life, so the activity of a busy city was exciting. Besides the sweltering heat of the coastal area, they had learned that there had been some fierce battles along the coast, particularly in the areas around Galveston Bay, in the city itself, and reaching as far south as Brownsville.

Therefore, they did not remain in Houston and kept inland as they rode south and west to the city of Victoria. Most of the families living here were Mexican *rancheros* who herded cattle, although some grew grain and hay. Still others grew cotton, and Victoria had become a major stop on what was called the Cotton Road extending to Brownsville. Over this route, cotton was transported into Mexico to be traded for arms and medicines in support of the war.

Rather than spending time in Victoria, John and Matthew headed northwest to San Antonio de Béxar, a city almost as large as Houston. Here, they visited the place where, some twenty-five years earlier, a crushing battle had taken place. As this location was now being used as a warehouse for war supplies, they were unable to go inside, but they learned details of the battle.

For thirteen days, forces led by the Mexican president, General Santa Anna, had laid siege to the city and especially to the Misión San Antonio de Valero that had recently become a fort. Because it had been a turning point in the Texas Revolution, Texas children had all been taught in school about the battle at the mission now known as the Alamo.

After a number of skirmishes in various parts of the city, on March 6, 1836, Santa Anna's forces, about 1500 strong, had overwhelmed the Texian soldiers and others garrisoned within the mission walls, who numbered less than 300. Greatly outnumbered, the Texians fought bravely but were defeated by Santa Anna's forces. Only three people were known to have survived this debacle.

When news of the defeat became known, there had been a surge of volunteers from Texas and nearby states who came to avenge the loss of almost 300 brave souls. About a month later, the forces of General Santa Anna met Texian forces led by General Sam Houston at San Jacinto. Here the tables were turned as Santa Anna's army was soundly defeated in less than twenty minutes, ending the Texas Revolution.

Since then, San Antonio had become a bustling city. Everywhere were bright colors, strange sounds and exotic smells. John was particularly taken by a lively form of music called *mariachi* that had come from Mexico. Musicians played at many events, strumming guitars and plucking fiddles and sometimes a harp. One band even had some trumpets.

One Saturday afternoon, as John and Matthew roamed a path along the river that ran through the city, they came upon a wedding party celebrating the marriage of a beautiful dark-haired señorita to her tall, handsome, new husband. This was unlike anything they had ever seen back in Crockett. As they watched, a band of musicians played festive mariachi music. Then a couple dressed in bright colors got up to dance, whirling, clicking their heels on the stone pavement, and making a similar clicking sound with something they held in their hands that John learned were called castanets.

Matthew whispered, "Let's see if we can get closer, John." The two approached the throng, but not wishing to intrude, they sat a little way off on the grassy slope and watched, taking in the gaiety of the occasion.

As they stood up to leave, John said wistfully, "It sure would be grand if'n I could find a gal so fine and have a dandy party like this. I wonder if my ma and pa had a fine party like this'n?"

Leaving San Antonio early one morning, they followed a well-traveled trail due west toward the small settlement of San Felipe del Rio, on the river that had become the formal border with Mexico.

Upon reaching Del Rio some days later, they reined in at a trading post to get supplies, hoping to visit with some of the locals. As they entered the post, the proprietor called out cheerily, "Buenos días, señores. ¿Cómo estás?"

John and Matthew grimaced in surprise and at the same time said to each other, "Do you speak ...?" and shaking their heads burst out laughing.

"I'm sorry," began John, now facing the proprietor and speaking a bit too loudly, "but we don't know much Spanish."

"Lo siento, I make de English. How I can help you?"

"We need some food. You know, comida?" he said, his hand making a scooping motion toward his mouth.

"Sí, ustedes, ah, you need de harina, how you say, flour?"

"No, uh," said Matthew. "Need corn meal, for johnny cake. Do you have hardtack? And jerky? Maybe some fruit?"

"Sí, tengo. Here is harina de maíz—corn meal. I habe de hardtack an' de 'yerky' también. Somet'ing más?"

They haggled, each trying to remember words in the other's language or signing clumsily. When they had just about given up, another customer entered the store. Observing the awkward exchange, he approached the counter.

"Con su permiso, señores. Perhaps I can be of assistance. I am Diego Alvarez, and I speak the English."

With sighs of relief, the two adventurers shook his hand and exchanged names. They accepted Señor Alvarez' offer and quickly concluded their purchases.

As John and Matthew loaded their supplies on the horses, Alvarez appeared at the door having completed his own business. "Where do you go, if I may ask?" inquired Alvarez politely, to which Matthew replied, "We want to ride along the Rio Grande. Now that we have seen big cities, we were hoping there was something exciting along the river. Somebody told us there are mountains west of here."

"But of course," responded Alvarez, "you must mean the mountains where the rio makes the big turn. The hombres who have been there call them Chisos. I myself have not ridden there, but I know hombres who have. They tell me of grand peaks and much beauty. Come, I take you to mis amigos who will know."

John and Matthew followed Alvarez to where several Mexicans sat lounging in the shade of some nearby trees. A few spoke passable English, and they invited the boys to sit. One noticed John's guitar, and before long John was strumming while the men tried to teach him a silly song about a five-legged cockroach, accompanied by riotous laughter.

Meanwhile, others gave them directions. They could go west on the American side of the river, but it would mean a long detour because the river widened into a lake at one point. By crossing from Del Rio, they could ride on the Mexican side and still follow the river. Then, when they could see the mountains rise, they should cross the shallow river back to the American side and climb to the Chisos. This would be more direct, saving them much time and hard riding in the sun.

After a pleasant hour or so, the boys departed, with many expressions of thanks.

"Cuidanse, tipos," called one of them, "hay muchos peligros," warning that along with the beauty, dangers also lay ahead.

CHAPTER 10

Back in Crockett, Mark and Lucas worked the farm side by side. Uncle Lucas had now been living on the Caldwell farm for some time and had almost become part of the family. The two men had grown close, and it didn't seem right to Mark that Lucas should be sleeping in a bunkhouse by himself. One day when Lucas had taken the buckboard into town and Mark and his father sat alone in the arbor, Mark asked, "Pa, what would you think about buildin' on to the house? Didn't you and Ma talk about this some before you left for the war? We could make a room for Uncle Lucas so's he can be here in the family."

"Good idea, Son, but with John away, can you handle it?"

"Well," responded Mark, "it would be easier if John was here, but there's a couple of fellows in town who are part of our farm group. How about I ask them for a hand?"

Mason agreed and, after some consultation with Lydia and Lucas, it wasn't long before a new addition had been built. In addition to a room for Lucas, the root cellar had been enlarged to store the foods grown on the farm and preserved by Lydia and Jennie. That also made it possible to give Lydia a small room upstairs for her sewing—a room that overlooked her beautiful garden.

Meanwhile, Lucas had decided to sell his farm, as he was now really a part of the Caldwell family. Being an "uncle" brought him much joy. He moved into the house and was now truly "in the family."

Catherine's brother-in-law Paul, who loved the outdoors, had discovered there was good money working in the lumber business and had moved to Crockett to become a logger. They owned a modest cabin and had welcomed Catherine and Matthew into their home and hearts. A loving Christian couple, they had missed their missionary wanderer. From Catherine's letters, they knew she had borne Matthew and suffered the loss of her husband, Matthew's father.

Seeing him for the first time, they had been a little taken aback that he displayed more of his father's ethnicity than his mother's, but they soon came to accept him into the family with warm hearts.

In Matthew's absence, the Caldwells made regular visits to Catherine at the farm where she lived with Alice and Paul. The ladies found they all shared an interest in fine needlework and quilting. Alice had a large quilting frame, and the ladies took turns assisting each other in making fine bedding for the colder seasons.

On one of these occasions, the topic turned to wedding dresses. Usually, a woman wore her nicest dress to be married, but in 1840, the British Queen Victoria had chosen to be married in a special white gown, and that custom had begun to catch on elsewhere. Alice and Lydia had each carefully preserved their gowns. As for Catherine, being a missionary entailed some austerity, and upon losing her husband in China, she had been forced to leave much behind to return to her homeland with her son.

One afternoon, when the ladies met at the Caldwell farm to sew, Lydia brought out a box and opened it to show them, carefully preserved, the beautiful ivory gown in which she had married Mason.

Made of fine sheer muslin, the gown's voluminous skirt had two ruffled tiers with bows at each side to lift the fabric into graceful scallops. The waistline dipped into a flattering V in front. The bodice was accentuated with a deep V of lace that continued over the shoulders and dipped to the waistline in back but was demurely filled in with lace. Long sleeves made of the same fine lace came to a point on the back of the hand.

Accompanying this beautiful gown was a veil of even finer muslin meant to be attached to a crown of fresh flowers and leaves.

Lydia sighed and said, "I had always held the hope that my own daughter would someday be married in this same dress. See, the seams are generous so they can be let out, but Jennie is already taller than I am, and the gown would be too short."

Alice spoke up and said, "I may have the answer for you. My grandmother had a beautiful ball gown from the old country when she passed, but it has not survived our travels very well. Still, I just can't bear to part with it. As I recall, the material is very similar, and if it matches closely enough, we could add an additional ruffle at the bottom."

"Oh Alice," countered Lydia, "that would be so generous of you, but of course Jennie is still only seventeen and way too young to even be thinking of marriage. She just finished her schooling, of course, and then there's the matter of her meeting someone. I'm happy right now to have her help me keep this house running and to continue her tom-boyish ways with her brothers."

With that, the subject was dropped and the ladies returned to their needlework.

CHAPTER 11

The farther Matthew and John traveled out of Del Rio, the more desolate it became with fewer and fewer settlements. The land grew more arid, with sparse vegetation, and the terrain began to rise. Several times, the boys asked themselves if maybe they should head back home, but having heard of this special place high in the mountains, they were determined to go on. After some miles, the river curved deeply south into Mexico forming what people called the Big Bend.

On their fourth day out of Del Rio, the terrain began to climb steeply. More than once they had to retreat to the river's edge to refill their canteens and to rest and water the horses. Their pace slowed too, because the sun bore down on them relentlessly. Once in a while, when the moon was full and bright and they felt safe in doing so, they slept during the day in such shade as they could find and rode by night.

As they climbed, the vegetation increased. Trees grew taller and thicker. Several times, they spotted grazing among the trees small white-tailed deer about the size of a dog, and once they came upon a mountain lion that had killed one and was dining on its prey. As they passed, the big cat growled and slunk off. John raised his rifle to shoot, but Matthew stretched out his arm and pushed the barrel down saying, "His belly is full; no call to shoot him if he doesn't come after us." John agreed, but they remained wary and did not see the cat again.

Finally, they could climb no higher having reached a high plateau in a crater surrounded by tall forbidding peaks. This area was filled with strange trees and flowers, where hummingbirds flitted and hovered.

Here and there a waterfall cascaded from one of the peaks, and brightly colored dragonflies darted and lit wherever there was a stream. While stooping to get water, they saw tiny frogs hopping up the trunks of trees.

Exhausted from the long climb, the boys dismounted, watered the horses, made a fire, and pitched camp. After a meager supper, because they were too tired to hunt, John sang a bit, as he often did in the evenings.

"John, I must say this about your singing. It's growing on me, not too fast, mind you, but it's growing." Matthew smiled as he continued, "Your songs are mostly of the Lord, and I guess that makes it a bit more pleasant to my ears. Truth is, John, you do have a gift. You may have gotten some of it from your mom's talent, but I think the big source is from the Lord."

Leaning into John, Matthew continued his playful jabbing, "There is one thing I must confess to you. As much as I like hearing you sing, once in a while, try to stay in tune with your guitar."

As they both laughed, Matthew stood up and walked over to a path between the peaks and called back to John. "Quick, come here, John! You gotta to see this." As John arrived at his side, Matthew continued, "There's the Rio Grande below us. How high up do you s'pose we are? Have you ever seen anything like this?"

"Glory be!" replied John sucking in his breath, "No, I never seen the likes of this. Look at that sunset!"

He confided softly to Matthew, "My ma and pa always told me to show respect for what God's made, but 'til we come here, I never saw mountains so—Matt, I don't know the words to describe it."

"I know what you mean," Matthew replied. "Sometimes my mother tells me about China, and she will say something is 'majestic.' If she were here, I think that's the word she'd say. I sure have never seen a place quite as grand as this. It reminds me of a verse she taught me once: 'I will open rivers in desolate heights, and fountains in the midst of the valleys: I will make the wilderness a pool of water, and the dry land springs of water'."[2]

Then John asked quietly and somewhat tenuously, "Matt, did you ever think about what Moses felt like up on that mountain when he met God? There's no burnin' bush here, but sure as shootin' God must be here."

Matthew agreed and yawning turned back to camp. "How about we turn in. I'm worn out from that long climb."

After a short pause, John said, "Matt, I been thinkin' about how my ma would do if'n she was here. She would say we should pray and thank God for gittin' us this far. And thank him for showin' us his wonders. And for keepin' us safe. We been travelin' a long time now, and sometimes, we bin forgettin' to give thanks."

The two young men stopped to pray, then after stoking the fire, quickly fell asleep under a full moon, serenaded by strange chirping frogs.

The next morning, when they awoke, the rocky peaks that had looked down on them the night before were totally shrouded in fog, casting a ghostly spell over the secluded valley. The searing heat of the previous day's ride was gone, and all was fresh and cool.

Energized, they stoked the fire, made coffee, and dined— if so grand a word can describe a meal in the wilderness— on jerky, johnny cake, and some tasty fruits. Back in Del Rio some of the men had showed them something called "strawberry cactus," and now they were grateful for its refreshing change.

Matthew pointed out that since it was so cool, it would be an excellent opportunity for some more lessons in the Chinese martial arts method he had learned from his father. John had been greatly intrigued by Matthew's ability to handle the two town bullies back in Crockett and asked Matthew to teach him. In the few short months since they had met, they had held practice sessions whenever and wherever they could. John was grasping the fundamentals and showing an aptitude for the discipline.

"Well, John, let's get to work on your skills. As I told you before, Cai Li Fo is not only effective for self-defense one on one but for defense when facing more than one attacker. In fact, that's probably its best use."

With that, Matthew continued: "Let's review. Cai Li Fo hand techniques consist of ten elements: slapping or pressing palm deflection, shooting arm bridge, back fist, sweeping, knuckle strike, upward power shot, claw, swinging power shot, chopping, and fist."

As Matthew recited, John repeated each Chinese name after him, and then John followed Matthew's lead in practicing each hand technique.

Next, Matthew proceeded to recite and demonstrate six leg techniques. As he caught John's attention drifting, he became the stern taskmaster and said, "I'm not done yet, John, pay attention, because there are eight techniques in how the hand and leg techniques are applied."

"Matt, how many years are we goin' to stand in this crater? I'll be too old to use them by the time I git to know 'em all." They both laughed as Matthew started his new lesson with Liu Tat kicking moves.

Following the lesson, they spent several hours in the secluded valley, exploring at the base of the peaks, taking in strange plants and unfamiliar wildlife. After two more nights in this wilderness and a lot more practice, they got up, ate, broke camp, and left.

From here, Matthew and John traveled north. This was a desolate and unsettled region, and it was frightening to them at times, being so alone. They traveled days sometimes without seeing another human face, but faith and courage led them on.

Descending from the Chisos peaks, they saw fewer deer but several times they saw vultures circling and knew that some critter had met its end. They were always on the lookout for other wildlife, both large and small. Jackrabbits they could roast for dinner, but they were happy to do without the company of anything much larger.

Once as they rode through a rocky patch where there was very little trail, Matthew's horse whinnied, shied, and almost threw him. He reined in just as John shouted, "Watch out; pull up!" Then they heard the tell-tale rattle of a viper. John, who'd been following behind, grabbed his rifle and fired off a shot, ripping the coiled rattlesnake.

"Thank you, Lord," Matthew breathed. "You've been merciful to us, and we are truly grateful."

After about five days' travel, they reached Fort Stockton. Here they relaxed and enjoyed their first baths in some time, plus food more appetizing than freshly killed rabbit or hardtack, though they both thanked God for providing for them on their desolate ride.

It had now been more than two months since they first left Crockett. To tell the truth, the constant riding through unsettled country had become somewhat lonely, although it had hardened the two boys into manhood. They decided it was time to head for home.

Leaving Fort Stockton, they rode east along some fairly well-traveled trails. Though they had passed encampments here and there, the few Indians they'd encountered seemed friendly or kept their distance, and they had been fortunate not to have any run-ins. The few settlers they met were mostly welcoming. Indeed, living in such isolation made the locals curious to hear from the travelers all they could of other parts.

Eventually, they reached a small town called Menardville. It was still early in the day when they reined up in front of the trading post, already trail-weary and dusty. Wanting nothing so much as a bath, a good meal, and to sleep in a bed, they decided to ask if they could barter their services in exchange, since by now, the money they had started with was quickly dwindling.

As they mucked stalls in the small stable behind the post, one of the cowpokes working there told John and Matthew of a lake two or three hours' ride from there, where the hunting and fishing were good and the water clean for a free bath.

"Jes' follow that thar trail over yonder, takes ya north. Y'all jes' keep a-ridin' 'til you come to a purty wide creek. That'd be Brady Creek. Then make your way east along the creek. Purty soon you come to a big lake. Got lots of fish there, if'n you can catch 'em, and this time of year, the water will be warm. You fellas know how to swim?" asked Pete while scratching a crude map in the dirt.

After several hours of work, the owner of the trading post called them in and fed them. He gave them extra food in exchange for their work, as they had decided to follow Pete's suggestion and head for the lake instead of spending the night at the post. With that, they saddled up and left.

With Pete's crude map committed to memory, they rode north in the afternoon sun. Sure enough, they soon came to a pleasant creek that meandered in an easterly direction. After another hour or so, they came to a lake. Tying the horses, they stripped down and plunged into the refreshing water.

After spending some time splashing and frolicking, John and Matthew sprawled on the grass beside the lakeside and relaxed in the sun.

"What's that on the tree over there?" asked John. "I bin seein' papers tacked to trees for a while now." He got up, put on the rest of his clothes, and went to look. It turned out to be a wanted poster for three thugs. It seemed these three had been visiting local ranches and farms uninvited. Anyone who tried to stop them was beaten as they stole pretty much all they could get into their saddlebags or strapped onto their spare horse.

One day they did more than beat a farmer. They beat his wife too. They were an older couple too weak to defend themselves. When the husband died from the beating, the sheriff nailed up a wanted poster that read:

Looking at the wanted poster, which had pictures of three mean-looking outlaws, John exclaimed, "Says here they were seen headin' east. Bothers me a bunch. If they git to Crockett, and Ma and Pa are alone ...."

Matthew interrupted, "Think good thoughts, John. We'll be home soon. We can warn everyone. I'm sure there's a poster in Crockett by now for all to see."

The two young men decided to camp beside the lake for the night just outside a small town. After a meal of freshly caught fish to go with what they'd been given earlier, they settled back, preparing to sleep under a moonlit sky. John began to strum the guitar and said, "Matthew, I got a new song I'd like to sing for you. It's about the Glory Land, and ...."

At this, a voice boomed out of the dark, "Don't know 'bout no glory land, but if'n y'all want to see any more of this land, you best be doin' what we be a-tellin' ya."

Leaping to their feet, John and Matthew found themselves looking into the faces of three armed men in the moonlight and recognized them from the wanted poster. Billy Lee started rummaging through the boys' saddle bags and supplies. Matthew cast a sideways look at John and said, "Been a while since we've been back to back. Ready?"

John took the hint and, as Macken and Hank surveyed the camp site, John slowly positioned himself back to back with Matthew. Macken and Hank thought they just had a couple of kids on their hands, so they weren't as cautious as if they had been older men. With Billy Lee busy, it just left two men. Matthew gave the signal by butting John; then quickly they were on the two. First they employed the palm deflection and back fist to knock the guns out of the outlaws' hands; then with a knuckle strike to the throat, Matthew stopped Hank. Hank grabbed his throat in pain and ran out into the trees gagging.

John, still a bit green in his training, managed to block one punch from Macken but not a second and got it in the stomach. Then, as Macken came at him, John took a stance, twirled and caught Macken across the head with his foot. John was pleased with himself and cracked a smile. That put Macken down, but in the meantime Billy Lee had pulled his gun out and drew down on the boys. "Pretty fancy footwork, boy. I guess I'll just shoot you in that foot."

Macken was up now but made the mistake of stepping between Billy Lee and John. John reacted by dropping down and, taking Macken's legs, spun him around just in time for the bullet to hit Macken. Matthew, with his greater speed, was on Billy Lee. Grabbing his arm, he slapped and pressed an upward power shot that took down Billy Lee. As Billy hit the ground, Matthew hit pressure points that locked the joints in Billy's shoulders and knees.

That ended the fight, but suddenly they heard rustling in the bushes. John grabbed a gun and started to aim for the sound. He heard a voice calling out, "Hold on there, fella, hold your fire. Friend comin' in."

John continued pointing his gun as he said, "Maybe you can let us see your face—and your hands."

The stranger answered as he stepped forward, "Well, here's my face, at least so much as you can see by the moonlight and your fire, but my hands are busy holding this vermin I saw runnin' from your camp."

As the man stepped into the light, pushing a subdued Hank before him, the boys saw that he wore a Confederate uniform.

"Name's Leander McNelly. I'm a captain with the Texas Mounted Volunteers, part of Company F, Fifth Regiment. Been trackin' these three for two weeks now. It's bad enough that these vermin are murderers, but one thing I can't stomach is a deserter. When they left their post because of their bein' cowards, a few good soldiers died. It's bad enough to lose men to the enemy, but when a man deserts his comrades, there ain't no excuse."

He paused to take a closer look at John and Matthew. With some passion still in his voice he continued, "I guess you fellas are right good. These vermin are mean as mean can be. What might your names be?"

"My name is John Caldwell, and this here's my partner, Matthew Lo."

"Pleased ta meet you two. You sure got some spunk."

With that, John relaxed and welcomed McNelly into the campsite. Matthew commented, "Well, this is more excitement than we bargained for when we started our trip from Crockett. What do we do with them now, Captain McNelly?"

McNelly, also now more relaxed, replied, "First, Son, let's get 'em tied up so's they can't get away again." With a bit of physical persuasion, the outlaw Hank finally told McNelly where their horses were stashed.

With a laugh, McNelly then suggested, "How about we drag 'em to town and collect the reward money? I git some pay, but I can keep the reward since there is one."

John and Matthew just looked at each other with wide eyes. McNelly continued, "We just have to split it three ways. Not bad for a night's work."

John answered, "No sir, Captain McNelly. Who'd you say you work for?"

McNelly pushed out his chest and answered proudly, "Right now I'm still part of the Texas Mounted Volunteers, but soon's I muster out of the army, I plan to go back and help reorganize the Texas Rangers along with a number of fellas I knew from before the war. Back then, the Rangers had legal authority in Texas to keep the peace, and we'd like to see it started up again."

During this conversation, the trio had tied up Billy Lee, Hank, and Macken and wrapped Macken's wound.

With that they saddled up and headed for town to collect their well-earned reward. On the ride into town, McNelly inquired, "I hafta ask. Where did you fellas learn to fight like that?"

Matthew replied humbly, "It's a form of martial arts called Cai Li Fo that my father taught me when we lived in China. It was developed in the 1830s by a man named Chan Heung, and my father studied with him. My father learned it because it is an effective self-defense system and is especially useful when fighting more than one opponent. I began to study with my father when I was very young. Since meeting my good friend John, I've been teaching him this technique so we can have each other's back in case of a fight. It sure paid off in this case."

"Yes it did, Matthew, yes it did," came McNelly's laughing reply. "It sure worked on these three varmints."

John and Matthew had taken a liking to McNelly, and once the outlaws were safely in the sheriff's custody, they exchanged addresses. McNelly said he didn't stay in one place very long but named a central location from which he worked. Then he added, "If'n you boys ever get a hankerin' to do some volunteer work, let me know. We're always looking for men who don't scare too easy."

Several days after the capture of the three outlaws, John and Matthew rode down the main street of Crockett, tired but happy. They had returned home richer both in finances and experience. Indeed, John and Matthew had left home three months earlier as boys but returned as men.

Stopping at the hotel, they strode into the saloon, where they were happy to tell the townsfolk about their experiences. The fulfillment they felt in taking bad men down was evident—not prideful, but satisfying. These were good-hearted young men who had discovered that they might have places in life as lawmen. They felt a bond with Captain McNelly and knew they would definitely contact him again.

Matthew suddenly began to feel anxious to see his mother, and took his leave of John, who, in turn, ached to get back to his own family. They shook hands warmly, mounted up, and rode off in different directions.

As John rode up to the farmhouse, Jennie spotted him from the porch and yelled "Ma, Pa, come quick! John's home!" Lydia raced from the kitchen, and Mason followed, still struggling with his crutch but stronger than he'd been before John left. Lydia grabbed her son in a hug, then stood back and said,

"Oh John, how you've changed! You're no more m' bairn. I declare, you're taller than when you left, and there's something more about you."

Mason joined them, shook his son's hand, and then wrapped him with the free left arm that had grown stronger in the previous months. "What you see, Lydia, is that our son has grown into a man, a fine, strong man." Turning back to John he said, "It's good to have you home, Son. We've missed you sorely."

All chores were quickly put aside, Mark and Uncle Lucas brought in from the field, and an early supper prepared so that all could hear John report on his adventures.

Mason sighed as he acknowledged the feeling that had been growing inside him the past year. He had come to realize that his carefree boy had become a man, and he would have to deal with the loss of his son to the world.

Lydia now had more to pray about. Her boy would need all the protection he could get from real danger as well as the cunning and sinful ways of the world.

The latter wouldn't be a problem, John knew. He had left as a boy who had grown up being told about God, but he had returned home a man who had come to know God in a very personal way. Matthew would be there to remind him, and he would be there to stand back to back with Matthew.

CHAPTER 12

Mason continued to heal slowly. It became somewhat easier for him to walk with his crutch, but his arm and side were still partially paralyzed. His joy at improving, however, was still over-shadowed by his memories of the flashbacks that brought him nightmares.

As life returned to normal on the Caldwell farm, there was more going on in town than just the two troublemakers Jeb and Jesse. Inside the jail, a young man was leaning his back against the bars of a cell. His face had blood on it, mostly dried but some still trickled damply down his cheek. Luke was a man in his early twenties who appeared to be a loner. He stood silent as he leaned on the bars. The sheriff was questioning him, if you could call it that. It looked as though this interrogation had been going on for a while.

"I'll bet ya know how to talk, friend, but I don't see your mouth workin' or my ears hearin'. Your kind ain't welcomed in my town. You got somethin' to say, or shall we say not to say about that?"

In a quiet voice Luke finally answered, "Sheriff, seems to me you're gonna believe whatever you want anyway, so the truth about how I feel won't matter to you nohow."

Luke had no sooner gotten the words out when Sheriff Culpepper smacked him again. The sheriff, appearing satisfied with his treatment of Luke, grabbed him up and threw him out the door into the street so that Luke landed at the edge of the boardwalk, yelling after him, "Ya know I can't hold ya, so why don't you git into some trouble so I can. And believe me when you do, I'll get you good."

The sheriff headed back into his office, leaving Luke lying in the street. Luke pulled himself up slowly and reclined painfully against the wooden edge of the boardwalk as he heard a female voice saying, "Can I help you, mister?"

Luke looked around and warily smiled as he saw a very pretty girl next to him. She was in a wheelchair looking down at him. Lela continued, "I see you've met our good Sheriff Culpepper. He doesn't take much to strangers ..." she coyly interjected, "your kind in particular."

Luke answered, "I wonder if he takes much to people in general."

"Well that's a true statement," she replied. "Got the personality of a polecat or rattler, take your pick." After a pause she continued, "Are you a polecat or ...?"

He seemed young to her, but his face seemed old for his age. What she could not know at this first meeting was that he had been through much for a young man. He just gazed at her, unable to fully comprehend her beauty. The wheelchair hadn't registered in his mind yet. All he could see was the pale golden hair that encircled her face like a halo and small braids fastened at each side with combs to keep it out of her face. Oh, that face! The fairest skin he'd ever seen, with a faint rosy glow in her cheeks and thick lashes that framed her delicate violet eyes.

Not answering right away he searched for words that wouldn't seem idiotic. Finally up off the ground, he mounted his horse. After a pause, he answered rather abruptly, "Some say I'm jus' a polecat, some say a rattler, but I'm used to bein' misunderstood."

Lela, thinking he might have taken her words a bit personally, started to say something. Luke didn't let her get the words out and finished, "That's what a war will do to you I guess."

By now he was on his horse. He stopped short realizing he had said too much and started to ride off without looking back. As Luke reached the end of town, he stopped. Turning around he saw Lela rounding a corner toward a door on the side of a warehouse. Luke rode up next to her and said, "I ain't used to people askin' to help me. I hope I weren't rude."

Lela half-smiled knowing what it's like to be put off and replied, "Just forget it, your business is yours. Just wantin' to help. I'm sure you figured there wasn't much I could do sittin' in this wheeled contraption."

Now it was Luke who was at a loss for words. He looked down as he pondered what to say. She made it easier for him as she continued, "This here's my place. If you get yourself cleaned up, I'll feed ya. That's the least I can do."

Luke was at a loss for words, but something drew him to this generous and stunning young lady. Luke hitched his horse as Lela went to a ramp that led to the door. She wheeled herself up the ramp and into the room she called home. Luke followed her in and, finding the sink, started washing as Lela pumped the water handle. Still groping for words, Luke stumbled, "You must have a dickens of a time when it rains."

Lela looked down to her chair realizing Luke was trying to make conversation and breaking out in laughter replied, "You must be popular with the ladies with compliments like that."

Luke turned red as he quietly said, "Well gettin' to know me is a bit of a chore; ain't too good with words."

They exchanged smiles, and Lela said, "Sheriff Culpepper don't seem to care much for you."

With a determined voice, Luke answered, "Maybe 'cause I'm new in town or, like he says, he don't take to my kind." He paused before continuing with a sense of seriousness, then added, "But soon I'm gonna be long gone from here. Got to be finishin' up some business here first."

Lela with some sadness in her voice murmured, "Must be nice to up and go when one pleases."

Luke's tone changed to a gentler demeanor, and he responded, "Yeah, but settling down some day—if I ever can, will be nice too. Had enough goin'."

Lela inquired, "What's stopping you?"

Luke abruptly ended the conversation, "Thanks for the hospitality, but it's best I git; got to dodge the sheriff."

Lela wasn't about to let that go but added, "You can stay for a bite to eat if," she looked up to Luke trying to meet his eyes and continued, "you can spare the time."

Lela appeared somewhat lonely and pushed back a bit. Luke smiled and gently answered, "If'n I stay much longer, you may's well invite the sheriff. He don't want me here too long, and he'll be lookin' for me, I'll bet on that." Luke stiffened up a bit as the thought of the sheriff seemed to bother him.

Lela, however, had other motives and told Luke, "Tell you what, if you hook up the buckboard for me, I'll ride partway out of town with you. I'll rustle up some food for you. Don't want you to starve out there. Besides, I don't get a chance to leave here often."

The loneliness on Lela's face was now unmistakable. She also clearly appeared to find Luke interesting. Luke looked at her with wrinkled eyebrows and asked, "How can you handle a buckboard? Sorry, don't mean to sound rude."

Lela explained, "Oh, I can handle one okay. Mr. Teasley, the blacksmith, usually hooks it up for me, and I get around a bit. Tiama, my horse, is real gentle."

At this, Luke burst out laughing and told her, "Gentle? Do you know what that name means in my language?" Still laughing Luke told her, "Thunder!"

They both laughed as Luke continued, "Well, you bein' kind to me and all, I'll do it if you let me pay for the food."

Lela sternly answered, "You'll pay by hooking up the buckboard."

Luke responded lightheartedly, "Okay, okay. I'll get your horse."

They smiled at each other, and Luke left not suspecting what Lela was thinking. As soon as Luke left, she quickly gathered some personal belongings, some pictures, an old ring, and some old clothes. She dug into a box from under the bed and pulled out her life savings and put the money in her purse. Not much for sure, but she was intent on something. All these things she threw into a bag and, wheeling out to the porch, threw it into the back of the buckboard as Luke was fetching Tiama from the blacksmith's. Then she promptly started on the food.

CHAPTER 13

An hour or so passed with talk mainly about the good Sheriff Culpepper as the two headed down the road. With the wheelchair safely stowed in the back of the buckboard, Lela held the reins and drove with assurance as Luke rode next to her. Lela had to have help getting in and out of the buckboard, but Luke was up to the task. Lela was the first to speak about personal matters, "Do ya know where you're headed?"

Luke cautiously answered, "I'm goin' to California. An army friend wrote me awhile back tellin' of the cattle ranches he knows of where help is needed. First I got to settle my conscience. Got to get some things straight so's I can sleep nights."

Luke had opened a door, and Lela cautiously started to push the issue. "Is it something that happened in that awful war that's pushin' you?"

Luke didn't answer but stared straight ahead. After an awkward pause Lela quietly added, "Sounds real nice. Is it dry there? You know, much rain? I don't want to get this wheeled contraption stuck in the mud."

As they laughed it didn't sink into Luke's mind exactly what she was saying. They rode along a bit, and finally Luke sat up with a start. Lela reined in quickly, and Luke turning to Lela stupefied shouted, "What you talking about. Gettin' your wheeled contraption stuck …?" Luke didn't skip a beat and with a hard look asked, "You lookin' to be goin' to California? You ain't thinkin' about taggin' along? I don't know nothin' bout you, it's a long, hard road, ain't no roads at all sometimes. It's tough to make your way west."

Lela didn't answer but started to pull her wagon under a tree. Luke was quiet for a time as he lifted Lela from the wagon and set her in her chair. Luke struggled for words as he couldn't put her pretty face out of his mind, but he could keep her wheelchair in mind. What was she getting at that seemed to bounce around in his head? He finally blurted out, "I don't even know your name."

Lela answered matter-of-factly, "Well, yes I want to go to California, Yes, I'm thinkin' about taggin' along with you. You can get to know me, you can tow me in my wheeled contraption behind the wagon along roads, or no roads. Yes, I'm tough enough—and—my name is Lela, Lela Elliott. What's yours?"

Now standing beside her Luke could only answer, "Luke, my name is Luke Geddes, and I want to—hey, wait a minute …."

Lela didn't give Luke a chance to go on, and in a matter-of-fact tone continued, "Luke Geddes, well that's a simple enough name. I guess I'll call you Luke, and you can call me Miss Elliott, does that work for you?"

Luke was getting his feathers ruffled and answered, "No it don't. I'll be callin' you nothin' because you ain't goin' with me. You *can't* be goin' with me. You have a home here, friends and family I'd guess, and I don't even know ya."

Luke was clearly frustrated. Lela answered Luke with sadness in her voice, "No I don't have friends and family in this town. As a matter of fact the town doesn't know what to do with me so when a house or room is vacant like the one I live in now, the town moves me in. I do little jobs here and there. I sew, I tend stores when someone needs to run an errand, and they pay me what they can. I can do all that in California. But I want to find something real, what I can do on my own, not beholdin' to anyone. I'm mighty good at sewin' and stitchin'. I'll start my own place and .... Besides, my friends don't want to be tied to someone they have to cart around if they want you over, and my family ...."

Lela paused to take a deep breath and reaching for an answer slowly told Luke, "My ma and pa left me on the door step of a family named Coy. Last I heard, my ma and pa are back East somewhere. I guess they couldn't live with a cripple. Somethin' went wrong with my back just after I was born. I was just a baby when they left me behind."

Luke started to hear the pain in her voice as a feeling of his own loss of family started to settle in. Lela continued with her story, "The Coys were very good to me. Cared for me as if their own. The war came, and Mr. Coy, being from Missoura, left to join the infantry there. He was killed in the Battle of Salineville in '63. Mrs. Coy, Ma, was taken ill and was sent home back to Missoura."

Lela not holding back tears continued, "There wasn't a way for me to go because she was too ill to take me. Said she'd come back some day to git me. Don't know if anyone there knows about me. So I was left here and just passed from pillar to post, one family to another. Most people just feel sorry for me, and I'm really, really tired of it, tired of the people and their sympathy. I need to move on from this place."

Luke calmed down a bit and didn't say anything for a long time. The silence between them was only interrupted by the sounds of the wind and birds. Luke, now trying to be logical, asked, "What if somethin' bad happens to me? I ain't even sure I'd make it all the way to California. If'n I get you there and somethin' does happen to me, who will look after you?"

Lela didn't buy the fact that he wouldn't make it to California. She looked deeply into his eyes and asked, "What is this thing that has you so fired up about? You got to clear your conscience. You talk like someone who has danger followin' him around. Why don't you tell me about it?"

Luke started to open up, some. "It was durin' the war. I was a good shot so they put me up in a tree to hit the blue coats from afar. If'n I saw an officer, even better. I'd lay him down. It was at the battle of Chickamauga Creek. There was this Captain advancin' up the hill and …."

Luke stopped short. He turned his eyes from hers as he continued, "Why am I tellin' you 'bout this? It would only make you git in trouble if you know too much. Besides, it ain't your business anyhow. Let it be."

Lela didn't ask any more and let Luke have his space. He was glad of that, and it showed as he softened up and told her, "I've got to find this man I'm lookin' for. They say he's got a farm near here. You might know him from his travelin' to town for supplies and such. His name is Caldwell, Captain Mason Caldwell."

Lela answered, "Sure I know him, him and his family. They're good folk. But don't see that much of him lately. He was shot up pretty bad in the war."

Luke jumped up, almost yelling, and said, "Where is he, where's his farm? How do we git there?"

Lela reacting sat up and with a surprised tone answered, "Not sure where it is. I know it's south of town some place. You know, we could ask Sheriff Culpepper."

Lela let out a laugh, but Luke didn't think it was funny. He stated, "You couldn't get me to ask him the time of day.

As far as he's concerned, there ain't no time of day that I would be in his town."

Lela in a more serious tone asked Luke, "Why don't you tell me some about yourself? Maybe by the time we find your captain, you'll calm down a bit."

Luke reluctantly started his story. His voice was stern and conveyed his pride in who he was. "I come from North Georgia, born from a white father and a Cherokee mother. Not sure how they met up, not important to me. My pa, when he was a mite younger than I am now, had to stand by as Jackson wouldn't honor what the Supreme Court said concerning the Indians in Georgia. Jackson took much of our land back in 1814 when he was a general. My pa married an Indian woman, so my pa became an outcast to the white man. Then when Jackson became President in '28, things got worse. Jackson wouldn't enforce what treaties there were, and Pa and Ma were burned out, stole from, and some kin and good friends were killed. My pa and his pride made him stay beside his Indian brothers as they were herded like cattle to Oklahoma. Our trail there became known as the Trail of Tears. Thousands of Cherokees died on that trail. The U.S. soldiers took all their cattle and grain. Soon after that I came along. What the soldiers did was one big reason I fought for the South. I left my home, my pa and ma, and all to fight the Yankees."

Luke started to speak more softly as he remembered some bad memories. "My pa taught me to shoot. I could hit a squirrel from 400 yards. When I told my major this, he moved me to the front lines. Told me, find a tree, climb it, and git as many Yankees as I could, 'specially the officers. I did my job pretty good.

"I fought in the Second Battle of Manassas and the Battle of Antietam, where I almost got m'self kilt. Then they sent me to Georgia where I was in the Battle of Chickamauga, and finally they sent my company back up to Virginny for the Wilderness Battle and the Spotssylvania Court House. But it was in Chickamauga that I come across Captain Caldwell."

Luke looked at Lela wondering if she cared, but he continued, "I saw somethin' there that was not to my likin'. At the time I thought best I mind my own business, but lookin' back now I see I was wrong. I need to make it right."

Luke took a breath and said, "That's all there is, you don't need more than been told ya. Now let's git goin'. I need to get my business done and git to California."

Lela, not done cajoling Luke, told him, "Luke Geddes, you can git to know me on the road to California. See, I'm already gettin' to know you."

Luke shook his head in frustration and, picking her up, all but threw her on the seat of the buckboard and started out looking for the road to Caldwell's farm.

Chapter 14

Since their return a few weeks earlier, the boys had regularly spent time in a ravine next to a hill taking potshots at a row of old bottles and cans. John wasn't the only one honing his skills in self-defense. Matthew had also become a better shot as the riddled cans and shattered bottles testified.

The two of them spent many hours talking—of adventure, travel, and of course improving their combat skills. There was also much talk of Captain McNelly. Their experience in helping to capture the outlaws opened their eyes to the reality that bad people existed everywhere, and they realized their skills would need constant honing.

"Your aim has improved, Matthew. That gives me peace of mind when I'm a-thinkin' I need someone to back me up like in the situation we jes' got ourselves out of. You sure are gettin' the hang of it."

Meanwhile, Luke was driving the wagon with his horse tied behind as he and Lela drove up to the ravine where John and Matthew were now sparring. Pulling off to the side of the road at the top of the ravine, he and Lela watched from a distance. Once they realized it was not a real fight, Luke slowly drove down into the ravine and quietly asked, "Hope I ain't interruptin' but maybe you can help me."

John looked over to the wagon and recognized Lela. Turning to Luke he said, "You a friend of Lela? Maybe a relative?"

John yelled over to Lela, "Are you okay, Lela, do you need …." Trying not to sound anxious, John paused then looked at Luke and concluded, "…help?"

Lela started to laugh and answered, "Nothin' I can't handle. This here's Luke Geddes. He is taking me to California."

Luke spun around and, throwing his hands up in the air, stated, "Who said so? You sure are head strong and becoming a pain in the …."

Luke stopped short and turning to John said, "Can't believe this woman. If'n she were a man, she'd be a bully for sure."

Lela was laughing as she yelled back, "I'm sure I couldn't bully you, Luke Geddes."

Luke gave up the argument for now and, as Matthew and John approached the wagon, said to John, "I'm looking for a man named Caldwell, Captain Mason Caldwell."

With a curious look John inquired, "And what would you be needin' to see him about?"

Lela started, "Well you bein'...." when John interrupted, "Yeah. My bein' a friend of this Caldwell man, I would ask again, what would be your business with him?"

Luke replied, "It's a personal thing, and I've come a long way to get this done."

John asked, "You mean this Caldwell fella some harm maybe? He did you wrong some way, some time ago?"

"No, no, I don't mean him no harm. I've got somethin' private to tell him."

John still not satisfied said, "I know this Caldwell fellow, so how about Matthew here and me go with you to his place?"

"I don't know where his place is. If'n you be knowin' the way, we'll follow."

John was satisfied with the answer for the moment and, turning his back to Luke and facing Lela, winked at her. Then he put his finger to his lips to indicate that she not say anything and ordered, "Well, let's be on the way; should be there in just a few hours."

John and Matthew gathered their things and saddled up. Luke climbed back into the wagon, sensing the hostility in John but figuring it was the only way he could get to see Caldwell. As they moved along, Matthew and Lela were careful not to let on who John was. They were mostly silent as they were all anxious to see what Luke wanted to tell Mason.

John pulled out his guitar and sang a song he'd made up, explaining to the others that it helped him relax when he felt "a little tension." Meanwhile, Luke found himself wishing he had a few drinks rather than a song to relax him. John sang:

Across the river where a man can rest.
Across the river a land at its best.
This rest don't last for just a short time,
But where comfort and blessings will always be mine.

Across the river I'll go when time finds me gone,
Where peace is heard in the evening song.
What will await this lost tattered soul
In this place, where I won't grow old?

I won't find gold on the other side,
I won't find silver on the riverside.
What I'll find is a promise foretold
Of a man who came, who came from old.

This man walks the streets on the other side.
He carries the marks in his hands and his side.
Because my sins he took to his cross.
I'll be goin' to that land that is across.

Crossing o'er the river will happen one day.
If you read the Good Book, it will show the way.
No matter the fate you choose for yourself,
You will cross that river you'll need no help.

If you cross o'er the river, don't be afraid.
He's waitin' for you it may be this day.
If you trust in the Lord and that's what you do
There's a home a-waitin' for you.

They applauded John as he made a bow from his horse.

Soon thereafter, they arrived at the Caldwell home. Uncle Lucas came up to them as they rode in. As the Caldwells came out to the porch, they greeted Lela and the stranger with a smile. Luke had climbed down from the wagon. His feelings were written on his face as he looked intently at Mason, who did not recognize him. Luke, however, stood at attention as Mason looked at him quizzically. By this time, John had stepped between his father and Luke. Matthew backed away, so as not to intrude.

Left alone on the wagon, Lela finally said, "Anyone know I'm here? If'n I could get a hand down, sure would like to join you. Just slap me down in my chair."

Matthew leapt forward to assist Lela down. Luke hadn't budged but just stared at Mason, clearly not happy about the half-crippled man he saw before him. John broke the silence, "Pa?"

Luke looked at John, and it suddenly dawned on him why John had been so protective and had questioned him so harshly.

"This here is Luke Geddes. He said he knows ya, Pa. Told us on the way here he knows you from the army. Was with you somewhere. Wants to have words with you. I know we always oblige people's concerns, so I brought him here."

Luke looking intently at Mason began, "Captain Caldwell, sir, I would speak with you in private if'n you don't mind."

John stepped in to say, "I think I should ...." but Mason interrupted, "John, this boy doesn't mean me harm. I feel I have a kinship to him from the army."

Mason turned his gaze to Luke and asked, "Seen some action, Son?"

Luke, standing tall, replied, "Yes sir, I fought in the Second Battle of Manassas, the Battle of Antietam, and finally at the end of the war Battle of the Wilderness, you know, the Spotssylvania Court House, but it was the Battle at Chickamauga that I need to speak to you about. I was a sniper there, sir."

Mason looked at him in amazement and asked, "A sniper? Aren't you a little young for that kind of bloodshed?"

Luke replied with a steady but mature voice, "Sir, I'm part Indian, and I've seen bloodshed most my life."

Mason was taken back; with a fatherly look he put his hand on Luke's shoulder and looking at his family and friends said, "You all can go in the house. The boy and I will just sit out here and talk awhile."

Mason slowly made his way, with Luke's help, to a bench under a tree that allowed them both protection from the sun and comfort. Mason looked hard and long at Luke, wondering what this young man could tell him of the war.

As they proceeded to the bench, Mason started to recall the Battle of Chickamauga Creek. It was in the clear predawn of September 19, 1863, when the regular brigade filed onto the Kelly farm in northwest Georgia, thirteen miles south of Chattanooga in the valley of West Chickamauga Creek. The battlefield was bisected by La Fayette Road. This provided good north and south movement, which connected to the fords on the Chickamauga.

The commanding General of the Battle of Chickamauga Creek was General Braxton Bragg. It was said that his physical debilities and personal deficiencies as well as his tendency toward insubordination didn't sit well with his commanders. Also his army having been driven out of Kentucky and Tennessee hardly endeared him to the 71,000 soldiers under his command.

Mason remembered the terrain as being densely wooded from Missionary Ridge all the way to Chickamauga Creek. Major General George Thomas described it in his official report as "original forest timber, interspersed with undergrowth and in many places so dense it was difficult to see fifty paces ahead ...."[3] No wonder Luke was called as a sniper. He could get at least somewhat above the trees.

Luke started to fidget a bit, and Mason not wanting him to be uncomfortable, said, "You come a long way, Luke? You passin' through?"

"Yes, sir, it seems a long way. I'm on my way to California, but I needed to have a word with you. I found out that you lived in these here parts from the hospital records."

With a light laugh Mason said, "Well, you went through a lot of trouble to find me, must be important whatever you got to say."

"What I got to say comes hard in my throat, sir. Please let me explain best I can in my own time. I don't want to leave nothin' out, and I don't want to overstate. What I got to tell you is best for me too. It's been a-worryin' on my heart for a long time, and 'fore I leave these parts, I just had to tell you."

By now Mason was really curious, but he held back, giving Luke his space so as not to press him. With a smile said, "Well Luke, take your time if need be, I've got no place to go, and if I did, with this leg it would take me forever to get there."

Luke didn't laugh or even smile at this but looked at Mason's leg with sadness evident in on his face and in his eyes. Then he said boldly, "Your leg is why I'm here, sir." Mason's look became serious as a searing memory flooded back to him.

Mason turned back to his own men as they moved forward in the underbrush. Just then he felt searing pain as a bullet tore into his back.

"What is it, Son? Is there something I need to know about what happened to me?"

With this question, Luke stood up and started to pace. Mason called after him and somewhat frustrated raised his voice, "Boy, don't walk away. If you know something, say it now. You aren't changing your mind now. I've had this mystery rolling around in my head for a long time about what happened to me. I need some peace, even if it hurts at first."

Luke stopped and turning to Mason said, "I ain't walkin' away, sir. I've thought this over in my head so many times. I just hafta find the words. I saw something I shouldn't have, but I kept my mouth shut. I am no better than the man who shot you."

Mason struggled to his feet. Visibly shaken, he quietly asked, "You know who shot me, Luke?"

Luke hanging his head answered, "Yes, sir, I do. Please forgive me for not sayin' somethin' when it happened."

Mason with mixed emotions replied, "Why didn't you come forward before? What stopped you from being an honest upright man and doing the right thing?"

Trying to get his composure back, Luke started to answer, "You got all rights to be mad, sir. I ain't got no excuse, but now I got to make it right. Here's the truth, sir. We were advancin' on General Rosecrans' position from the other side of Chickamauga Creek, in the vicinity of Crawfish Springs. Our commander, General Polk, as you might recall, got us crossed to the west side of the creek toward Missionary Ridge. When you called your men forward, my company came in behind you as you advanced.

"What you don't know, Captain, is that a Reb by name of Corporal Sam Pike and I were in the same company, but it wasn't your company. Ours was from the Department of East Tennessee under Major General Simon Buckner. We were merged into Bragg's Department of East Tennessee, givin' no notice to any of the field commanders such as yourself. You see, Captain, I was in the headquarters area fillin' my bags with ammo when I heard the generals talkin' about this merger. They acted fast, sir, and there just wasn't time to git the information to you before your company attacked.

"You called your men forward. My company was comin' in behind you as you advanced. My orders was to get up to the tree line and climb the limbs so as to do my job. When

I got up into the tree, what I saw was Corporal Pike comin' up through our ranks pretty fast. Then he stopped as he got up to your men. There was a lot of yellin', shootin', and commotion comin' from your company.

"Pike raised his rifle and shot you. When he turned, he somehow saw me lookin' down on him. I know the only reason he didn't shoot me was because there was a lot of men around. He yelled to me to climb down. When I did, he said it was an accident and for me to keep my mouth shut. He said the war will be over soon and no one's gonna care anyhow. I knowed it wasn't an accident because of where his rifle was aimed. There were no Yankees beyond you; they were still on the other side of the ridge. He also told me he would find me when the time came if'n I didn't keep quiet. I believed him, sir, because he rode with Cantrell and with Bloody Bill Anderson."

Luke paused to catch his breath. During the previous rambling he had begun speaking faster and faster. After calming down a bit, he continued, "Pike was as bloody as Anderson. He told me things when we were in camp—stories about his time with Cantrell and Anderson—that still git me sick inside. Even with the blood I've seen, he is someone I don't want to deal with. My fear is what was keepin' me away so long, sir, but my conscience burns within me. It has overcome my fear."

Mason stared at Luke with disbelief written all over his face, his body frozen. He could not move or talk. Luke was not sure what his next move should be. Looking to the house, he saw that everyone had respected Mason's request that they wait inside—although John had been peering out of the window during this dialogue between his pa and Luke.

Luke took a deep breath to muster his courage and addressed Mason with a mature voice, "If'n it'd make you feel better, sir, I'll wait for you to go get your rifle, and you can shoot me. I was a coward once but not no more. I deserve what you give me. In the army, I would be shot or hanged anyhow."

Mason slowly sat back down and told Luke, "I don't know how I feel right now, Boy. It took a while for you own up to what you did and come forward. But to forgive you may not be important. Even if I'd known who shot me before, it still wouldn't heal my body. Maybe now my mind and soul can start to heal."

No words passed between them, but Mason was visibly distressed. Finally after digesting Luke's discourse, Mason added, "I was sure I hadn't seen you before. At least now I know why. Even if I had known about the merger, I suppose it would've made no difference about knowing this Pike either."

A lot of emotion was running through Mason, and Luke had no words for him anyway. Finally Mason looked at Luke and asked, "Where do we find this Corporal Pike these days?"

Luke answered honestly, "Sir, I ain't seen him since the battle. I don't know who he might be hooked up with now, and I'm thinkin' it's best I don't find out."

When Mason next looked at Luke, his eyes held new respect for this young man. He had to admit it took a lot of guts and real manhood to come forward now. Mason stood up and yelled toward the house, "Lydia!"

As Lydia and John raced out to the porch, Mason continued, "Have we enough food to feed our guests?"

Looking at Luke his face displayed very little emotion as Mason continued, "We want to make them feel welcome."

Luke wasn't sure just how to react. He had no way to know if Mason would forgive him or not. He couldn't read Mason's expressionless face and just stood there with the weight of the world taken off his shoulders even though he didn't know if he was out of the woods or not.

CHAPTER 15

As the family and their guests sat around the table that evening, enjoying the food prepared by Lydia and Jennie, Luke was mostly silent as he was still not sure where he stood. He ate slowly, feeling very much out of place. No mention of the conversation between Mason and Luke took place at the dinner table. John had come to realize that Luke was not there to harm his pa in any way and started to make small talk with him. "How'd you meet Lela? You have a mutual acquaintance?"

Luke dryly replied, "If'n you call Sheriff Culpepper a mutual acquaintance."

Lela with a slight laugh added, "Yep, the sheriff was kind enough to throw Luke right down in front of me."

Mason joined in, "Nate Culpepper, huh. Not a friend of this family, I ...." Mason's voice trailed off.

Luke added, "Y'know, he acted as if he wanted me out of town because he had it in for me. I never knew him before. Maybe he knows someone who knows me. Maybe bad news travels faster than Lela's gentle horse."

No one got the joke; Luke and Lela smiled at each other. A thought occurred to Mason, "Maybe he has something to do with our conversation."

Again, no one asked about the conversation. Mason added, "I know the sheriff had some relatives in the war. I believe he said it was a cousin."

Luke stated, "It was a big war with many men, sir. Be a needle in a haystack in findin' out who it might be."

Mason wryly told Luke, "Yeah, but it would be something worth finding out."

Luke replied, "If'n I could get close to the sheriff, maybe I could poke around a mite. But the closest I could git to him would be his fist or the butt of his gun."

Mason felt bad for Luke as he realized he had begun to develop a fondness for the young man. Mason had endured much pain over the years, and forgiveness came hard even though he knew it was the Lord's will to forgive. As dinner concluded and the women set about cleaning up, the men retired to the porch to enjoy the evening quiet.

Luke rose to go, saying, "I guess we'd best be on our way, don't want to overstay our welco...."

Mason firmly interrupted, "No, you stay awhile. You can stay in the bunkhouse."

Luke got the hint, Mason wasn't done with him yet.

At this everyone retired. Lela shared Jennie's room, and Luke headed to the bunkhouse.

Morning came with signs of rain and a chill in the air. Mason was relieved to see that Luke hadn't taken off during the night. At the breakfast table Mason told him, "We'll be going to town today; maybe you should join us. Lela can stay with the womenfolk, and they can talk woman talk."

Luke was feeling relieved that Mason had decided not to shoot or hang him, but he also realized that Mason wasn't about to let him go quickly. "I can git my supplies for my trip to California. Thanks for the offer. I'll help hook up the horses to the wagon."

Luke with humorous tone continued, "Hope the sheriff's gone fishin'; don't want to run across him nohow."

Looking at Lela with a smirk on his face he added, "If'n it rains, don't be gettin' your wheeled contraption stuck in the mud."

Everyone got a laugh out of this, but Lela and Luke just smiled at the joke. As they started out, Mason half-smiled at Luke, the tension between them subsiding. Mark, Luke, and John headed toward the barn to hitch up the wagon. Uncle Lucas elected to stay back and handle the chores. Besides, he wasn't a slacker, and now that he truly felt part of the family, he took it to be his duty.

Lydia finally broke her silence. "Mason, what is it Luke was so fired up to talk to you about?"

Mason looking into her tender eyes told her, "Nothin' to worry your pretty little head about. Just war stuff, stuff a tender heart like yours needs not to hear."

"If it has to do with you, it's important to me. I want to share what your heart tells you. I love you Mason Caldwell."

"I'm blessed indeed. You will find out in due time, when I can share it all with you."

Lydia knew her husband well enough not to press it further.

The men left, and there was little conversation among them. John was in no mood to sing or say much. He knew better than to ask in front of everyone what was going on between his pa and Luke. He only knew that Luke wouldn't be hurting his pa. As they arrived in town, they pulled up to the general store and everyone except Mason got down from the wagon and went inside.

Sheriff Culpepper approached Mason asking rather coldly, "You doin' business here in town?"

Mason half-ignoring him answered tersely, "Yup."

Culpepper with a smirk on his face and a nasty tone asked, "How you feelin', Captain? You're a lookin' a little under; the cold weather gittin' to ya?"

Not getting ruffled, Mason looked at Culpepper and stated politely, "Cold and rain always put you under a bit."

"Cold and rain is in every man's life now isn't it, Captain?"

Mason, still trying to be congenial responded, "Yeah, Sheriff, I guess forgiveness is hard for everyone. You—me ...."

The acute tension between them clearly signaled animosity of long-standing, a sign that something grievous had taken place between them in the distant past.

Just then Luke stepped out onto the porch of the store. He froze for a moment as the sheriff looked at him almost shouting, "You pushin' me, Boy? Thought I told you to move on. You ain't welcome here. I guess you want to see the back of my hand again or a little time in my jail to let you know I mean what I say."

As Culpepper reached for Luke, Mason now with boldness in his voice said, "Sheriff, you best not be touching my new house guest. You've got nothing to hold him on; there's no need making something up. Whatever you come up with, he was with my family and me. No judge can go against our witness."

Culpepper was at best frustrated. He glared at Mason with hate clearly visible on his face and in his eyes. With the supplies loaded and Mark back from the bank, they started for home. Mason was uneasy about the encounter with Culpepper, wondering why he wanted to push it with Luke.

CHAPTER 16

They arrived back at the house just in time to unload the supplies before the rain started to fall. Mason related the story of his encounter with the sheriff and decided it was time to tell of his relationship with the sheriff. The family as well as Luke and Lela were all present during this recitation.

Giving his attention to Lydia, Mason said, "The sheriff sure has a lot of hate for me, no forgiveness in his heart, Lydia. Do you remember the time we were in town and there was a robbery at the bank? We happened to be in the crossfire of the shooting because someone behind us was shooting toward the bank. Remember what happened?"

Lydia looked around the room at everyone and, bringing her attention back to Mason, quietly responded, "Mason, we need not talk of it here and now. We don't want to tell of such things to our children. And also we have guests, and besides I don't want to speak of the killing and all. I ...."

Mason, trying to appreciate her tender soul interrupted, "Sorry. It seems I may not be thinking, but I feel it's time that everyone should know. Even the strangers here will find out someday I'm sure, but the important thing is, I want it to be me telling it to my children first. They need to hear all the truth." He then started to tell of the tragedy that happened that day so long ago.

"As we arrived at the hitching post in front of the general store, I got out of the wagon to tie up the team. As I did, I heard gunshots coming from the direction of the bank. When I looked in that direction, I saw two men running out the door. It was plain to see they were robbing the bank because they were toting money bags and wearing bandanas across their faces.

"Then there were gunshots behind us as someone was shooting toward the bank putting us in the crossfire. I was mighty concerned, mostly for you, so I pulled my rifle from the wagon as they started down the steps into the street and started shooting at the robbers. As I took aim, a man came running from around the water trough, and just as I shot my rifle, one of the robbers grabbed him and pulled him in front of him. My bullet struck and killed the man. I just didn't react in time.

"Eventually the robbers were caught, and they were blamed for the man's death, but I have to live with killing an innocent man. Trouble is, I come to find out later that the man I killed was Patrick Culpepper, the brother of our sheriff. Culpepper isn't going to forgive me for sure."

No one spoke a word. Blank looks masked their faces, but it was now clear what had caused the animosity between Mason and Nate Culpepper. Mark was the first to speak up, "Pa, you never spoke of this before. We coulda been there for ya if you'd told us."

Mason in a calm voice answered, "It would have done no good for you to know. You were just young-uns when this happened. I talk of it now only because I have an uneasy feeling about the sheriff. I don't expect he'd do anything anymore, but for some reason I just got this bad feeling inside."

John spoke up, "I sure would like to know if'n he had anything to do with who shot you." Mason and Luke looked at each other with total surprise.

Luke said, "Didn't say nothin', sir."

Mason answered, "Me neither, Son."

Now it was too late; there was no choice but to let everyone know what Luke's business was with Mason. So Mason gathered them around the table and related the story Luke had brought to Mason, including who did it. The family was in total disbelief. Because everyone wanted a resolution immediately, questions were asked that couldn't be answered—such as if the bank robbery incident could be related to a man no one knew but Luke, who in turn had shot Mason during the war. The men were ready to go get

Pike, especially John who was up and pacing the floor with a determined look on his face and in his eyes.

The problem was, no one knew where to find him. Mark looked at John and said, "Well, you brought it up, Little Brother. Maybe the sheriff knows somethin' about Pa. It's a long shot but, us just sittin' here doin' nothin' ain't sittin' well with me."

John was just as anxious as Mark to get to the bottom of this. John had never had a great liking for Culpepper and even less so after he refused to defend Matthew.

CHAPTER 17

Something new was brewing with Culpepper as the Bolin brothers sat in his office. It seemed the two troublemakers had something in common with the good sheriff. They were the sheriff's henchmen. It was no wonder they were never in trouble for being in trouble.

The sheriff told Jeb and Jesse, "Got a letter from my cousin this mornin'. He's headin' to Dallas, about 160 miles away. I've been writin' letters but just keep missin' him. Says he's been movin' around a lot since the war. Also said he found out we have some unfinished business. Someone told him there's someone in these parts that has survived the war. Someone he don't like so he wants to tie up some loose ends."

Jeb and Jesse looked at each other confused—not an uncommon condition for them.

Culpepper continued, "I want you two to ride to Dallas and find my cousin. Bring him here so's he can git done what he needs to git done. He's gonna be stayin' at the St. Nicholas Hotel. It's owned by a lady by name of Sarah Cockrell."

Culpepper sternly warned them, "You keep your mouths shut 'bout where you're a goin' and why. No one is to know that my cousin is around. If'n you screw up, you'll answer to me. Got it?"

The Bolin brothers had done dirty work for Culpepper before and knew he meant what he said. Jeb spoke up, "Yup, Sheriff, we know what you mean. You can count on us for sure. What is your cousin's name, Sheriff, so's we know who to ask for?"

The sheriff abruptly answered, "Pike. His name is Sam Pike. I'm gonna give you this letter to give to him. Don't read it or let it out of your sight. If'n I find out you know what's in this letter, you can count on not findin' a place to rest before I find ya. First thing you do when you see him is to tell him, 'This is from Sheriff Culpepper.' It has instructions in it for him to come here with you. That's all you need to know. If'n you don't lag, you can get there and back in eight to ten days, twelve at the outside. I'll be waitin' right here."

Jesse, being the older, snatched the letter from the sheriff's hand, shoved it into his vest, and the two Bolin brothers saddled up to leave town, ready to do the sheriff's bidding. Culpepper, however, in his haste to get them on their way forgot to seal the envelope.

After three days on the road to Dallas, Jesse couldn't contain himself any longer. Looking at Jeb he pulled the letter out of his vest and remarked, "The sheriff forgot to seal up this letter. Let's take a look see. Ain't gonna hurt to see what Culpepper is fired up about."

Jeb replied, "Then again it could hurt a lot if'n we find out what's in that letter. It ain't none of our business, and I ain't tanglin' with the sheriff. You best keep that letter out of your head."

After four days, they reached the hotel and, finding Sam Pike registered there, sat in the lobby to wait for him. When he strode in, the desk clerk pointed him out to the Bolins, who approached him with caution. Knowing the sheriff, they didn't expect Pike to be all that friendly toward them. He was clean looking, but the scars and ravages of war had given him a sinister appearance. His leather vest, army hat, gray pants and a gray shirt left no doubt he had fought for the South, and he could care less who knew it.

Jeb greeted him nervously. "Ah, Mr. Pike?"

Pike looked hard at him before answering.

"Maybe – maybe not. Depends who wants to know."

Jesse quietly answered, "We got a letter for you from Sheriff Culpepper, an' he wanted it delivered direct to you, sir."

Pike leaned into Jesse and sneered, "Do I look like an army officer to you?"

Now unnerved, Jesse answered, "No sir, I mean Mr. Pike."

Still in Jesse's face, Pike continued, "Then don't call me 'sir'. I earned my stripes. Didn't have to go to school or be a big rich man to get my rank."

Jesse and Jeb backed off as they answered together, "We sure understand, Mr. Pike."

Pike calmed down some and taking the letter started for his room. Jeb and Jesse followed. When they got to the room, Pike opened the letter and, assuming that Jeb and Jesse knew the contents and circumstances, started to read out loud.

Sam,

I bin tryin to git ahold of you to let you know that Caldwell is still alive. I see in your letter to me you knowed that already from askin at the hospital. What I want to tell you is he is here in Crockett, and you bein my kin and all, I know you want to finish what needs to be done. Remember my brother Patrick was your kin too, us 3 bein cuzzins. You need to come here soon as you can. I'll be waitin for you.

Nate

With that, Jesse looked over to Jeb and, signaling with a nod of his head for Jeb to follow, started to leave the room. They had heard enough, and Culpepper's warning resounded loud and clear. "It ain't none of your business."

"Y'all goin' some place?"

Apologetically, Jeb answered Pike, "Well, we just want to belly up to the bar and then get back to our camp. We got no money to stay in this place, and I know the sheriff wants us to leave early in the mornin' to get back."

Pike sternly ordered them, "Meet me here at nine in the mornin'. I want my hot breakfast a-fore we head to Crockett."

The boys all but tripped over each other as they headed out the door and to the bar. With relief covering both their faces, no words were spoken. They had already heard more than they wanted to know.

CHAPTER 18

Luke and Lela had found a home at the Caldwells' for the time being. Luke slept in the bunkhouse, and Uncle Lucas had moved back there also to allow Lela to stay in the room built for him. Luke was still there as they were waiting to find a way to resolve the issue with Pike and Mason.

Matthew's mother, Catherine, had grown close to Lydia and became a frequent visitor to the farm. It seemed that every time Catherine came over, a spark appeared in Lucas' eye. With the passage of time, he had begun to heal from the loss of his beloved Anna. It was apparent to most, and especially to Catherine, that he had, one might say, a weak spot for her.

One day while the family was inside, Lucas sat outside on a bench under the jasmine-covered arbor making conversation with Catherine, wanting to know her better.

Casually he said, "As for me, Mrs. Lo,..."

She interrupted, "I've been here enough times that Catherine would be just fine."

Lucas answered with a little blush, "And the family calls me Uncle Lucas. I'd be pleased if you called me Lucas."

With that out of the way Lucas continued, "You say you have family here. Yet you say you ain't from these parts."

Catherine explained, "No. My sister came here almost ten years ago. This was after I went to China. We came originally from Illinois. My late father worked for a newspaper there called the *Prairie Farmer.* It was started in 1841 and helped a lot of immigrants that came to farm there. I didn't much care for farming but got some respect for this beautiful earth that God gave us."

Lucas had edged a bit closer to Catherine, and she hadn't moved away. *A good sign,* thought Lucas as she continued.

"We had this preacher come to our church service one Sunday, and he talked of a people across the big Pacific Ocean. It took my heart like a storm. I knew I had to go, but I had to be very careful how I let my family in on it. One day I said, 'I want to do some traveling.' My father asked, 'Goin' to New York?' I told him 'Not quite, Daddy.' I told him about going to China when I became of age. Well, it took the better part of a year before I got their blessings. He wanted me to make sure this just wasn't a romantic whim of some sort. Away I went, met my husband at a revival, and well you know the rest."

Lucas was even more taken by this woman. He wanted to know more about her and asked, "What of your husband, we knowed he died."

Her answer came with a deep sigh that signaled a heavy heart. "I arrived at the town of Ningbo in 1843, a seaport city in the northeast of Zhejiang province. Ningbo was one of the five Chinese treaty ports opened by the treaty in 1842. This was during the Qing dynasty. I met my husband, Kim-Kwong Lo, at a revival meeting. We knew our hearts were bonded by the Lord and soon married. Matthew came along not long after that. Then we set out to serve the people of China and bring them to Christ, and moved to a small village just outside of Ningbo.

"There, we built schools and hospitals, as well as our churches. Kim even helped to start a publishing house. In February 1858, the Church of England Missionary Society arrived at Ningbo and helped Kim with his mission work. They also helped with the publishing house, but our town leader took offense. Although Buddhism was not near as big a force as it was nine hundred years ago, Liu, the town leader, held to Buddhism very strongly because it was the religion of his ancestors. Liu had my husband Kim put in jail and falsely accused him of many things. Liu was the law in our village, and Kim was taken from the jail and killed by Liu and his comrades. I ...."

She stopped short, no longer able to hold back the tears. Unable to speak, she just hung her head as the memories came flooding back. Looking back at Lucas, she added, "I tried to keep our mission going for a few years, but when it became too much without Kim, I decided to come back home."

Putting his arm around her, Lucas said gently, "I'm very sorry, Catherine. Didn't mean to bring up bad memories. Please forgive ...."

She interrupted, "It's okay, Lucas. He is with the Lord, and we will all meet again in glory. Just as you and your beloved Anna will one day."

They smiled at each other as he finished, "Well, I sure am glad you're here now; everything is gonna be just fine." The affection Lucas and Catherine had developed for one another was evident as they looked into each other's eyes.

Meanwhile, another conversation was taking place inside the house. Mason and the other men sat at the kitchen table talking. Lela sat some distance away in her chair sewing. What was it that drove Pike to shoot Mason? That was the question for which everyone needed an answer.

John asked, "Who is this Pike, and what is his reason for shootin' Pa? Where did he come from? I know one day he and I will cross paths. I'm not gonna ask questions, I'll just take care of what needs to be done."

Mason stopped him, "Then I lose a son to an anger that sends him to prison and to be hanged for the death of a man who is worth nothing. No, Son, this will have to be justified by the laws that we fought for."

Matthew, who had learned the tragic story from John, quietly added, "John, we will find out what this about. We need to be in the law, not above it."

By now, signs of fatigue and stress were showing on their faces due to the mental anguish of trying to figure this all out. Matthew continued, "If by chance Culpepper and Pike are in cahoots, we need to find out. I can only wonder if that is true though it doesn't seem likely. Like Luke said before, figuring out if Pike and Culpepper know each other would be like finding the needle in the haystack. But true or not, either way we need to know so we can plan our next move. Question is, how do we find out?"

Mark chimed in, "Well, first we hafta find someone who knows both Pike and the sheriff, or we have to see them together. And if'n we do catch them together, we hafta see if'n it's just a case of a stranger meetin' the sheriff."

With Mason's lack of trust in Culpepper came a thought. "Those two varmints that hang with the sheriff, the Bolin brothers, they may know something."

Luke added, "Well, first we have to find out where Pike is. I have a thought. Maybe the army knows. I'll get a letter off to my friend in the discharge office."

Mason looked at Luke warmly and said, "It might be, Luke, you can get redemption for your silence."

Luke looked at Mason with understanding and answered, "Yes, sir, I'll face him if need be, sir, I owe it to you and your family." He paused and quietly added, "I owe it to myself. It's time to quit living in guilt."

Luke looked over at Lela, who had been silent, and added, "Ain't goin' to California with this burdenin' my heart."

Lela looked at him hoping to see more than he was letting on. Luke with a grin finished, "I guess me and the sheriff might cross paths, and that I'm not lookin' forward to nohow."

Everyone laughed along with Luke, and the tension was relieved for the moment.

Mark, who had been quiet for several minutes, told everyone about a plan he had hatched, "What we'll do tomorrow is, when you post your letter, Luke, we'll git those two brothers here to the ranch. I have an idea that more than likely will git them here. And Luke, you must avoid the sheriff. So I'll post the letter to your friend at the discharge office for you, then meet you at the livery stable."

"Stayin' away from Culpeper is what I do best, and for sure I'll be doin' my best." Luke replied.

Mark and Luke just nodded at each other. They knew that Jeb and Jesse had some kind of relationship with the sheriff. If they could get any information from them, they might find out if Culpepper was connected to Mason's shooting. Mark knew that, when dealing with greedy men in need of money, playing to those lustful desires made a plan more likely to succeed.

They had to get Jesse and Jeb to the house. Mark knew how to do it, but it was important that John and Matthew not be around lest the Bolin brothers suspect another takedown like the previous one.

Mark told John, "Well, Brother, how would you like to help out around Matthew's house? I ain't havin' you two around when the Bolins show up."

John with a smile answered, "Anything to git them varmints here."

With that, John went to fetch Uncle Lucas so they could let him in on the plan. The Bolin brothers did not know Luke, so the trick was to first get the three of them together where the sheriff wouldn't see them.

As daylight broke, Luke and Mark left to execute the plan. Arriving in town, they rode directly to livery stable. Conveniently, the livery stable was very near the dilapidated shack the Bolin brothers called home. Their usual carousing the night before insured that Mark and Luke arrived before the Bolins were up to face another day of laziness. This wasn't difficult considering these two rarely arose before noon.

Mark posted Luke's letter, and then he and Luke patiently waited for the Bolins to come out to the water pump. Finally, as Jesse and Jeb came out, Mark started his conversation with Luke, "Well, good to meet you, Mr. Geddes, We'll be seein' ya at the farm later this afternoon. Glad to have you join us. The pay is extra good as we got a lot of fixin' to do before we can bring in the new steers next week."

"Thanks much, Mr. Caldwell. Sure can use the money for my move to California."

Looking on, Jeb and Jesse overheard all this. Mark looked at the brothers and asked, "I seen you fellas in town from time to time. You all keepin' good jobs here 'bouts?"

Jesse answered first, "We keep busy."

Jesse looked at Jeb, and they both laughed. Mark decided to get to the point. "If'n you fellas are lookin' for some good money, I'm a-lookin' for some good hands to do some work for a couple of weeks. Pay is real good. A dollar a day, room and board, and if'n the work gets done quicker than grease in the summer sun, there's an extra ten dollars. I got to git this work done mighty fast so as not to lose the steers I'm bringin' in."

Jeb and Jesse looked at each other and walked off mumbling to one another. Mark looked at Luke thinking he hadn't gotten through to them. Jeb, however, spoke up, "You sure it won't be more than a couple of weeks?"

Jesse added, "Ya see, we got promises to keep with …."

Jeb quickly interrupted, "We just don't want to make this a drawn out time. We got other interests and need to move on."

"I can appreciate your time must be valuable to someone, and I don't want to be interferin' so I'll keep my promise. No more than a couple of weeks at most."

As they shook hands, Mark gave them directions to the ranch with instructions to be there first thing the next morning. Luke and Mark knew they would tell Culpepper, and that worried them. What if the sheriff told them not to go? All they could do was return to the ranch and wait it out.

Of course, Jeb and Jesse did go to the sheriff and related the news to him. Jesse told Culpepper, "Anyway, Sheriff, we need the extra money, and it can't hurt nothin'. If'n ya need us, we can help you when we come back at night. We have room and board, but one of us can come check with you to see if'n you need us back here."

Culpepper didn't much care as a rule what these two did, but the Caldwells? *Why the Caldwells?* he wondered. Feeling uneasy, he started asking a few questions. "Has anybody else been asked that you know of?"

Jeb answered, "Well, there was this stranger watering his horse at the livery stable. He's gonna go work for Caldwell. They went their separate ways, and we went back into the cabin, so we don't know if'n anyone else was asked."

Culpepper asked, "What does this stranger look like?"

Jeb answered, "Well, Sheriff, he wasn't much taller than Jesse here, had a full brimmed hat and a clean face. That's all I remember."

Jesse added, "You know, I noticed his boots, they were dusty but gray. Seemed strange that they were not boot black or brown like all ours. Also his shirt had a small tear in it. Like someone grabbed him or somethin'."

Culpepper asked, "Was his hair long and black with two braids?"

Jeb answered, "Yup, it's as you say, Sheriff. I remember that now. He pulled his hat back to wipe water on his head."

Culpepper turned and slowly walked toward the wall. He wondered why Luke would be working for the Caldwells. Maybe it was just a coincidence, but Culpepper wasn't one to trust anything or anyone at any time. He just didn't have a good feeling about this.

Jeb and Jesse looked at each other, and Jesse asked, "You know this fella, Sheriff?"

Culpepper in a thoughtful voice answered, "Yeah, I know this fella, but what I don't know is what he's up to. Boys, I got somethin' I need for you to do."

With that Culpepper explained his plan. "Do what is expected of you at the ranch, but ask around if'n this stranger or anyone else workin' there was in the army. If'n they were, find out where they done their service. I know ol' man Caldwell was in the army, but find out especially if'n this stranger was servin'. Then you get back to me and let me know what you find out. I 'specially want to know about this stranger. Git his name and, if'n he was in the army, where he may have done battle and find out what side he fought on."

And so the battle of wits started. The Bolin brothers started off to the ranch at sunrise, although it wasn't easy for them to watch the sun rising before them.

CHAPTER 19

The days passed long and hot. Rain would have been welcome, but it didn't look as if the few clouds there were would comply. Jeb and Jesse found working for a living a bit much and tried to find ways to slack off. Uncle Lucas didn't give them much to do knowing they were being used because he didn't want them to walk off the job before the necessary information had been obtained. Meanwhile, everyone seemed to be hanging in—for now.

One evening after the Bolin brothers had labored in the back forty with Luke and Mark for most of the day and were now taking supper in the bunkhouse, Mason, Mark, Lela, and Luke sat on the porch talking about California and adventures west of Texas.

"Well, I'm a farmer and a rancher," said Mark. "I am a man of the earth, and I feel like my pa does about havin' land you call your own. No man can take it, no man can tell you what to do. Farmin' and livestock; ain't nothin' wrong with that."

Luke looking at Lela said, "I'm hopin' California will make me feel like that someday. Can only find out by tryin'. But I'm needin' to get rid of the travelin' itch and head for California."

Lela chimed in, "I'm itchin' with the travelin' itch too. We can itch together."

This brought a laugh from everyone except Luke who just shook his head. This time, however, there was a hint of smile and maybe a glint in his eyes. Just then, they heard the rattle of a buckboard and looked up to see it coming down the road to the house. Mark got up to greet Uncle Lucas and Catherine, who had been in town shopping.

Uncle Lucas seemed anxious to talk to Mason. Sitting down on the porch and dividing his attention between Mason and Luke, he reported, "There's a stranger in town. He hangs with the sheriff more than just a mite. They seem pretty close. The thing is, he looks mean and ornery. I inquired with my friend Josiah at the barbershop while Catherine was at the general store. He said this stranger is a cousin to Sheriff Culpepper."

Luke prodded, "Can you describe this man to us, Mr. Neiter?"

"Sure 'nough, tall man, maybe over six feet, wears a leather vest, army hat, Confederate soldier for sure, gray pants and a gray shirt …."

Luke continued to prod, "Did he have long hair with grayin' sides, and did you notice on his vest if'n he had a lot of fringe and a big silver button tied with rawhide on each of his pockets?"

"Yeah, Luke, all what you said is true."

Luke stood up and, looking down at Mason said with agitation, "Pike! He's here, Captain."

Luke started to pace and rubbed his head as he added, "Why come to Crockett? Does he know I'm here? Is he still wantin' you? I'll bet for sure this ain't no coincidence. Do ya think your friend Josiah is right sayin' he's the cousin of Culpepper, the cousin who was in the army?"

Mason stared off into space.

Mason's memory traveled back to that day in the Chickamauga underbrush. This time, just before he was shot, he was certain he saw a flash coming from the man who shot him. Could it have been the sun reflecting off a silver button on the man's vest?

Snapping back to the present, Mason looked at Luke. "Don't know who he's after Luke. I do know we had better be ready for what I 'spect might be comin' next."

About this time, John and Matthew appeared, having worked at Matthew's cabin for the day, and a few moments later, Lydia called to say that dinner was on the table.

"Catherine, will you and Matthew stay and have a bite before Matthew takes you home?" They nodded. Over chicken and dumplings, Mason related to John and the rest of the family what Uncle Lucas had told them. Now something would have to be done for sure. Mason, Luke, and everyone else had had as much worry and concern as they could take. It looked as if the day of reckoning would come at last.

CHAPTER 20

The next day a stranger came to the door of the Caldwell household. Pretty little Jennie answered the door to find a handsome, well-dressed, young man. He was not the usual gun-totin', high-booted, spurs-a-jinglin' cowboy she was used to seeing in town—not a man dressed to herd cattle. She was smitten right from the start. He was also taken aback by her beauty and just stared at her.

After finally collecting his thoughts, with a polite but bold voice he stated, "My name is Jonas Coy. I'm comin' through this area lookin' for the town of Crockett?"

"Well, Mr. Coy, you are close to Crockett. May I ask you what is your business?"

Just then Lydia appeared and remonstrated, "We should not be too hasty in asking questions of a stranger, young lady. Let the young man feel at home and get to know us before we start asking personal questions that I'm sure are not any of our business."

Turning to the young man she asked, "I heard your name is Coy. Is that correct? Would that be from Missoura?"

"Yes, ma'am. Jonas Coy. I most surely am a-comin' here from Missoura, ma'am."

Jonas was not shy about his calling. His only interest was to serve his Lord, so he continued, "I'm lookin' to start a church gatherin', and seems Texas is a good place to start. I see where David Crockett was here in these parts and the town is named after him. I admired the spirit of Colonel Crockett and his always lookin' for new territory. I guess I feel the same way."

Taken by the boldness and honesty of this young man, Lydia started to ask, "Tell us Mr. Coy, are …."

Jennie jumped in. "You a bit hungry? It's comin' on to supper time, and we got enough food if'n you'd like to stay. You are surely welcome to join us."

Lydia looked at Jennie with a knowing smile, "Took the words right out of my mouth."

The look in Jonas' eyes made it clear that a home-cooked meal was far more tempting than his campfire cooking. He answered, "Well ma'am, I don't want to be a bother."

Lydia smiled with the warmth of a mother looking at a lonely young man as she told him, "It is no bother. The menfolk should be getting in shortly, so get yourself washed up. We will be serving in a short while." With that, she gestured toward the pump at the side of the house.

Jennie was very pleased that Jonas would be there for supper and said rather shyly, "We make a mean apple pie if'n you like that kind."

Jonas responded, "Be pleased to have a samplin' of that."

Romance seemed to be in bloom as the two looked at each other for more than a moment.

Because Lela had now been with the Caldwells for some time, the boys had built a ramp for her. This allowed her to be more mobile and no longer dependent on anyone. Lela was feisty and had her pride.

She was just coming through the door, having wheeled herself in from the garden, and saw Jonas as he turned to go wash up. She said, "I saw a strange horse at the post, now I see the stranger."

Lydia smiled and explained, "This here's Jonas Coy. Mr. Coy, this is Lela Elliot."

Lela looked intently at Jonas and said, "You from Missoura by chance?"

Jonas replied, "Sure strange that everyone keeps askin' about Missoura."

Lela continued to question Jonas, "Do you know Henry Coy?"

Jonas perked up and with a quizzical look answered, "There is a Henry Coy that was my uncle. He was killed in the war."

Lela pressed further, "And a wife named Mary?"

At this Jonas looked at her with some reservation and asked, "Sure 'nough, we supposed to know you? Do you know my uncle and my aunt?"

Lela quietly continued, "Two of the kindest people a person could come to know. Why, we are almost cousins."

Lela then told how she had been left on the doorstep of Henry and Mary Coy—weeping gently from time to time as she told the story. She looked upon them as her father and mother. Listening to Lela made Jonas proud of his aunt and uncle even as his heart went out to Lela.

She finished her discourse, "I wish I could see Momma Coy once more. Sure would do my heart good."

Jonas looked at Lydia trying to find the strength to say what needed to be said. Finally, summoning his preacher voice and with much warmth, he stated, "Well, Miss Elliot, you will see her again but it will have to wait till glory. She went home to be with her Henry and with her Lord."

Lela tried to hold back the tears, but it was no use. Lydia came over to her and, leaning down, held her tight. As Jonas recalled his own memories of Henry and Mary Coy, thoughts that had given him much joy over the years, he got up slowly and left the room, allowing Lela private time to reminisce.

As Jonas headed over to the pump to wash for supper, the water hid tears that filled his eyes. By now, the other men had come in from the field and headed for the pump for some much needed cleaning up. Dirt and sweat make for a pretty messy combination. One by one, the men introduced themselves and made small talk with Jonas.

Soon they all headed into the house for a long-awaited supper.

Jonas, of course, was asked to say the blessing for the meal and, at the end of his prayer, he concluded, "And Lord, I feel a love in this house, yet I also feel a heaviness at work that needs to be lifted. Whatever the darkness, Lord, bring light. Whatever decisions need to be made, let them be made with your will and with your wisdom. In Jesus' name we pray. Amen."

Those at the table looked around at each other wondering if this Jonas could reach into the future. It was evident that Jonas had a true spirit for the Lord, and he would need it when the time came to build a church in their dusty but pleasant town. Mason found peace in Jonas' prayer because he knew he would need the heart of the Lord in his walk toward forgiveness.

Meanwhile, as those at the Caldwell home enjoyed dinner, the Bolin brothers were back in town reporting to Sheriff Culpepper. They started to tell what they had learned about Luke but hesitated as Sam Pike walked in. Culpepper smiled as he told Pike, "Well, Sam, here are the two who will help us finish what we need to git done."

Looking at the brothers, Culpepper prodded, "Continue on boys."

Jeb answered, "As we were sayin', Sheriff, we know that Mr. Caldwell doesn't go out of the house too often. It seems only to inspect the fences along the road after the work's been done."

Jesse barely let Jeb finish and, feeling satisfied that they had followed instructions about Luke, added, "This braided man you asked about was in the army. Says he fought for the South. Some battle 'Chick-a-muggin' or somethin' like that. Sometimes he's the man that takes Caldwell in the wagon for the inspection."

Pike asked, "This the man you described to me, Nate?"

Culpepper slowly replied, "Yeah. Jesse, you know this guy?"

Pike leaned into Jesse and continued his questioning, "Did you ask his name when you had him here?"

"No," replied Jesse.

"Well, Cousin Nate, this here guy's name is probably Luke Geddes. He saw me shoot Caldwell."

Jesse getting wide-eyed and starting to back away stated, "Yeah, that's his name all right."

Aahhh. Shoot Caldwell? That was all Jesse and Jeb needed to hear, and they started toward the door, but Pike stopped them, "You boys ain't goin' nowhere. You're gonna help us. Now I hafta take care two problems, and this time no witnesses. Now let's figure a way to do that."

Culpepper said, "I wish I'd a-had somethin' to hold him on. We coulda took care of this quietly."

Jeb and Jesse had finally begun to grasp was going on, and the two of them were feeling more scared than worried. They already felt uneasy about Pike and were now wondering if the sheriff, who had badgered them but never hurt them, was a lot worse than they had expected. It finally dawned on them that this was something they couldn't get out of, and they slowly walked back to where the sheriff and Pike were sitting. Pike and Culpepper started to hatch a plan. They needed to draw Luke and Mason out somewhere, somehow. Little did they know that might not be as hard as they thought because Caldwell had a plan of his own.

The Bolin brothers headed back for the farm. They had been instructed that one of them was to come back to town as soon as they learned when and where Mason would be inspecting the fences. When they returned to the farm, Mark noticed their nervousness. Returning to the house, Mark quickly called the rest of the group together in the kitchen for a meeting. They would have to engage the brothers in conversation and draw them out, to find out what they knew.

The next morning as the work for the day was assigned, Mark said to Jesse, "Well, you boys did a lot of mendin' of the fences on the west side next to the tree line this past week. They need inspectin' for sure. Do you think we should have a look at them? I'm not sayin' y'all done a bad job, but you know that them steers are sturdy animals, and it won't take much to punch a hole in a fence if'n it ain't hung right."

Jesse looked at Jeb and nervously answered, "Well, sir, maybe we can take your pa out to do some inspectin' say day after tomorrow. Knowin' how busy you are with all the farm things you got, you don't need to be comin' along, we can git him there oursel'es."

Trying to act matter-of-factly Jesse added, "Maybe Luke will come with us. Jes' in case we need some help, he might want to advise us to do more fixin' in case we messed up."

Mark got it. The plan was in place. He answered, "See no problem with that. Glad you boys are willin' to help, but Luke has some things I need for him to do here first. He'll ride out and meet you there about noon."

Jesse, with a half-smile, answered, "Yes sir, Mr. Caldwell, no problem for us, we'll be here."

Jeb added, "Me and Jesse hafta go to town and finish a job we started yesterday evenin'. That be okay with you, Mr. Caldwell?"

Mark could hardly hold back a laugh knowing his plan was being put in force by unsuspecting minds. Mark answered, "You boys go ahead. While you're there, relax and have a drink. Put it on our tab."

The boys left thinking they had pulled off a big one. Reaching town, they headed for the saloon just in case someone who knew Caldwell was watching. As they entered the saloon, they grabbed a kid and told him to get the sheriff for them. When Culpepper got there, they related the plan. Culpepper was pleased and patted the boys on the back while telling them, "You do this job good, ya hear. I'll make it good for you boys."

Changing his demeanor, he assumed his usual mean look and added, "And keep your mouth shut! You'll know the wrath of Pike if'n you don't."

The boys didn't have to be told twice as they stated in unison, "You can count on us, Sheriff."

CHAPTER 21

Morning came and tension was high. It would have been better if there had been another way to involve the law, but since Culpepper was the law, their plan would have to do. If only they'd had more time. They had already sent for the marshal out of Dallas, but unfortunately it would take him several days to arrive.

Mason and Luke had had their fill of killing in the war, but John was not satisfied. He had really never accepted the fact that his father would never be the whole man he once had been. John knew this weighed heavily on Mason's heart. This would be a time of testing for John. His love for his father had no bounds, but revenge is an ugly sin, and he knew it. How would he deal with this when the time came?

Lydia didn't like this idea at all. She told Mason, "Leave this to the Lord, Mason. Forget this, and Pike will leave, I'm sure. I love you, and if you don't come home to me I'll—just...."

Lydia's tears started to well in her pretty eyes as Mason answered, "I am laboring with all I have in me and finding it very difficult to forgive. It's a struggle for me, but one thing for sure; he isn't going to go away. I'm sure this is coming from a family pride he shares with his cousin, the sheriff. Culpepper will never forgive me, and I'm not going to be looking over my shoulder any longer. The revenge isn't coming from me; it's coming from them. I saw pride at work during the war. It can be real ugly. It just doesn't seem to go away. Taking pride in your Lord, pride in your country, pride in your family, that's one thing. But hateful pride is a sin that was born in Satan, and that's what we're seeing here. Leave it to the Lord? Maybe he's asking me to help him. I don't mean he needs my help, but from where I sit, my spirit tells me I'm doing the right thing. Maybe the Lord is leading."

Lydia knew more words wouldn't help. She just held Mason and prayed silently.

After breakfast, Mason tenderly embraced his wife, then met the Bolin brothers at the barn and, with Mark's help, got into the back of the wagon. The Bolin brothers couldn't figure why they were leaving so early. What Mason had planned, however, was to get John and Matthew to the rocks near the tree line before Pike got there. They just needed to know the exact location. They rode off to the west side of the farm to do the supposed inspection.

Halfway there Mason said, "Just ride slow and easy when we turn off the road."

Jesse answered, "Okay, Mr. Caldwell, we won't be goin' fast."

The brothers proceeded slowly, unaware of the plans the Caldwells had made. As the wagon turned off the road about a mile from the fence at the fruit tree orchard, Luke, John, and Matthew suddenly appeared in front of the wagon. Jeb started for his gun as Jesse reined in the horses.

John yelled, "Don't think about it, Jeb. How about you git down off'n that wagon after you throw your gun down."

Jeb answered, "Yes sir, Mr. Caldwell, didn't know it was you. You come up so fast."

Jeb threw his gun down as Jesse said, "We got no quarrel with you Caldwells. We work for you. How come you drawed down on us?"

John came around the wagon as the boys jumped down. Getting a bit hot under the collar, John stated, "It seems someone has a quarrel with us."

Not wanting to start something they knew they couldn't finish, the Bolin brothers moved slowly to the edge of the road.

John continued, "You boys ain't interested in what condition the fence is in. You couldn't care if a colt could run through it full speed. I could guess who put you up to this, but how 'bout you fellas tellin' us what might be on your mind? You know confession is good for the soul—and maybe your health."

Jesse looked at Jeb and said, "Maybe we'd be better off sidin' with the Caldwells. At least they don't seem as mean as some people we know."

John started to go after Jesse but Mason called out. "No, Son. It's not our way."

Turning his attention to Jeb, Mason continued, "You boys are doing someone else's dirty work. I tell you what. We'll just turn you in to the marshal when he comes through here in the next few days, and when we tell him you stole money from us.... Well, I'm sure we can find something on you boys that will convince him."

With that Mason took out some money and handed it to John, who got the hint and started to put it into Jeb's pocket. Mason continued, "Y'know, when we tell the sheriff and Pike it was you that turned them in, and they find you boys in the same jail with them, well I guess you know what will happen."

Jeb looked at Jesse and said, "Look, Brother, we need to make a deal. I ain't gonna be tanglin' with those two sorry hombres."

Jeb told Mason, "If'n we help ya, will you not say who is helpin' ya? We just want to be on our way some fur piece from here and out of this mess."

Mason sternly told them, "All right, no jail, but you will testify or be in this up to your necks. Now what's waiting for me up the road at the fence line?"

Jesse told Mason and the boys about the plan to ambush Mason and Luke when they showed up.

"There's a place that the fence line meets up with the trees. It's there that he's a-plannin' to ambush you and Luke."

Mason told them, "I figured that would be the place because it's the only place we had you fix the fence."

They loaded the brothers back onto the wagon and, taking their ammo from them, returned their unloaded guns, gun belts, and holsters. John and Matthew quickly rode ahead. Fortunately, they had plenty of time thanks to Mason having left much earlier than the Bolins planned. Once they had the right location, the plan was for John and Matthew to plant themselves in the rocks near the tree line. Luke would ride behind the wagon but at a distance. The rest would have to be left up to fate, faith, and the will of God.

As they approached the fence, Mason had them turn off the road and come up from the south rather than approach straight in. This direction would put the rocks behind the tree line. The time of reckoning was at hand.

Mason told the Bolins, "From my position, any wrong move, or I catch you trying to jump from the wagon, I'll put a bullet up your backbone, and you will know what I feel like when I try to walk."

Jeb and Jesse sat motionless; they knew that when things started to happen, they could be a target from either side. Jeb pulled the horses back about twenty feet from the fence. They sat there, and Mason told Jesse, "Get down slow like and come to the back of the wagon, and Jeb, don't move. Luke is a crack shot."

Jesse did as commanded and lowered the tailgate. Mason slowly got to the ground as they heard the unmistakable voice of Pike, "Welcome, Captain Caldwell. Not so good to see you again. Gotta say though, you sure are full of a will to live. I guess I will hafta end that for ya. How about you come over to the fence line? Leave the gun in the back of the wagon; we don't want any accidents—besides, I'd like to see you hobble some, makes me feel all warm inside."

Pike had a big satisfied smirk as he called out, "Toss the gun, Luke, and keep your hands where I can see 'em. You know, kid, you're as big a turncoat as if'n you had joined the Yankees. Couldn't keep your mouth shut, could ya? Well, I'll take care that right quick. Come closer so I can see your pitiful face as my bullet rips you."

Luke was still a good fifty yards or so away and was looking for his backup. He knew he had to do as Pike said or Pike would get suspicious. There was a blessing here though. Pike had come alone, and this was a big mistake.

John's voice came out from behind the rocks, "Yup, you must be that Pike fella I heard about. You look mean enough, but I must say, you sure are a coward. Shoot a man in the back? Good thing you're a lousy shot. How 'bout that, a coward and a bad shot? I'm a-hopin' you might like to take a shot at me. I got an idea. Let's you and me figure a way to face off and get down to the...."

Mason, standing behind the wagon with his crutch, interrupted, "No, John. This man is going to face a judge and a jury. We have all the witnesses we need, and I want to see him crippled— but only in the sense that his freedom will be a jail cell. I'm not about to lower myself or my family down to his unholy hatred."

Pike made the mistake of starting to pull his gun on Mason. A gunshot rang out, and John yelled, "Please do that again, Pike. You ain't got any idea how bad I want to shoot you right now."

With that he aimed at Pike and slowly started to squeeze the trigger. Pike tossed his gun and started to raise his hands as Mason yelled, "John...."

Mason paused looking at his son with pleading eyes. "Please, John, don't make yourself like him. I beg of you, Son, don't let hate have its way with you."

John met Mason's eyes. With a shaking hand, John paused, then slowly lowered his gun. The tension was high, and it was all John could do to stand down.

At that moment, Matthew appeared and, binding Pike securely, put him on his horse. The Bolin brothers wanted nothing more than to ride off into the sunset, but Mason having climbed back into the wagon assured them that it would be healthier for them to just ride back into town with the rest of them. This, however, presented another problem—the good sheriff. Jesse and Jeb had by this time explained to Mason and the others that Pike and Culpepper were cousins. How do you bring the sheriff's own kin to town and put him into the jail?

John had an idea that he quietly told Mason and Matthew. He then took off at a gallop headed for town. Stopping in front of the sheriff's office, he quickly jumped from his horse and ran into the sheriff's office. Seeing him, Culpepper was very uneasy.

John cried out almost hysterically, "Sheriff, somethin' happened. My pa went to see some mended fences with the Bolin brothers, and when they didn't come back, we went lookin' for 'em. I think there must be a problem 'cause we can't find 'em. You know how bad those brothers can be."

The sheriff seemed somewhat relieved, thinking Pike had done his job. The thought occurred to him, *Maybe he dragged the bodies somewhere and buried them.* Looking at John as if he cared, he said, "I'll git my horse and head out to find your pa. You'll hafta go with me to show me where to start lookin' and see if there is any evidence of foul play."

John answered, "Well, Sheriff, I'll go with ya, but I gotta get some water for my horse. I been ridin' him hard. I'll meet you here in just a moment."

John left the office and, as planned, the wagon appeared from behind the jail. Matthew, pulling Pike by the ropes binding him, entered the office with Mason and the Bolin brothers following behind. Then John came back in, taking a position behind the sheriff. Culpepper gaped at them and wasn't sure what to do, but Mason made it quite clear, "Put this man in jail, Sheriff, he tried to kill me. Again!"

Culpepper didn't know what to do, as Pike said nothing. Finally he answered, "Well, I got no proof so I can't just lock him up."

Culpepper was smart enough not to draw down on them as John, pulling out his gun, said, "That's not the right answer, Sheriff, so you can join your cousin in the cell."

A perplexed Culpepper wondered how they knew that Sam was his cousin. He looked hard at the Bolin brothers. The fear on their faces said it all as they backed away. Culpepper was speechless for the first time as John took his gun and put Culpepper and Pike in the same cell, as Mason had instructed him.

"The marshal will be here tomorrow. We sent for him awhile back. He will do his job; that I'm sure of."

Mason was concerned that they might not have enough evidence to get Culpepper for conspiracy, so he knew it was necessary to keep the Bolin brothers on his side. The question was how. Nudging the brothers ahead of him, he went outside with Matthew and John.

Mason then told the Bolins, "You boys are going back to the farm with us. Luke, I hate to ask you, but can you stay here until the marshal shows up?"

Luke snapped to attention and proudly answered, "Captain Caldwell, sir, it would be my honor to serve you, thank you for the opportunity."

As Culpepper and Pike sulked in the same cell, the anger that welled up in them was enough to melt the jail bars.

The Bolin Brothers, having been escorted outside, started to run. Matthew was just a little too quick for them. They seemed to have forgotten the last time they'd had a run-in with him. Matthew drop-kicked Jeb at the same time he reached for Jesse. This spun Jesse around, putting Matthew off balance, but Matthew was quick on his feet. Jesse took a swing at him. Bad move as Matthew grabbed the incoming punch and, twisting himself around, flipped Jesse to the ground. Jeb, watching, didn't dare get up. Recalling his previous shellacking, he decided not to get into it. Besides, John had drawn on him.

Jesse found himself looking up at Matthew as Matthew had his foot on his throat. Throwing his hands over his head, Jesse gave up. Matthew's composure actually relaxed every one.

Well, not quite every one. Mason, who'd had enough of this, said with an angry voice, "You boys aren't very bright, that's for sure, but if you want to survive this ordeal, be advised that I—we—will not tolerate your stupidity. You will be really hurting if you try that again. Now let's all get home before the womenfolk run out of prayers for us."

nce back at the farm, Mason related the story to the women including Lucas and Catherine, who were also there. Amid sighs of relief, there was much hugging and laughter.

Something nagged at Mason, however, something that didn't feel right. Had he been wise to leave Luke alone there with those two? Could Culpepper and Pike have other friends who might come to break them out? Lela had similar misgivings as she looked at Mason and said, "Mr. Caldwell, it's Luke, you see, I feel...."

Seeing her hurt and interrupting her, Mason turned to Lucas, "If we lock the Bolin boys up good and tight, can you spell me and take turns guarding them tonight?"

Uncle Lucas answered firmly, "I'd be right pleased to help, Mason. After all, I'm too old for the wrestlin' matches. Now, you did say they would be locked up tight, right?"

Everyone laughed as Mason asked, "John, Matthew, would you be good enough to go down to the jail and spell Luke from time to time?"

John replied, "Of course, Pa, we was thinkin' the same. Matthew and I talked about it on the way back here."

Lela looked at Mason with a tear and a smile.

So it was that the Bolin Brothers were tied up securely and put in the root cellar where there were no windows and only one well-secured door. The room was small and uncomfortable, but that didn't bother anyone but the Bolins.

As John and Matthew prepared to head back to town, Lydia warned them, "You boys be 'specially careful. I've been bending the Lord's ear so much lately for you all, I'm not sure if he's still awake. I'm sure I tuckered him out."

Catherine added, "Remember, Matthew, what you learned from your father. Look, think, and don't waste time figuring it out. You trained well, so let your instincts and our Lord go with you both."

John and Matthew honored their mothers with a bow.

CHAPTER 22

ohn and Matthew were no longer kids who looked for adventure as if it were some kind of game, but now men who had come face to face with the world. At stake were their families, who must be protected, and justice, that must be done to honor both Mason and their own beliefs.

They wasted no time heading back to town. As they burst through the door of the jail, Luke quickly pulled his gun but relaxed as he recognized them. John and Matthew noticed that Luke was writing something. Luke smiled and said, "I wonder if California is gonna be a good move for me. You know that California was mostly sidin' with the Yankees, and I don't think they'd take a likin' to me. I'm wonderin' if'n I write my old sidekick from the army, he might have an idea where a man can settle down from this war."

It took no time at all for John to come up with an answer for Luke. John ventured, "Texas ain't exactly the end of fertile land and cattle. What's wrong with this great state?"

Matthew added, "Got a point there, John. Maybe a man with money saved from his army pay could get a little hunk of that land."

Glancing up at the two and scratching his head, Luke agreed it was certainly worth looking into.

Morning came and so did trouble. Two of Culpepper's "friends" came into the office to see what was going on. Matthew had gone off to get some food, and John was checking on the horses, leaving Luke alone in the jail as the men came in. Luke told them to leave, explaining that the marshal was coming to handle matters.

The men left but went around to the back of the jail. There, they quietly called out to Culpepper. "Sheriff, what's goin' on?"

"It seems there was a misunderstandin'. We was jumped by this renegade soldier. Thinks he is some kind of hero or something. Has something against my cousin here from when they served together."

Dan, one of the men, asked the sheriff, "What can we do to help?"

"You need to break us out, quick, before his partners come back. Git in there and draw on him now."

Luke, thinking it was Matthew and John returning, didn't look up as the two men rushed into the jail, guns in hand, and took him by surprise. They freed Pike and the sheriff. Culpepper grabbed Luke and started to beat on him with his gun. Just as he started to put it to Luke's head, Pike stopped him saying, "No gunshots, we need to git out of here, now. And know this, Luke, I'll be huntin' you down."

With that, Culpepper struck Luke over the head with the gun butt, and he collapsed on the floor. The four men ran out the door, heading for the corral and their horses. John, coming out from behind the barn, spotted Pike and Culpepper. They saw him too and started shooting. John ran for cover but not before a bullet hit him in the thigh. Fortunately, it passed through the flesh only, and he was able to make it behind the corner of a building next to the corral.

From this vantage point, he held his ground and fired back, preventing Pike and Culpepper from getting into the barn and to the horses. As Pike and Culpepper were pinned down next to the barn but needing to get inside, Dan and his partner watched this unfold from the corral and had a change of heart. Dan told his partner, "We don't need to git shot, I'm a-thinkin' it be best we be gittin' outta here."

With that, the two disappeared. Just then, Matthew rounded the building and spotted John, who yelled to him, "Don't let them get to the horses! Go around the other side and keep them from goin' in."

Matthew moved quickly as John gave him cover fire, but it was too late as Pike made it inside the barn. Luke's voice was heard saying, "Hey, Sheriff, didn't hit me hard enough. I guess I'll hafta shoot ya."

Culpepper looked up to see Luke coming from the walkway. As Luke started toward him, Culpepper drew down on Luke, but John put a bullet into him. Culpepper went down writhing on the ground obviously in much pain.

By now, Luke had reached the entrance to the barn as Pike came out. As Pike started to mount his moving horse, Luke grabbed his leg and pulled him from his saddle. Pike started for his gun, but Luke kicked it out of his hand. Quickly getting to his feet, Pike pulled out a knife. Luke drew his own knife, and the two faced off.

Matthew arrived, with John limping behind him, and John started to level his gun at Pike. Luke yelled to him, "No, John, this is my fight. This should never have got this far. I shoulda took care of this when it happened. Let me get this done one way or the other."

Pike expressed his feelings too, "Brave talk, half-breed. Let's see how you do up against a white man. Good with the rifle but let's get this done man to man with just these blades."

Luke stared into Pike's eyes and told him, "You're a coward, Pike, and you been mean all of your life, and I'm gonna cut the mean right out of ya."

Pike lunged at Luke, and Luke sidestepped but not fast enough. Pike's blade caught Luke along his side. Luke grabbed his side as Pike turned and came at him again. This time Luke dodged him and swung his knife, only to be pushing air.

Pike laughingly gave Luke a dig, "You move good, but you ain't gonna be movin' at all when I git through with you, Boy."

Pike came down on Luke with his knife, and Luke grabbed his hand. At the same time, Pike grabbed Luke's knife hand. They pushed at each other with each trying to turn the other. Pike was not only the taller but also the stronger of the two. He tripped Luke up and they both went down, but the momentum gave Luke a chance to put his foot in Pike's belly, flipping him over and away. Here the quickness of the smaller man came into play as Luke rose up ready for another round.

Pike was getting frustrated. Trying to make Luke angry, he said, "Come on, Luke, come on. Come git me, half-breed, you ain't man enough, Boy."

Luke stood about five feet from Pike when all of a sudden Luke put both hands down to his side and didn't move. It was as if he were in a trance. It seemed his Indian brothers had taught him a thing or two. Luke steadied his body and focused his mind. Pike stared at him but only for a moment. Thinking this was his greatest opportunity, Pike lunged at Luke. Luke dropped to his knees just a fraction of a second before Pike reached him and came up with his knife, driving it into Pike's belly. Time seemed to freeze for a second, then Pike fell on his side.

As Pike lay dying, Luke looked him in the eyes and said, "I wish I could hate you, Pike, but I'm a-feelin' only pity for ya. I pray that God has mercy on your miserable soul."

As John limped over, Luke said to him gently, "It won't heal your pa, but at least he won't have to live in the pain of rememberin' and not knowin' what happened to him. I've done the right thing now."

With that, the fight was over, and Pike lay there as his lifeblood left his body.

Culpepper was carried to Doc Thompson's place as John limped along, clinging to Luke for support. Nate Culpepper was not doing well, and John pondered how he could keep himself from finishing the man off.

Doc Thompson bandaged John's wound, then stepped out of the room to treat Luke while Matthew waited with them.

This left Culpepper and John alone. John looked at the sheriff and after a few minutes finally said quietly, "I'm tempted to rip your heart out for causing all this. You have messed up my pa's life and had no real cause to do it. You knowed he was trying to help and protect his family. You're a rotten man, Sheriff, and should be put down like a mad dog. But, I'm gonna honor my pa by not touchin' you. I'll honor my God by lettin' him give you what you got comin'. I'll let the law deal with you."

Satisfied that Culpepper was too weak to leave Doc Thompson's office, they returned to the Caldwell farm where they related the events of the day to those at home. The relationship between Pike and Culpepper, and how Luke was involved, was explained to everyone, as well as what would be done to make things right. The men especially felt relieved that the mystery had been solved, and the women were relieved that their men were out of danger. Relieved indeed, but not jubilant—especially Mason, even though he now knew who had shot him and why—answers to the questions that had haunted him for so long.

He knew he still had to deal with Culpepper as well as his half-useless body. Lydia tended to John, whose leg had been bandaged by the doctor. Her eyes were on her husband as Mason told them, "We did what needed to be done, and by the grace of God, we returned with our lives intact."

Turning to John he added, "I'm proud of you, Son. How you took control over your emotions and not giving in to revenge made me very proud. I know your leg will heal as will your heart."

Luke, content that he was still alive, was just plain tired and wanted to rest. Lela watched him with tears in her eyes, but no words had passed between them since the men returned home. Doc Thompson had done a good job of patching Luke up, but that didn't ease Lela's concern for her wounded hero. She didn't know how to say what she wanted to say.

Finally, wishing she could jump out of her chair and grab and hold onto Luke, Lela stared into his eyes and said, "Luke, you'll need someone to look after you. You've been hurt real bad and I feel I should—I'm the one who can. Luke, I'm— I'm—just happy that you're.... Oh, Luke, come close to me. Hold me, Luke, let me feel your arms assuring me you're here and not a vision."

Luke went to Lela and, holding onto his wounded side, got on his knees and embraced her. Luke's emotions were foreign to him. He had never been able to get close to anyone because of constant rejection as a half-breed. Maybe, just maybe, someone could love him. With his new friends and the warmth of this loving family, he suddenly felt the kind of peace he had longed for as far back as he could remember. He recalled the family he loved and missed. Life was beginning to have a new perspective.

At the dinner table, everyone slowly unwound and settled into light conversation. Pastor Coy heard what happened and came to the Caldwell household to inquire if the family needed some pastoral service. Instead, he found he was the one ministered to. The love emanating from this family blessed him mightily. Even more was the blessing of seeing Jennie.

As all rejoiced that everyone was home safe and sound, Mason spoke the blessing for the evening meal. "Father in heaven, we accept this food as a gift from you...." Here Mason paused as he felt a deep connection to his Lord.

"Bless it to the health of our bodies that we may serve you in all we do. We celebrate life as a gift from you. I have to add the word thanks, but it doesn't quite cover what I feel inside. I'm surrounded by love, more love than I can express to you or that I deserve. Your coming to our aid this day, protecting us from more harm and sorrow that would break more hearts if we weren't here is beyond what I could ask. So with humble hearts, we all thank you, and honor you for your faithfulness in answering the prayers of your children, especially those prayers of my beloved wife. Now, Father, we ask this of you. Your wisdom for answers to what still needs to be done to put a final end to all this pain. In the name of your son, Jesus, we speak our prayer."

A chorus of "amens" resounded from those at the table. As the food was passed around, Uncle Lucas was the first to speak, "You know, we still got those varmints out in the root cellar to take to town, the sooner the better as far as I'm concerned. Puttin' them in jail would please me a whole bunch. I hope we ain't been feedin' them too good. They're gonna miss this fine home cookin' when they get into the jail cell."

Laughter and "serves 'em right" were heard around the table. When Matthew volunteered to get the Bolins back into town, Mark agreed to assist.

Plans were made, and in the morning Mark and Matthew headed to town with Jeb and Jesse tied up in the back of the wagon. John needed rest as much as Luke, but despite protests from his mother, he insisted on saddling his horse and riding into town sometime after the others had left in the wagon. Upon arriving in town, the first thing John did was to go the doctor's office to see how Culpepper was doing. The sheriff was awake but barely moving.

Doc Thompson told John, "You ripped him pretty bad. The bullet broke some ribs and put a hole in his lung. He isn't gonna be movin' a whole lot very soon, and even if he does move, he ain't never gonna be breathin' normal again."

The other news was that the marshal would arrive in town the next day.

With the Bolins locked up, John stopped to check in with Mark as he and Matthew secured the jail. There was now a strong bond between John and Matthew, and they both seemed to enjoy the feeling of being lawmen. As the truth got out about what Culpepper and Pike had done, the townsfolk offered no resistance to having their sheriff locked up. In fact, most were actually glad to see Culpepper gone.

It seemed the sheriff had but very few friends, and two of those friends had disappeared.

The next morning, John again insisted on riding into town. He and Matthew were sitting in the sheriff's office with Mark. Their faces lit up in surprise when they looked up to see their old friend McNelly walk in.

"You boys ain't learned to stay out of trouble, have ya? Well that's good because I bin lookin' for a couple of good men."

John replied in surprise, "Didn't know you were a marshal, Captain McNelly."

"I'm not. Just fillin' in for a spell. We've been busy reorganizing the Rangers. I'll tell you about it as soon as we finish our business here."

With that, Matthew and John related the story of Mason, Pike, and Culpepper to McNelly from beginning to end with all the gory details. McNelly told the boys, "Judge Grayson will be here in about a week, and we will have a speedy trial for Culpepper. So are these two varmints goin' to testify?"

John answered, "Yeah, but my pa made a promise to them that if they testify, he would ask the judge for leniency for them. Could you help my pa in keeping his word?"

"Your pa is a generous man. Good heart. I know Judge Grayson, and I'll see to it that he will do as your pa asks."

Jeb and Jesse heard all this, and they smiled and sighed in relief.

The days went by too slowly. Mark and Matthew took turns with McNelly watching the prisoners in the jail—not that the Bolins had friends likely to break them out. Everyone just wanted to get this thing over and done with. In the meantime, Culpepper had started to heal somewhat.

Five days after McNelly arrived, the stage pulled up, and Judge Grayson alighted. The next day, the courtroom was filled with people from one end of the county to the other. Culpepper's breathing was raspy, and the pain from the shattered ribs didn't help much as he sucked in air to fill his one good lung. Not many felt much sympathy for him, however. Over the years, the sheriff had rubbed more than one person the wrong way.

The trial was short and sweet—for the Caldwells at least, not so sweet for Culpepper. He was convicted of conspiracy to murder and sentenced to prison for a very long time. What he had to look forward to was meeting up with men who, shall we say, have long memories of how they came to be in prison. The Bolins were set free as promised but on the condition they leave town and never come back to Crockett.

Mason had found forgiveness for Luke and, more than that, they seemed to have developed a special bond.

Mason saw a young man who had come into manhood by stepping forward and doing the right thing. John and Mark recognized this as well and welcomed Luke as a brother.

Life returned to normal as the family resumed working the farm. It became evident, though, that the farm pretty much belonged to Mark and Mason. Seeing McNelly again had given John and Matthew an epiphany about their future.

Before leaving town, McNelly told them, "You both have courage; you have the spunk that it will take to tame this wild territory. We are small in numbers right now, but we are strong in our desire to protect and help those who can't stand on their own.

"You know we're working to reorganize the Texas Rangers. Right now we're just a group of volunteers with no particular name. Most of us served in the army, and now we want to come home and keep the peace here. We're men who are able to handle any given situation without definite instructions from a commanding officer or higher authority. This ability, however, must be proven before a man can be a member. You boys think it over and git back to me. You know how to contact me."

CHAPTER 23

By October, Luke was still undecided about what he was going to do. On the one hand, there was the idea of moving on, as that was about all he knew and what had been his life. On the other hand, he had a strong desire to keep the wonderful relationship he had developed with his new friends—and maybe a certain wheeled contraption and its scrappy occupant.

Pastor Coy was courting Jennie, if one could call it that, as she was very eager to be courted by him. He had established a small congregation at the edge of town and seemed to be well liked by his people. Of course, more than a few of the pews were regularly occupied by the Caldwells as well as Uncle Lucas, Catherine, and their extended circle.

They were soon to be Mr. and Mrs. Neiter. He had asked, and she had accepted. It was expected that Jonas would be doing the matrimonial honors. Matthew was pleased to see his mother happy again, and everyone else showed approval as well.

Several times Lydia had noticed Mason retreating to the barn at odd times. She began to wonder whether something was wrong, so one day she stole quietly after him. Peering in she observed Mason with a makeshift cane in place of his usual crutch, slowly and carefully making his way close to the stalls where he would have something to grab if he stumbled. Smiling to herself, she stole away as quietly as she had come. *He has his pride*, she thought. *If he'd wanted my help, he'd have asked. I must let him be. Whenever he's ready ….*

John and Matthew were another story. They had taken Captain McNelly up on his offer to join the group of volunteers. Gone now for more than a month, they were not expected home any time soon.

The day dawned with a brisk wind that would keep most folks indoors but there was a knock on the Caldwells' door. Lydia opened it to find young pastor Jonas Coy standing there. Wondering why he was there so early, she didn't have to wait too long to find out.

"Pastor Coy, is there something urgent that brings you here at daybreak?"

"I have somethin' I would like to ask Mr. Caldwell if'n you don't mind, Mrs. Caldwell, and if'n I don't get it said soon, I'll probably not get it out."

Lydia suppressed her instincts, knowing what it was about and summoned Mason. She left the room with a grin that could almost be heard. Jonas looked at Mason, trying to stand tall, and with his best manly voice, began, "Sir, I have come to ask a very important question. I have been courtin' Miss Jennie for awhile, and I, uh, well you see, I, uh...."

Mason interrupted him, "Jonas, Jennie is a big girl now and, I think, wise enough to make her own decisions. You don't need to ask me for her hand in marriage."

Mason, funning a bit with Jonas, added, "If, of course, that's what you're here for, and if you are, ask her yourself. But if it makes you feel better, as far as I'm concerned, it's okay with me and her mother."

Jonas could only sigh with relief as Jennie came into the room. It was all he could do not to stumble all over himself as he gazed into her eyes with a comical look on his face. Mason, a wise man, left the room. Jonas reached out to Jennie and took her hand. Jennie was not aware of the conversation that had just taken place, but was she reading the expression on Jonas' face correctly? With a quiet voice, Jonas then started to propose to her.

He had rehearsed this a hundred times, but the words that came out just poured from his heart as he said, "I been wantin' to ask you for a while, Jennie. I guess I was just too afraid you would not want to, ah, well, I don't know what I would do if you said no but...."

Jennie interrupted impatiently, "Say it, Jonas, just ask, so's I can say yes."

With that she threw herself into his arms. From her commotion, the rest of the house came in to see what had happened. It was now official. Marriage was the rule of the day.

Then there was Luke. He hadn't yet saddled up for California or other parts that might await him. Over and over he mulled the questions in his mind. *What's holding me back? Lela for one thing. Do I love her enough to take her as a wife? Would she be a burden? Does that even matter? Does she truly love me enough for that? Another thing. Do I really want to go and leave these fine folks who have accepted me as I am? Dare I now say I have a family here in Crockett?*

As he sat in the kitchen pondering these questions, Lela, who had been sitting next to him, saw the uncertainty on his face and figured he needed to left alone. She quietly said to him, "You got a deep-thinkin' look on your face, Luke. I'm gonna go inside and leave you to your thinkin'. If you want to talk to me, I'm just a stone's throw away."

As Lela left the room, Mason entered. Luke turned to him. He felt he needed to talk to someone, and who better than someone experienced in life's challenges? Actually, who better than Mason, who was now the father figure in his life?

"Sir, I bin hankerin' for a life that doesn't have so much violence in it. I figured herdin' a bunch of steers couldn't be too bad after the bad things I've seen and especially all the things I've done. California still has a lot of call to me, and I don't want to pass up the opportunity to git settled down."

Mason was pleased that Luke had come to him for advice and counsel. "Luke, getting settled down is only half of the problem. This nation is full of opportunity, and I'm sure you will find something. You know, cattle and farming are good for the soul, but you still got adventure in you even if you don't know it. You didn't survive this war to not make your mark in this great land."

These words lifted Luke's spirits. For the first time he felt like "I ain't just some half-breed."

Mason continued, "I have a friend in the cattle business. His ranch is up in Dallas. I'll send you up there with a letter if you'd like. It's a newer ranch, and it's gonna need a lot of hard work to get it going. That should be an adventure to a strapping young man like yourself."

Luke would have preferred to stay on with the Caldwells rather than move to another part of Texas, but he knew that wasn't possible. First and foremost, it was a farm, not a ranch. Farming wasn't what he had in mind, and he knew there wasn't enough land to support another family. A family? A family means getting married. It means having children. He thought of Lela. It was all so confusing. He knew he had to move on, but with her? Without her?

Luke told Mason, "Well, sir, I much appreciate the offer; it's mighty kind of you. I sure would like to be a-thinkin' on it. I know I must be movin' on shortly, and I don't want to be a burden any more to you and your family."

Mason smiled warmly at Luke and answered, "Well, son, you take all the time you need. Measure out the good and the bad, the future, and where your heart is. I would say best you pray on it. We will all pray on it, and, Luke," here Mason paused for emphasis, "you've never been a burden."

Luke smiled back as Mason headed outside leaving Luke alone to ponder his dilemma. The nights were cold now, so Luke went out to the barnyard to cut some wood as the women came into the kitchen to prepare lunch. He wanted to make himself useful, and a little strenuous work had always helped him to think.

As Luke was chopping wood, he heard Mark yelling and shouting as he came riding in. Dropping the axe, Luke ran toward the road leading to the corral and called to Mark, "What's so excitin' that you can be heard a mile away?"

As Mark came close he told Luke, "The Jensens are sellin' their land and asked if we want to buy it? Ain't no good for farmin', maybe just for cattle. Farmin' is where their heart is, so they just want to move on to California."

Luke started to laugh. "Well, someone is goin' to California."

"They got a bunch of money from a relative that passed on back East and are sellin' their land for a very, very low price. They would even take payments through the bank if'n someone came up with some money up front."

Luke thought to himself, *Is this a sign? Or better yet, I'll bet I know who's been prayin'.* They went into the house where Mark sat everyone down and told them about the Jensens.

"We been neighbors so long they said we had first chance to buy their place. They remember the kindness you and ma showed them when they ran on hard times and needed help."

Mason was silent for a moment, but Lydia, who usually didn't get much involved in these sorts of things, looked at Uncle Lucas and said, "Well, Lucas, you've been talking about living in town, and Catherine is living with her family. What are you going to do when you get married?"

Lucas answered, "I got some money from sellin' my place, and I could probably buy their spread, but I'm too old to be herdin' cattle. I know that land, and it ain't good for crop growin' so cattle would have to be its crop."

Lydia answered with a smile on her face, "I know a young man who is strong and has proved he can take on a challenge."

Everyone looked at Luke who just stared back with his mouth open. Mason now brightened and, looking at Lydia, said, "Well, we get a bit forward with people's lives, and we get to be pushin' a bit don't you think, Mrs. Caldwell?"

Lydia knew when she was called "Mrs. Caldwell," she could be in a mound of trouble. She answered a little sheepishly, "I, well, you're right. I don't mean to be a busybody and …."

Luke quickly chimed in, "Mrs. Caldwell, you just might have an idea, but I need thinkin' and prayin' time on this. It ain't such a bad idea 'specially if Uncle Lucas would be considerin' me."

"As I recall, Luke," said Mason, "the Jensens had a line shack some ways from the main house. Just something for you to add to your thinking and praying."

No comment came from Lucas, but a slight smile appeared in his eye. Lela almost had tears in hers. What a wonderful gift it would be to be with people she loved who had become her family. Of course, there was a problem. Who said Luke would want to take her along? She had thrown herself at him since they'd first met and now truly realized he needed alone time. But how much time? She couldn't even guess. She started to leave the room toward the porch. She didn't want them to see her when the tears started.

Those remaining at the table fell silent, each lost in thought. Lucas felt it would be a good thing for him and planned to discuss it with Catherine in the morning. Mason looked at Luke with a half-smile knowing Luke was drawn to the idea.

Mason asked Mark, "Did the Jensens give you a time when they would need to know our answer?"

"Soon, Pa. They're meetin' up with some family members from back East who are comin' in on the train in about seven days. They're all hankerin' for farmland in California, some place called the San Joaquin Valley. Hear tell they got a lot of fertile land there. Maybe even thinkin' of growin' cotton."

Mason was happy for the Jensens and told Mark, "Ride out to the Jensens' place and let them know we'll give them an answer within the week. I'm sure a decision will come about by then."

Mark left to do as Mason had asked. Lucas left and headed for the barn. Luke was already there. Lucas approached Luke quietly and sat next to him. After a few minutes, he finally said, "Luke, I like you, Son. Don't have children as you know, and so I guess I don't know how to express my feelings. I just want to say, I like you, and I know you're an honorable man. You will be welcomed in my life no matter where life sends each of us."

Luke was touched and looking at Lucas told him, "I'm mighty fond of you, Uncle Lucas. Your words mean a whole lot to me." With that, Lucas returned to the house and left Luke alone in his thoughts.

Suddenly Luke felt very alone. He prayed in earnest, *Lord, I bin a handful for you and maybe even a pest from time to time. I ain't never really got to know you very well, and I guess this here family got me to thinkin' more about you. I know you got me out of some troublin' times, I can see that now. I want to say to you; I can handle a good fight with a real live enemy better than the fight I can't see that's goin' on inside me right now. You got somethin' to say to me, let me know soon. I ain't good at waitin' but most of all I ain't good with this kind of inner battle.* Luke went back to his firewood and swung the axe with a vengeance.

Lela who had been watching from the porch, heard none of the conversation but prayed that what was in her heart would reach Luke.

CHAPTER 24

Coming into town was always an adventure for the Caldwells. As he frequently did, Luke joined Mason and Mark on this trip. Between the two wagons, they were able to haul back a sizable load.

The morning chores had been completed and lunch was over when they left the Caldwell farm. Luke had talked Lela into coming along this time just to get her out for a spell.

While Luke was at the lumber and hardware store, the others were at the general store filling the list Lydia had given to Mason. Here, Mason saw a new shipment of fabric for dressmaking. He knew how much Lydia enjoyed sewing, but she spent much of that time mending or making new clothes for the children as they outgrew the older ones, or for others.

He told Mark, "Your ma looks out for me in so many special ways. She is always mending and fixing, but I think it's time she deserves something new that she can make just for herself."

At this, he looked at Lela and said, "Lela, you're a good knit and sew person. Could you, would you help me pick out some material that Lydia can use to make herself a dress? I'd be stumbling around here trying to see what colors she would look good in—though I must admit, to me she looks good in anything."

He stopped himself as he felt a blush coming on. Lela, with a smile ear to ear, answered, "Mr. Caldwell, it would be a pleasure to help you. I know just the color that would please her, and yes, havin' time with Mrs. Caldwell is always a joy for me."

With that they went over to the table and started their search. Meanwhile, a face peered through the window of the store. A boy about six or seven years old was eyeing the candy in the jars displayed in the window. As many a young child has done, he just kept staring, proving that our sweet tooth starts long before we realize. With this young man, the sweet tooth seemed to be quite intense. Mark saw the boy's wide eyes and beckoned for him to come inside. As he came in the door, Mark observed that the boy was dressed in very different attire not seen in this territory. His pants came just below the knees, he wore long stockings, and his shoes were a bit fancy for ranch and farm country.

Mark, having a generous heart, thought this kid just might need a piece of candy to brighten his day. Unable to resist the temptation on the chance that a piece of candy might be within his reach, the boy slowly entered. As he approached the counter where Mark was standing, the storekeeper, Mr. Harris, turned around and started to shoo the boy out, as he hadn't seen Mark motion for him to come in.

Mr. Harris told the boy, "Get goin', Samuel. You know better than to beg from a stranger."

Mark interrupted, "No problem, Mr. Harris. The treat is on me. I beckoned him in."

"Okay, Mark, but be aware that this boy knows better, I know that for a fact because...."

Mark interrupted, "Maybe I should know better too, but you know me, Mr. Harris. I ain't growed up yet."

Mr. Harris grinned and just shook his head. With that Mark turned to Samuel and told him, "Now you pick out a real juicy one. I'll be joinin' you in a bit."

Suddenly, Samuel reached out and, taking Mark's arm, held tight without saying a word. He didn't even go to the candy jars. Mark was beside himself and wondering what the problem was. He pried Samuel loose and bending down asked him, "Did I offend you, Boy? All I wanted to do was to git you a piece of candy and make you happy. I know that if someone offered me some candy, I'd be fishin' in that jar."

Samuel finally spoke, sounding rather foreign to Mark, because Samuel had a very thick British accent, "You see, sir, no one's been so nice to me. They are always making fun of my mum and me."

Mark looked over at Mr. Harris, who started to explain, "Mark, Samuel and his ma are here from …."

Before he could finish, a pretty young woman walked in and pulled Samuel away from Mark. A decidedly awkward pause followed, especially for Mark.

Eventually, Mason, who had been watching this unfold, spoke up. "Are you the boy's ma?"

With a pronounced British accent she answered, "Yes, this is my boy Samuel. What's going on here? Did he do something wrong?"

"Oh no, ma'am," responded Mark quickly. "You see, I saw him standin' at the window and thought he might be wantin' some candy. I'm at fault here, ma'am. The boy ain't to blame for nothin'. Just trying to be friendly and kind."

Emma Livingston, putting Samuel behind her, told everyone in a somewhat huffy tone of voice, "We will take our leave now. Sorry for any inconvenience we may have caused."

Not missing a beat, Mark told her, "No, ma'am. Just wanted to do an act of kindness."

Emma was not impressed and told Mark assertively, "Well, it is only right to consult with a parent when giving a treat, especially when it comes to a boy this age."

Mark was not accustomed to being spoken to like that, especially when he was only trying to being friendly. With a trace of annoyance in his voice, he told her, "Well, lady, whatever your name is, in these parts kindness is somethin' honorable. We like to think of it as making friends too. You got a problem with makin' friends?"

By this time, her feathers were getting ruffled and she retorted, "Where I come from, manners are preferred over boisterous dialogue and perceived honor."

Mark was starting to fume and pointed his finger at her as he started to yell, "Perceived? What in the dic...," but before he could start his diatribe, Mason chimed in, "Hold on, everyone. This is gonna go places we aren't wanting to go. Let's all calm down and have a civil talk. Starting with you, Mark. You know better than to get upset when you don't know all the facts. Maybe Mrs. aahhh," Mason looked at Emma and with kindness in his voice continued, "Might we know your name? Maybe we can start with that and be civil from there."

She replied, albeit somewhat haughtily, "Emma Livingston."

Mason smiled and said, "Emma, that's a pretty name. We don't hear that name around these parts much. Well, this here's my son, Mark Caldwell. My name is Mason Caldwell. And this is Lela Elliot. May I ask where you're from, Mrs. Livingston? I'm guessing from your speech you're from England; am I correct?"

Emma, following Mason's lead, had calmed down and answered, "Yes, that would be correct, Mr. Caldwell."

Mason, still trying to keep things calm, continued, "It seems you're some ways from home, young lady. Is your husband nearby? Maybe we could go fetch him for you."

A long pause ensued, but before Emma could answer, Samuel, who had come out from behind his mother, said, "You see, sir, my father isn't with us—he is...."

Emma abruptly interrupted, "It isn't of any importance. We really must go now; we've got to get back before the night falls. We haven't a torch to guide us."

With that they started to leave. Mark was suddenly reluctant to let her leave and followed them out. Catching up to them, he stepped in front of her, so that they had to stop so as not to bump into him. Mark took off his hat and with a very different attitude than he had earlier, looked down at her and quietly said, "Miss Emma, I want to apologize for my rudeness. I sometimes git a little riled when confronted with something I don't understand, that is with the candy and all."

This was not exactly what Mark had in his mind, and his voice almost had a quiver in it. He continued, "If you would be kind enough to let me make up for my actions, I'd be right pleased if I could walk you home."

Emma still wasn't sure of Mark, but something made her feel more at ease with him than she previously felt. She was silent for longer than Mark would have liked, but he was trying hard not to get his dander up again.

Finally the tension was broken when Samuel, looking at his mother, said, "It's getting dark, Mother, and I know you always tell me I have to be home before it gets too dark—and ...."

Samuel paused as he looked at Mark and added, "Mr. Caldwell has been very kind to me, and I think he would protect us if a ruffian tried to harm us."

Mark was amazed at this young child's command of words. He would himself never have put them in that order. Looking at Samuel, Emma said, "We are not in the habit of putting someone out of their way. Besides, the fact is we have managed very well so far, and I'm sure we can continue to do so."

Mark sensed her putting him off and with a firmer voice answered, "Just tryin' to be neighborly, Mrs. Livingston. Don't mean no harm, I'll be on my way. Hope your walk ain't too far."

At that, Samuel grabbed Mark's arm and clung to him. Emma was mystified by Samuel's action and started to pull him away.

"Samuel, what has come over you? What are you doing? Please stop embarrassing us—and Mr. Caldwell."

Samuel released Mark and slowly backed away. Emma told Mark, "I truly apologize for Samuel's actions, I don't know what has come over him."

Mark, who intuitively seemed to know what the problem was answered, "Apologizin' ain't necessary. I'm thinkin' Samuel is just a bit scared of the dark. Maybe he's feelin' the dark is bigger than it is because he's in a place that he ain't familiar with and needs some reassurin'. You folks do seem far away from home."

Emma gave in, not all that reluctantly, took Samuel's hand and with a quivering voice told Mark, "It is true, Mr. Caldwell, we are a long, long way from home. Samuel and I would be most appreciative if you would walk us home, if it isn't too much to ask."

Mark didn't say another word, letting Emma have her space. He just walked with them as they proceeded down the boardwalk.

CHAPTER 25

Back at the farm that evening, Lydia noticed a definite change in Mark. He stood at the fence on the edge of their property staring out into nowhere. His mind was in town and on an English lady. Mark's imagination wandered as he pictured himself with Emma. This wasn't possible because Samuel indicated he had a father. That made it clear she was not a widow and therefore was not available to him. Nevertheless, he thought, *Isn't she just the prettiest little filly ever?* Those questions and others raced through his mind as he tried to sort them out. As he surveyed the farmland so dear to him, he asked himself why he felt so restless.

Suppertime came, and Lydia sent Jennie to fetch Mark. She approached Mark a bit curiously as Mark, obviously frustrated, was kicking the dirt around under his feet. Finally Jennie, not one to back off where her brothers were concerned, called out, "Mark, supper's on the table."

Mark didn't answer and continued to kick at the ground. Jennie again called out to him, this time impatiently, "Mark, supper's on the table!"

Mark turned slowly and looking at her didn't say a word but just half-smiled. Turning back to his fields for a moment, he sighed and started to follow Jennie back to the farm house. The silence around the table was deafening. Lydia was not sure what to say, but Mason just smiled and very slowly shook his head.

Lydia, observing Mason's actions and seeing Mark just picking at his food, finally broke the silence. "So, Mark, how was the trip into town? Anything new and exciting that I would be interested in? Sure missed going there today, but staying caught up here is a chore in itself. Besides, your pa gave me a wonderful gift. I'm going to make the most beautiful dress in the territory."

Mark looked at his mother and cracking a half-smile told her, "There's not much to say."

After a long pause as Mark pondered the right words, he finally reported, "There's some foreign folk from England that was shoppin' at the store. Never heard anyone talk so funny before."

Mark stopped and went back to picking at his food. Lydia asked, "Well, did you meet these folks?"

Without looking up, Mark answered, "Yeah, I did, Ma."

Lydia still digging, "Can you tell me a bit about them, Mark, or do I have to pry it out of your pa"?

Mark getting a bit frustrated just added, "It was a lady and her son. Seemed like nice folk. She don't seem to know much about our ways, she is a bit stubborn, she is .... Well that's it, Ma. I gotta get out to the barn, forgot to throw the hay for the horses."

With that Mark quickly got up and ran out the door. Lydia looked at Mason with wide eyes and said, "Throw the hay? What do we have hired hands for? What's gotten into that boy?"

"What's gotten into that boy is that he's no longer a boy."

Lydia gave Mason a quizzical look as he continued, "My love, can't you see a man who is taken aback by a beautiful young woman? Don't you remember me fallin' all over myself when I first saw your beautiful face? Well, Mark's been like this since we got in the wagon to come home. That English lady is quite a looker, and with her strong-willed temperament, she tapped Mark to his core."

Lydia glowed as she recalled when Mason first laid eyes on her and when she on him.

CHAPTER 26

As the weeks sped by, it seemed to the Caldwells and the Neiters that each day grew more hectic. Jennie was now betrothed to Jonas and planning their wedding. Mason and Lydia's little girl, now grown up, would soon be leaving home.

Uncle Lucas' pending marriage to Catherine would mean other changes in living arrangements. Finally, John and Matthew had decided to go into the world as peace officers with Captain McNelly.

Luke had come to a decision too, his days of unrest over. He had taken Uncle Lucas up on his offer to become a rancher, so Uncle Lucas had bought the Jensens' ranch.

That left Lela. How should he approach her? His heart was hers, and he knew it but how to tell her? Would she love him for who he was? Would she accept his moody, grumpy, and sometimes brash boldness when speaking his mind? Most of all, could she live with his being a half-breed? Good questions to ask himself. Luke also wondered if she would be concerned whether he would be able to handle a cripple. Would he understand and be able to handle her independence? After all, she'd had to fend for herself over the years and not rely on someone to take care of her. It wasn't long before fate provided the answer.

With Lucas' decision to purchase the Jensens' ranch, he and Catherine decided they should marry sooner rather than later. A date was chosen about one month away.

This sent the ladies into a flurry of activity. Although Lela tried to spend a part of every day with Luke, there were times when his work simply left no time for her. Lydia was also concerned that Lela's attentions to Luke had become somewhat unseemly. In addition, on those days when the three ladies met to sew, it seemed unkind to leave Lela at the Caldwell farm by herself. So for some time now, she had been invited to join Lydia, Catherine, and Alice in sewing—an activity for which Lela had shown uncommon talent.

Therefore it came as no surprise that when the nuptials for Catherine and Lucas were announced, Lela spoke up quickly, "Miss Catherine, it would give me the most pleasure if you would allow me to make a weddin' gown for you. I've been seein' the catalogs down at the general store, and I have some ideas if you'd let me tell you."

"You understand, Lela," Catherine responded gently, "that I am not marrying for the first time. A white gown would be inappropriate. I can just wear my Sunday-go-to-meeting dress."

"Oh, I understand, Miss Catherine. I had in mind somethin' in a lovely fabric that I saw in Mr. Harris' store. It would go so well with your dark hair. And I saw a most becomin' hat that would frame your face to match."

So while Lucas consulted with Pastor Coy and arranged for a ceremony at the church he had founded, the ladies tended to the myriad details of a wedding. Lela appointed herself to make Catherine's gown in a lovely shade of soft sage green—a gown that could later be worn for any number of occasions.

In addition, a message had been sent to Matthew to see if he could arrange leave from his training to attend his mother's wedding—and John too if that would be allowed. It was.

As Luke, Mark, and Lela were in town that October day, a light drizzle was falling that portended heavier rain to come. The two men needed supplies and couldn't let rain stop them though they had thought they might get back home before it became heavy. Lela had insisted on going along as she needed to purchase the fabric and other sewing supplies to work on Catherine's wedding dress. As the men knew only too well, she was persistent in having her own way, so she tagged along. Luke placed her wheelchair on the boardwalk near the store and put her in it.

He told her, "Now don't be rollin' off this boardwalk. Sure 'nough, you'll be in trouble if'n you do. Get your shoppin' done and wait back here. We won't be long pickin' up the tools from the hardware store and leather straps we need from the blacksmith."

She replied with a sigh, "Luke Geddes, quit treatin' me like a child. I can get along just fine without your orders."

Luke just looked at her and, shaking his head, walked away. He felt pain in his heart though, hearing her say she could get along without him. Why should that bother him anyway? As if he didn't know.

He and Mark left Lela and headed for the blacksmith. Lela finished her shopping and started to roll out of the store. As she did, the wheel of the chair struck a piece of wood blown from the roof by a gust of wind that preceded the rain. This thrust her chair around, and down the steps she went.

As the rain started to fall in earnest, people had rushed indoors, so there was no one around to help her as she lay in the mud. Her words came back to haunt her. *I can get along without your....* Maybe she did need him to give some order to her life. Suddenly her independence started to fade into tears as she struggled to pull herself into her chair.

Then it happened. The rain turned to deluge, blinding a man on horseback who rode straight at Lela unable to see her. Just as the horse was about to trample her, a hand came from nowhere and grabbed the horse's bridle. This stopped the horse and surprised the rider, who immediately pulled back on the horse's reins.

Luke reached down, pulled Lela from the mud, and held her tight in his arms. He looked into her tear-filled eyes as he carried her up the steps to the boardwalk and told her, You're a stubborn woman, Lela Elliot, maybe you're right. It might be you can do without me to pull you out of the mud, snow, hail, and rain." The rain hid the flood of tears rolling down her face. She had nothing to say.

A few weeks later, on a chill but sunny day in mid-November, the families, neighbors and close friends from the town gathered at the Free Will Baptist Church. Lucas had lived in the area for many years, so most of the townspeople knew him and, pleased that he had found happiness again, were delighted to join him in celebrating his joy.

No one paid attention to the weather as a tall, smiling, and proud Matthew Lo escorted his mother Catherine in her lovely dress down the church's central aisle to where a grinning Uncle Lucas waited to make her Mrs. Lucas

Neiter. Pastor Jonas Coy read the words. The happy couple exchanged vows, and he pronounced them man and wife.

After the ceremony, all those in attendance had been invited to the Caldwell farm for a festive reception, as the cabin of Alice and Paul had been deemed too small. Then Lucas helped his new bride into the carriage, and they rode away together to the ranch that was to be their new home.

The house previously owned by the Jensens had been quickly made ready with everyone pitching in. Lucas had already moved from the Caldwell farm and helped Catherine move her belongings from the cabin she'd shared with her sister and brother-in-law.

Mason's earlier recollection had been right. There was a small line shack on the property, and Luke set about cleaning it and making it ready to move into. After giving the newlyweds a week or so of private time together, Luke would follow and start a new life as a cattleman and rancher.

Two days later, Mason, Lydia and Jennie, along with Catherine, Lucas, and Luke stood in the Caldwells' front yard as John and Matthew made ready to ride off, excitement blanketing their faces, as they anticipated new adventures to serve and protect. Their mentor, Captain McNelly, had been passing through and had joined the boys for the trip back to camp.

Lydia, with tears in her eyes told McNelly, "Keep an eye on these rascals. They seem too eager to get into a scrape," to which McNelly answered, "I can only tell you, Mrs. Caldwell, I been watchin' these two 'rascals,' as you call them, in their trainin'. They're fine young man who've learned our methods well, and those regulations are made to keep our recruits in line, so you need not worry."

Mason felt proud, but now he reflected back on his war days and the young men who'd served with him who held that same pride. He told the boys, "You listen and listen good to Captain McNelly and your other officers. I know how you feel right about now, but don't go takin' foolish chances. Be ready, be careful, and always go with your Lord."

Each of the mothers, Lydia and Catherine, hovered and fussed over her son. With that, the three rode off yelling goodbyes and waving to family and friends.

Luke standing beside Lela said to her, "Life has given me a new chance, and this family has given me redemption for the pain I caused them. A man couldn't ask for more than that."

Luke paused as he looked down at Lela. She waited for the rest but it didn't come. A shiver of dread ran through her, and hope faded that she and Luke would ever be together.

As Luke climbed up on his horse to head back to the fields, he groped for words and finally said, "Don't be getting that chair stuck in the mud."

Lela tried to smile back at Luke as she hid her thoughts and aching heart.

Mark also headed for his beloved fields, content to be a tiller of the soil.

Mason, with his arm around Lydia, turned to her and looking ever so lovingly into her eyes, softly told her, "Love has prevailed this day. It is a day to rejoice in the Lord for his countless blessings. But I rejoice more in the woman he has given me. I could never find a purer love this side of heaven. You have loved me through my faults, my failures, and all my complaining. I can never give you all that you deserve, but I will do my best to honor and love you as I'm called by God to do."

Lydia, putting her hand on his face, only looked at him with the tenderness of her heart and answered, "We have traveled the road together, we have always traveled this life together, and" then softly added, "we will continue to travel it together when we are in Paradise."

CHAPTER 27

Since Christmas, John and Matthew's lives had become decidedly busy working with Captain McNelly and the volunteers. It seemed that bad guys rarely took time off, as was the case with their current assignment. After reporting to Captain McNelly in Jacksonville, John and Matthew were assigned to escort Jack Collins, a man accused of murder, back to Huntsville. The problem was that Collins was notorious for his lack of respect for the law. This animosity wasn't just hate, but pure malevolence.

Collins' father had been killed while trying to rob a bank. The son never got over that and vowed to take it out on anyone with a badge. He had proved this by killing the sheriff in Henderson, Texas. As he surveyed his two youthful escorts, they didn't make him feel he was being treated with respect. After all, wasn't he bad enough to have a seasoned old timer rather than a couple of raw recruits? Little did he realize that nothing could be further from the truth.

Collins sneered at the boys and asked them derisively, "Got nothin' better to do but to hold my hand? Don't hold too tight. I may have to help you grow up a bit. Don't like the law, never did since you killed my pa. You think you can get me to Huntsville? Think twice."

John was the first to answer, "Well, Mr. Collins, we don't respect you either, so I guess we start out even. But if you're likin' to try us, you best be thinkin' hard as to what you're gonna do."

Matthew added, "Mr. Collins, we may look young, but do we look foolish? What makes a man like you think you can go on forever and not get what's coming to you? We're going to be all over you. 'Bout time someone should have a Jesus talk with you. Of course, I guess going to prison will help get the Devil out of you."

"I doubt it, son. The Devil done learnt a lot from me. Tame me? No one else could, so don't get your hopes up. Better you have no hopes at all."

It was January, so the nights were still cold, and sleeping on the ground didn't help much. A blanket under you, a blanket on top of you, and a saddle for a pillow does make one a bit homesick. It was even too cold and uncomfortable for John to play a tune, although that didn't make Matthew especially unhappy.

Of course one of them had to be awake at all times to watch Collins. From the warning they had received from Captain McNelly, this guy was as bad as they came. At one point, Collins actually turned over, grabbed Matthew, and tried to seize Matthew's gun. Matthew, however, not trusting him to begin with, didn't have his gun on him. Matthew had placed his gun just far enough out of reach that with his own speed he knew he could get to it before Collins could.

Not anticipating this, Collins had started a wrestling match with Matthew. It took but a few seconds before Collins, who still had his handcuffs on, was face down in the dirt. John didn't even wake up.

In the morning John looked at Collins, who was cuffed to a tree, and turning to Matthew, commented, "I see you had a bit of a tussle and was polite enough not to wake me. I appreciate that, Matthew."

"You were to the point of snoring, John, and looked so peaceful. Mr. Collins was good too, he didn't even grunt. Of course that would have been pretty hard with his face in the dirt."

The boys delivered Collins to the prison in Huntsville and collected the bounty from the prison warden.

"Glad you boys weren't harmed or got into it with Collins. He would as soon kill ya as look at ya."

"He tried," John said looking at Matthew and continued, "My partner was a mite too fast for him."

Both Matthew and John smiled as they waved goodbye to the warden and headed back to Jacksonville. What had they learned from this encounter? Collins was just another example of the "bad guy" element. There were many more like him out there—and probably would be 'til the end of time. It was becoming more and more clear to them that there was a cloak of evil that could descend on men at any time. Keeping the peace brought a new emotion to them both. First, it stirred memories of how they were brought up by God-fearing, Christ-believing parents.

Second, dealing one on one with these criminals—murderers, thieves, and the like—brought on an emotion of sorrow for all mankind. Both young men discovered they actually felt pity for these men. How and why had they become like they were? Where were their folks when they were growing up? Life was hard enough in the wilderness, carving out a home from forests and from barren land. Why would these men take from those who have worked so hard to make a life for themselves and their families?

"I'm not sure what makes these men so ruthless, John. They just hurt people and have no regret for their actions. I find myself feeling sorry for them."

"I would guess that like me, Matthew, you were taught to love all men as God's Word tells us. That's the commandment we have from our Lord. Remember what Luke said when he killed Pike? 'I wish I could hate you Pike, but all I feel is pity for ya, and God's mercy on him.' Luke was on his way to feelin' the Spirit movin' in him."

John with his head lowered thoughtfully continued, "I remember the time Luke and I were talkin' about his killin' in the war, bein' a sniper and all, how he had remorse for what he done. Although it was his duty, he said it hurt him to his soul and wanted to find peace and forgiveness. He said he knows somethin' inside of him was askin' not to hate. I guess we need to keep that Spirit workin' in us too, so's we don't git hard-hearted and start to learn what hate is while servin' to keep the peace. The best thing for us is to keep ourselves in prayer."

"I agree, John. Best we stay in prayer not just for staying safe but to keep our hearts and souls going in the right direction."

With that the time had come to be bedding down, but before they did John decided to sing a song.

"Remember that song I wanted to sing to you before we were interrupted by those first three thievin', murderous vermin? Well I'll serenade you now if'n you don't mind."

Matthew wasn't quite ready to hear the angels sing just yet.

"Let me clean my ears first, John, or maybe I'll just let them stay plugged up."

Not to be deterred, John picked up his guitar and with a grin, began,

Walkin' down the roads and these dirty ol' streets,
A thought came to mind seein' dust on my feet.
The Good Book says I'll be walkin' on streets of gold
Ain't no dust, ain't no dirt gittin' under my soles.

Glory Land is comin' just 'round the bend,
And when I die, I will ascend.
I'll be walkin' on down great streets of gold.
Yes, I'll be a-walkin' as the Good Book told.

Chorus
Glory Land, oh Glory Land,
That's the place of my very last stand.
Face to face with the Man I trusted,
I'll face the Man that was so blessed.

What wonders are there in the Glory Land?
For sure not this dirt and not this sand.
Whatever it is let me say only this
I know for sure it will be so grand.

It's marchin' through that Glory Land,
The very last place we'll make our stand,
With the Lord walkin' at our side.
Glory Land, oh sweet bye and bye.

Chorus

At this point, John looked at Matthew with a grin on his face as he finished:

> *Angels will sing much better than I*
> *And carry a tune that will make you cry.*
> *Matthew, you best not be a-laughin' at me,*
> *Even though I know you agree.*

Matthew did laugh at this last verse and told John, "I do agree, my brother. Maybe by the time you walk in Glory Land, you'll be able to carry a tune."

They both laughed as they laid their heads down. Sleep came a little easier now that John had brought some levity to their conversation, but still, they continued to think of the sorrows this world has on this side of Glory Land.

Chapter 28

A few weeks passed. Luke was now living on the new cattle ranch with Uncle Lucas and Catherine and feeling happy with the decision to stay on with the new family he had acquired through love and honesty. It was something he had always looked for and had finally found. One afternoon Lela rode out to the ranch to visit Luke. It had become difficult for her not seeing him every day. Although she had not said anything to anyone about it, the Caldwells knew better.

As Luke and Lela sat on the porch of the ranch, Luke told her, "Well, won't have to worry about getting stuck in the mud on the way to California, will we?"

Lela, trying to look cheerful, responded, "No, Luke Geddes, I guess I'll have to stay out of wagon ruts around these ranches."

They smiled at each other, but neither of them uttered their usual laugh. Lela continued her act, wondering if it might be best for her to leave all those she had grown to love and to head to a new place, maybe far away, to start over.

With the marriage of Lucas to Catherine having taken place in mid-November followed just a few weeks later by Christmas, Jennie's wedding to Jonas was set for late March.

Lydia and Jennie Caldwell were in flurry of activity. For Jennie, it was to be her day of days, so no detail would be spared. First, they unpacked Lydia's gown for a fitting. It was in fact a few inches too short on Jennie and needed some other small alterations. Alice was true to her word. She unpacked the ball gown from her grandmother and brought it to the Caldwell home. There was more than enough lace and fabric to lengthen the gown, and after a bit of conversation among the ladies, it was determined that the rest of the gown could be used to make paraments and altar linens in the church.

Lela brought her considerable talents to the alterations, and in a few short weeks, Jennie was arrayed in a most beautiful gown.

"We must be sure to keep it up here in the sewing room, Ma," said Jennie. "You know it's considered bad luck for the groom to see the bride's gown before the weddin' day."

"Pshaw," replied Lydia. "That's an old superstition. Still, there's no call for Jonas to be comin' up here to this room at any time."

Meanwhile, Jonas was faced with a small predicament of his own. He was the pastor of the local church, but he could hardly perform his own nuptials. Jonas, however, was nothing if not creative. As soon as Jennie accepted his proposal, he had sent a telegram to the seminary where he had studied for the ministry asking if any of its graduates had found callings in northern or eastern Texas.

Not long afterward, a letter came back from one of his professors that brought him great joy. His former professor and mentor, Elias Craddock, was now the pastor of a church in Nacogdoches, Texas, which was just a little more than fifty miles from Crockett, an easy trip via stagecoach. Quickly another letter was dispatched, and soon a reply resolved Jonas' quandary. Pastor Craddock remembered his former student and said it would bring him great pleasure to officiate at his wedding.

Mason increased his "walks" first to daily and then two times a day. One evening as they readied for bed, he confided, "Lydia, my love, I don't think I could bear it if I were unable to walk well enough to give away my one and only daughter at her wedding. I've been practicing in the barn, and I've asked Mr. Harris at the general store to order me one of those fine walking canes."

Lydia merely smiled a knowing smile and said, "I'm sure Jennie will be pleased and proud to have you give her away."

Soon after John and Matthew had delivered Collins to the territorial prison, they had been given leave, to spend some time at home with their families.

While in town one morning a few days after arriving home, they noticed a commotion in the main street of Crockett and went to investigate. Now that they were trained members of the still unnamed volunteer force, they were always alert for problems. This commotion didn't look very good. In the middle of the street, three men were beating and kicking a young man who could in no way defend himself.

As John and Matthew intervened, the men started in on them. Big mistake. John started using the oriental skills that Matthew had taught him on one man, while Matthew took the other two down with ease. The young victim was beaten too severely to get up, and none of the townsfolk seemed to want to help.

John grabbed his opponent and, slamming him into hitching post, said, "Real brave, three of ya takin' on this kid. Hope you got no hankerin' for more trouble than you can handle stranger."

With that the man took a swing at John. Another big mistake. John grabbed his arm and twisting around, pinned the man in a painful arm lock just short of breaking it.

"You done, stranger?"

Matthew just watched. He had done a number on the other two, who just sat on the ground thinking twice about getting up. John asked, "What brought on a whippin' like this that three of you ganged up on one poor guy?"

Thinking Matthew and John would sing a different tune at his answer, one relaxed and with a smirk answered, "Well, this man ain't a man, if'n you know what I mean."

"No, I don't know what you mean, want to explain?"

"Well," answered the big man, "He's got lady-like tendencies, you know. He's a man who likes a man in a manly way. We heard him say he would rather be with a man than with a woman."

This was the first time either John or Matthew had had any experience with men desiring other men as they would a woman, though they had read of such things in the Bible. Both were at a loss for words as they looked at each other confused.

Finally, Matthew looked down at the two on the ground and told them, "Maybe your parents didn't teach you respect for all of God's children so this must be the reason for this whipping as far as you're concerned. Well a human being is a human being. You three have violated the code of—aahhh—well—aahhh, the Great Commandment to love your neighbors, accepting all God's creatures in love."

With that Matthew looked at John and just shrugged his shoulders. It sounded good to him, and apparently to John also, who let loose of his combatant friend and said, "Yeah. That's it, all right. Now go on, the three of ya. Take off and don't let us catch you at this again, or you're likely to wind up behind bars."

The three bullies scrambled up and took off. The young victim still couldn't get up, so John and Matthew assisted him and ushered him to Doc Thompson's. On the way they asked, "What's your name, and what brings you to our town?"

"My name is Bo Willis, and I'm just headed through from the East. I didn't think people here were as nasty and not understanding as they are where I come from, and no use takin' me to the doc 'cause I'm sure he won't help me once he makes his mind up that I'm not what you'd call normal."

John answered with a laugh, "Doc ain't too normal himself. Er, no, no—aahhh, I don't mean in your way. I, ah, mean that, ah, well, it's just after all he's seen, he just rolls his eyes and does his job."

John decided not to say any more since he now had his foot in his mouth. They dropped Bo off with Doc Thompson and stepped outside to discuss this new experience of life. Are there, they wondered, answers to this way of living?

"You sure got a gift for words, Brother Matthew, you sure told those three about how to treat God's children," came John's words as he was trying to break the ice.

"Well, I guess that's the best I could do not knowing if I would say something stupid. Maybe it's a question for Jonas as it comes right from the Bible, but the Book doesn't say too clearly how we should handle it. For ourselves, maybe, but not about others," Matthew finished.

In the meantime, Doc did the best he could with Bo and, calling John and Matthew in, told them, "Bo here is going to need some rest so he can heal from all these deep bruises. His one arm is swollen, and I suspect he may have a fracture. I would feel pretty bad if he was left alone and these fellows come a lookin' for him again. Is there anywhere you can take him?"

Matthew had an idea, "Why not take him to Uncle Lucas' place and let Mom nurse him? Those bullies don't need to know where Bo is, and with Luke there, he should be safe even if they did come calling; I wouldn't want to try to start something with Luke around."

John agreed readily, so they got Bo's horse and rode off toward the Neiter/Geddes ranch, slowly for Bo's sake. As the Caldwell farm was on the way, they stopped to give Bo a chance to rest and introduce him.

Mason, the kind man that he was, listened to what had taken place in town, and putting his hand on Bo, told him, "Sometimes men are just mean because they don't understand; sometimes they're born that way, and sometimes they are just ignorant. I hope you find it in your heart to forgive them one day. I know how hard forgiveness can be, but it sets the heart free, believe me."

Bo managed a smile and replied, "Thank you, Mr. Caldwell, for not judging me. I'm grateful there are some who aren't like those I mostly meet."

The three rested for a while, and Lydia prepared them a nourishing lunch. Leaning down to Bo, she said, "I'm glad to have made your acquaintance, Bo. I hope you find peace on this side of heaven. Please know you will be in our prayers. I have a feelin' we haven't seen the last of you, and that would be just fine with us Caldwells."

Bo was taken aback by the love he received from these strangers and didn't really know how to thank them. He gathered his thoughts and said, "I would be honored if you let me call you friends. I don't have many, none around here for sure."

Mason answered, "We'd be honored to call you friend, and yes, you likewise do the same."

Lunch over, John, Matthew, and Bo mounted up and rode away toward Lucas' and Luke's place. Arriving at the entrance gate, they looked up and saw a sign above the entrance reading,

ROCKING EAGLE RANCH

That took the boys back a notch and left them wondering how that name came about, or indeed, if they were even in the right place. They had returned to their duties immediately after Catherine had moved in with her new husband, so they'd not heard any news from the Neiters since the wedding. As they rode up to the house, they were relieved to see Uncle Lucas nailing boards to a new room at the side of the house.

As he approached to greet the men, John jumped off his horse and yelled to him, "Well, Uncle Lucas, probably thought you could get away with not seein' us for a spell. That's not likely."

"Well, I'm never away from seein' ya. Those ungodly faces couldn't be forgot no matter what I do."

With that they embraced warmly, their mutual love evident in their faces. Bo drank it all in as it was an unusual scene for him. Lela came wheeling out onto the porch and gave them a warm and happy greeting. Catherine followed Lela, and by then Matthew was on the porch hugging his mother as she said, "I hope you boys are staying safe and not getting into any fights."

Bo just looked at Catherine and didn't say a word. The boys helped Bo down off his horse and took him into the house. No one said anything, but by the looks on their faces, they had a lot of questions.

Settling Bo on the couch where he could stretch out, John was the first to speak, "This here's Bo Willis. He got himself beat up pretty bad, and Doc Thompson wants him to rest and heal up. He might have some broken bones. We had a long ride, and for now he needs rest. He is...."

Bo interrupted. "This ain't a good idea. I appreciate the kindness John and Matthew have shown me, but I couldn't impose anymore. I'll just get to my horse and be on my way. Don't want to bother anyone no more."

Bo squirmed some and grimaced with pain as he tried to get up. He was totally overwhelmed by all that had been going on. Also, he was not comfortable taking a handout and didn't want to start. Matthew stopped him and said, "How are you going to ride with all that pain? Besides, if you don't do what Doc told you, you're gonna just hurt yourself more."

Frustration and embarrassment were evident in Bo as he said to Matthew, "Maybe you'd better tell why I got beat up. Maybe they would like to put me on my horse and get rid of me."

Those in the room looked at each other in bewilderment at Bo's statement. Just then Luke came in. "What's going on? I saw the horses from the corral and was wondering who our visitors were. I thought I recognized John and Matthew's horses but the third I didn't."

Catherine chimed in with, "John, Matthew, how about you introduce your new friend to Luke?"

With introductions out of the way, Bo continued his discourse, "Where I come from they just say I have a gender problem. I'm not much on women, and I—well, I'm tired of trying to explain."

Catherine answered, "Bo, I think most of us know what you're trying to say. Let me try to explain it. What Bo is experiencing is a feeling that women don't interest him. He has feelings toward other men that most men have toward women. Does that pretty much sum it up, Bo?"

Bo looked down and answered, "Yes, ma'am, it pretty much does."

Silence fell over the room for a moment, but the boys then told how they had actually met Bo. He was feeling pretty overwhelmed by now, as if he was about to get beaten up all over again.

Uncle Lucas spoke. "Well Bo, I'm a man of few words, and I'm a-gonna say this. You're welcome to stay here 'til you heal, and then whatever decision you make, I'm sure we all will support it. Now I ain't got a lot of space, but the bedroom that is half-built is closed in, and we can get you a bunk, and that is about as much privacy we can give you for now—if'n that works. And we insist that it will work, because we ain't gonna toss you out. So you rest here while we get that room ready for you."

Bo was too tired to say anything. He sensed that these were caring folk who genuinely meant what they said, so he gave in and simply said, "I'll find a way to repay you all. That's a promise."

A cot and bedding were rounded up, and they made Bo as comfortable as possible given his injuries.

Once Bo was settled, John and Matthew cornered Luke to ask about the name Uncle Lucas and Luke had given to the ranch. John was first to bring it up. "A name like that don't make much sense to me. I ain't never seen an eagle in any kind of chair."

Matthew added, "Well, maybe the eagle is trying to lift the chair and drop it on some old cows so they can rest while they're a chewing their cuds."

That brought a laugh, and Luke, smiling and grinning, told them this story.

"You see, my tribe has always had a feelin' for the eagle. It flies free and isn't troubled by what it sees or does. The eagle has strength in both body and character, and I'd like to be like that. After what I've been through, I feel I've earned at least a small part in that eagle's life. God has been good to me. Since I been talkin' with Jonas about how God loves to be there even for people like me, I feel like I can take flight anytime and enjoy what life has in store for me. Also I feel strong, and so the work it takes to keep this ranch going doesn't bother me, but Uncle Lucas, well there's another story."

Matthew and John looked at each other wondering what that meant. John asked, "Uncle Lucas is pretty strong for a man his age. Are you sayin' there is a problem with him?"

Luke explained, "John, Uncle Lucas is doin' good, and he is strong, but he is havin' problems with his walkin'. His legs are gettin' weak, and he won't admit it to anyone, but we can see it when he walks. It looked like it might even be his knees. So I told him this. 'Uncle Lucas, you know I don't know much about ranchin', so I'll make you a deal. You sit in that there rocker and you supervise me in what to do next. Of course you will ride from time to time to do the supervisin'.

"Then Lela, well you know how she shows up at the oddest times. She overheard our conversation and said, 'What I see is a rocker and an eagle.' Well the name stuck."

One could hear the howling a mile off. Luke walked away from the boys as they continued to laugh, but John wasn't going to let this go. He loved the old man. When it came to Uncle Lucas and his ailment, John was going to get him some help as soon as possible.

CHAPTER 29

The sun filled the sky, and the beauty of creation unfolded in all its majesty. Mason and Jennie stood alone in the front room of the Caldwell farmhouse waiting for the music to start. As Mason looked at Jennie, arrayed all in elegant white, a sheer veil held by a crown of fragrant white blossoms, it finally struck him that his little girl was no longer a little girl. He saw the beauty of a young woman with a glow about her that warmed the very place where they stood. He had known this day would come, but how does one prepare for it? How does a loving father look at this child of his and accept that she will soon be gone from his home?

The best Mason could do was to comfort himself knowing she would never be gone from his or her mother's hearts.

With warmth in his voice he said to Jennie, "You are a beautiful young lady, my little one, but I want you to remember, you will forever be my little girl. We have raised you to keep the Lord first in your heart. We couldn't be prouder of you, and we are pleased that you have found a true man of God to spend the rest of your life with."

"Pa, I want to be your little girl always; please don't let that ever change. You have been my strength in so many things." Trying hard not to cry, Jennie concluded, "I know you will always be there for me if I need you."

As Mason and Jennie embraced, they heard the first notes of music. Together they walked slowly and carefully from the house. At the steps, Jennie preceded him down and turned to assist him as he cautiously made his way down the few steps.

Using his new cane and leaning as much on Jennie as she on him, they turned toward the garden along the side of the house and walked slowly into the arbor lined with roses, irises, and other colorful flowers. The air was redolent with the scent of the jasmine and honeysuckle that covered the arbor, and the flowers created a pathway leading to Pastor Elias Craddock and Jonas.

John had gathered a few of his fellow musicians to play for the wedding. His pride in his little sister was evident by the look on his face as he watched her, a vision in white. Looking joyful and beautiful, she smiled lovingly at him as she walked past. It was evident that he had been practicing for some time because his strumming had never sounded so good.

Upon reaching the place where Jonas stood before Pastor Craddock, Mason gently placed Jennie's hand into Jonas' hand and waited.

The pastor began to read the familiar passages, "Dearly Beloved, We are gathered here together in the sight of God and this company to join this man and this woman in holy matrimony," followed shortly by "Who gives this woman to be married?"

Though Mason's face was lit with a proud smile, there were tears in his eyes as he said, "I do."

Then he looked directly at Jonas and spoke, "I pass our daughter on to you, Jonas Coy, asking that you will care for her as her mother and I have. Let the two of you become one with the Lord, keeping him first in your hearts, and you will both always walk in his light. We are proud to call you son."

Following the ceremony the assembled guests, who included not only family but neighbors and members of Jonas' church, rejoiced with the young newlywed couple. Also present were some of the townsfolk, Mr. Henley, Mr. Harris, and Mr. Teasely to name a few—good folks who never saw Mason as a cripple but as a man of integrity who always gave a helping hand to those in need. The Caldwell family was loved by all. As everyone celebrated together, there was a feeling of oneness, a time when strangers came to know each other and became friends.

As always, there were one or two who hit the jug a bit too much, but it didn't take John, when not playing the music, or Matthew to simmer things down. All in all, it was a day that would be long remembered.

During a brief lull in the festivities, Jonas, Jennie, and Pastor Craddock returned to the house with Mason and Lydia, where together they opened a large leather-bound Bible, a gift from Lydia and Mason to their only daughter. Finding the pages in the middle of the book for recording significant events in the family, Pastor Craddock made the first entry, recording for all time the joining of Jennie and Jonas as one.

CHAPTER 30

A week passed. John and Matthew had returned to headquarters again.

Bo was pretty well healed and able to get around with only a bit of a limp. Recuperation had given Bo time to reflect on his relationship with his new acquaintances, especially with Uncle Lucas. He even called him Uncle from time to time to gauge his reaction. Lucas didn't mind, especially if it helped Bo to heal.

One morning when the air was fresh with the new spring, Lucas sat in his rocker as Bo sat in the chair next to him. Uncle Lucas was telling Bo how he'd come to know Luke through Mason.

"You see, Bo, Luke has had his share of trouble and just wanted to settle down. I was needin' to get back on my own again and not continue to be a stick-in-the-mud at the Caldwells'. God works in mysterious ways it seems, and after I lost my Anna, he brought Catherine into my life. It seems God is in the hookin'-up business."

Bo's only reaction was to be happy that Uncle Lucas had found joy in his new life.

"Good to see you got hope, Lucas, but that's a hard stretch for me. I suppose if you got enough though, maybe things will work out."

Lucas smiled at Bo, and patting his shoulder, exclaimed, "Keep looking, Bo. There's a heap of hope out there just waitin' for someone to grab and hold on to."

At this moment, they heard a wagon and looked up to see Jonas and Jennie coming down the road to the house. As they drove up to the house, Lela came out and greeted them with a smile and a wave.

Lucas whooped, "Dag nab it, if'n it ain't the preacher and his bride. Probably makin' their courtesy calls after the weddin'."

Bo shrank back and his heart sank. He hadn't met them yet, and his defenses went up automatically. All he could remember was the bad experiences he'd had with preachers. *Will I be judged if they know who I am, and "what" I am? Surely, he is going to introduce me to these two.*

How agonizing it had been to talk with preachers in the past. To a man, they didn't seem to know how to deal with what he was going through or how to help him to identify his feelings. He was even told he was a sinner bound for damnation. How was he going to face another preacher? Bo quickly entered the house and went to his room.

As the others entered the house, Catherine called out to Bo to come out. He didn't, so Catherine knocked on the door. Bo just said, "I'm not feeling too good, I'm going to rest a spell."

Catherine figured it was best to leave him alone. Bo paced the floor as he said to himself, *Another self-righteous man of the cloth. What does he know? I figure he'll be the one who will turn these folk against me. Why am I here? Why should I even bother to think that for once I have made some understanding friends?* His past experiences hadn't given him much hope of forging friendships with people unlike himself. He feared they would soon turn against him. A sadness came over Bo, as he had been through this before, though he was hoping that this time it would be different.

As Catherine offered refreshments to the others, she said, "Looks like you beat the rain. I know we are in for a really wet one this time. Might just plan on staying a spell. Besides, we have plenty for dinner so we would be pleased if you would join us."

Jonas answered, "I couldn't remember any time I turned down a delicious home-cooked meal. That is, I mean, not that Jennie isn't a great cook," he added hastily.

After a laugh from everyone, Jennie continued, "It looked like you have a house guest. Maybe we can meet him still. He kinda left us in a hurry."

Catherine responded, "You will, he's just restin' for a spell. He'll be out for dinner."

An hour passed. Bo was still in his room, getting more and more uneasy about meeting Jonas and Jennie. Meanwhile, dark rain clouds billowed outside. Luke had been in the field but headed to the house as the clouds appeared, making note of Jonas' wagon as he passed the barn. Entering the house and greeting everyone, Luke said, "Well, Lela, what you got for this hungry man to eat? I'm starvin."

Lela wheeled over to him and swatted him with the spoon she held in her hand. Everyone knew she was always having fun with Luke. He bent down and took the spoon from her saying, "Keep it up, and I'll have to take you to the woodshed and see how tough you are when I...."

Lela interrupted, "I dare ya, you big bully. I'll get Tiama to be a kickin' the dickens out of you."

This brought a laugh from the others, who poked fun at Luke and called him a big bully.

When the meal was on the table, Catherine again knocked on Bo's door. This time she told him in a warm but firm voice, "Bo, I think you need to come out now and eat your lunch. You need your strength if you're gonna heal properly."

Bo reluctantly came out with his head lowered, not meeting the eyes of Jonas and Jennie.

Catherine made the introductions. They exchanged greetings and sat for the midday meal, but there was a quiet tension in Bo that everyone else felt as well.

Jonas said grace, and everyone started to enjoy the meal before them. Most of the table conversation revolved around about cattle and the farming business. That suited Bo fine, especially since his situation hadn't come up. With the meal out of the way, however, Bo finally looked over to Jonas and asked somewhat accusingly, "Pastor Jonas," Bo paused as he looked into Jonas' eyes, "so you're a preacher man?"

"Yes, Bo, I'm what some would call a preacher man, or a pastor if you like, but I would be obliged if you just called me Jonas."

With that, Bo still didn't relent and in a strong and urgent voice continued, "What does the Bible say about a man that took to another man with carnal desire?"

Everyone stopped breathing, and there was dead silence. Jonas felt as if he had just been shot between the eyes and just looked at Bo trying to figure out where this was going.

After a long pause, Bo with some indignity, continued, "You see, Mr. Preacher Man, as some around this table knows, I'm that kind of man. I ain't had a lot of good words from the pulpit about this. All I ever heard was I was a sinner and never heard or felt a lot of love."

Jonas was a young man but gifted with the Holy Spirit. He could hear the pain, loneliness, and anger, in Bo and with a quiet voice told him, "Well, Bo, I can tell you what the Bible has to say about a man lying with another man, and I can tell you what the Lord said about it."

Jonas now looked directly into Bo's eyes and continued, "Do you want to hear it, or you just already made up your mind and don't want to hear it? Your anger seems to precede your question."

Bo started to settle down a notch, realizing he'd opened a door that would be hard to close—especially by just walking away. He told Jonas, "I'm guessing you're right, 'cause I already made up my mind and know what you're gonna say, but since I asked, go ahead and see if you can convince me of something else."

With that, the others started to get up to give these two some space but Jonas told them, "Everyone, please stay. This message is meant for everyone because there is so much confusion on this. I learned this from a wise and Spirit-filled man in the seminary I attended. He knows God's Word more than anyone else in that seminary. I was blessed to have him as my teacher. So please listen so you all can give an answer if need be to some of the more ignorant folk you know."

Jonas turned his attention back to Bo as he continued, "You have a right to be angry and hurt by what you may have heard from the pulpit and from other people, 'cause it was more than likely wrong. Some folk are just ignorant and scared of what they think of people who are different from them or the way they think everyone ought to be. That's not what you'll get from me, 'cause I'll be givin' you truth for sure. Shame on those men of the cloth you've met before. Too bad they don't know better, and everyone else for that matter. First you must understand and, remember you asked, so here it comes."

Jonas didn't wait for an answer but looked more deeply into Bo's eyes and gave his answer, "According to God's Word, it is a grave sin for a man to lie with another man. The Old Testament tells us this. But, remember this if you don't remember anything else. Having those feelings, is not —you hearin' me?—is **not** a sin. Being a man that has these feelings nohow makes you a sinner. Understand? But know this too. If you act on them, then you are sinnin' just like if a man cheats on his wife, or a wife cheats on her husband, or like a man who murders another man or steals from him. All sin is sin, and one ain't any different from another because they all hurt the Lord and go against his law and his Word, and his love I might add.

"Know this too. God is the one who determines what is and what is not sin, not man. Now here is the most important thing you must do. You will have to settle your relationship with the Lord first. I ain't in the judgin' business and no one in this room, or in this world, has the right to judge you. What you decide, what you do, and how you act is up to you. You must always remember that you are loved by our gracious Lord, and I'm willin' to bet by those of us who are in this room."

Jonas paused but for a moment then added this guarantee, "Bo, we all—and this includes you—are *'saved by grace through faith, and that not of ourselves lest any man should boast,'*[4] and also *'God so loved the world that He gave His only begotten Son that whoever believes on Him should not perish but have everlasting life.'*[5] This, Bo, is the only message you should be gettin'. So you must, as I have said, first get your relationship straight with God and his Son. Then the rest is up to you."

Bo was visibly shaken by this as he tried to digest it. It was new to him just as it was new to him to have these folks accept him for who and what he was. Bo looked a little lost but didn't feel quite as alone as he had before. Jonas reached over and put his hand on Bo's shoulder. At that everyone just sat quietly, as they too had learned something they had never known.

The rainstorm had passed, and a late afternoon sun peeked through the clouds. Jonas escorted Jennie to their wagon, and Lela left soon after.

CHAPTER 31

Everyone was at rest at the Rocking Eagle Ranch except Luke. He was out at the corral just hanging on the fence gazing up into a star-filled the sky. He said with a whisper,

"Good Lord, I bin a thinkin' about this stubborn female a whole bunch. Now why would I want to go and do a thing like that? That could mean a possible weddin'. Yes, Lela is stubborn and sometimes downright bossy all right, but she ain't mean. No, not a mean bone in her body. Maybe she'd be a good thing for me. I sure know I need much help, kinda get bossy myself I'm sure. Little stubborn too. As if you ain't knowin' that. This feelin' is awful strange to me—I don't understand all that's happenin' inside me. Oh, this is all so confusin'."

That night, Luke tossed and turned. His sleep was filled with troubling dreams. As the next day dawned, he was restless and almost cranky. Bo, Uncle Lucas, and Catherine were already sitting around the breakfast table when he appeared. The food was ready, but there was dead silence from Luke.

Uncle Lucas commented, "Luke, you're mighty quiet this mornin'. You ailin'?"

Luke made no response but ate quickly and left for the barn.

When Luke had moved to the ranch with Uncle Lucas and Catherine, Lela had missed his daily presence intensely. She had taken every opportunity to ride over to the Rocking Eagle to visit, and this day would be no exception. Lela had thought long and hard since that day in the rain wondering what Luke had meant. Was he saying he wouldn't be there when she needed him?

Luke heard the sound of her wagon as she came up the road. She saw Luke at the corral and called to him. As he usually did, he approached the wagon to help her down and into her chair. Once she was seated in the "wheeled contraption," she usually wheeled herself with little effort as she was strong from having had to push herself around in the wheelchair for many years.

"Luke, you all right? Is there somethin' that's a-botherin' you?"

Luke didn't answer her, so she tried to follow him to the corral. The previous day's rain had left its muddy afterlife, and Lela struggled to wheel herself over the soggy earth to him. He turned and watched her struggle then started toward her as she confidently stated, "It's okay, Luke, I can get to ya, just give me a minute."

Luke threw his hands in the air and, frustrated, blurted out, "Dang, woman! I ain't never met a female as stubborn as you. That's the reason I didn't want to take you to California with me. Look at you, stuck in the mud." And without missing a beat, no pause, he blurted out,

"Will you marry me?"

With that Luke just stopped cold, looked at the sky, and under his breath said, *I went and did it. I went and did it. Oh my Lord, now what do I do?* At this point, Lela was almost in front of him trying to push herself out of her chair so she could grab hold of him.

Luke reached down, grabbed her, pulled her into his arms as he said, "I ain't much, couldn't promise much, but if'n you can accept me the way I am, I'll do my best to make you a happy woman. I'll do my best to take care o' ya."

Lela replied, tears flowing, "I was comin' to tell ya that I was plannin' to leave this place. Head for California myself. Don't know how I'd get there, but I just couldn't stay here and look into your eyes and feel the pain of —you—me— the future without you. Oh, Luke, I've been waitin' for that question a long time. I have answered that question many times in my heart, but, Luke, my dear Luke, I ain't a whole woman, and to have you saddled with …."

Luke quickly interrupted her, "You are more than a whole woman to me. You take care of me like no one ever could, or ever wanted to. Don't say no, Lela. I ain't never been feelin' this way before. I don't know what to say if'n you say no."

Lela, wrapping her arms tightly around Luke, softly said, "Yes, Luke Geddes, yes. I'll be all I can be to you. I've loved you for what seems forever, from the time you was lookin' up at me from the dirt in front of the jail house. I ain't gonna let you go."

The air was damp and a bit cold, but Luke and Lela didn't notice. They just held tightly to each other and sealed their love with a long kiss.

As noon approached, Catherine called for the others to come to lunch. Soon, the five of them were seated around the table, but no one spoke.

Finally, Lucas could hold back no longer. "Luke, Lela, what in tarnation is ailin' you two? By now you would be goin' after each other tooth and nail. You look like you got somethin' to say but the cat got your tongues. You two are usually slappin' each other around by now. Usually all your laughin' and carryin' on is what keeps us old folks awake around here."

Lela was the first to answer. She didn't look up from her plate but with an uncharacteristically shy voice answered.

"Well, Uncle Lucas, this big tough guy got soft and asked me to marry him."

With that Lela went back to eating. Though not totally surprised, all were taken aback and sat there dumfounded. Slowly, the smiles started across their faces as they looked at each other. Luke just sat there looking down at his food. He wasn't about to say anything. But by the same token, Uncle Lucas wasn't just going to sit there without getting the facts.

He asked, "Okay, Luke, get it out. What about it? Come on, Luke, spit it out."

Lela still didn't look up from her plate. Everyone sat watching and waiting for an answer, but Luke and Lela just continued to ignore everyone.

As each one continued to prod and push, Lela finally gave a flippant answer, "Well, if Tiama is included, I said then that would be fine with me." Luke put his arms around her and started to laugh. The rest joined in, and congratulations came flying across the table.

Meanwhile, back at the Caldwells, a new and interesting chain of events started to unfold. It seemed that Mason's military past wasn't going away. This time, however, it wasn't a bad thing. A young black man rode up to the ranch and, dismounting, shouted to Mason, who was sitting on the porch.

The young man called out, "Cap'm Caldwell, sir, ma name's Henry Bartholomew Hawkins. I reckon you jes' be wonderin' why I come to you."

Mason looked at the young man and agreed. "I'm wondering all right, Henry Bartholomew Hawkins. I can't recall who you are, but you look just a mite familiar."

"I come to be a-thankin' you. You saved me; that is you saved my life. Do you be rememberin'?"

Mason smiled and answered, "Well, you ain't that scrawny Yankee that ran up that hill to take your colors and got yourself shot by any chance"?

"Yes, sir, Cap'm, that's me all right."

"Well you've grown a bit since I saw you last, haven't ya?"

"I have, Cap'm. But I found you out through the hospital records after this war ended and am here to be a thankin' you."

Mason laughed and looking up as if talking to the wind but loud enough for Henry to hear, "Good Lord. I guess nobody has any privacy any more. Reminds me of Luke's detective work."

Henry looked confused and said, "Sorry, sir, I don't be knowin' any detective with a name of Luke, I ain't knowed any detectives at all."

Mason laughingly replied, "No, Henry, just that another man found me the same way. It seems you can find anyone these days if you have a hankerin' to do so."

Mason continued, "I remember you, Henry. I should have shot you, you Yankee blue coat, but you were so young and looked so helpless. Brave too. Didn't mind riskin' your life to get that flag. Didn't I cover you up with some branches and leaves?"

Henry smiled and with a lift in his voice answered, "Yes, sir, Cap'm, you surely did. Do you remember what you said?"

"Not a whole bunch, you want to refresh my memory?"

Henry did, "You said, Boy, I'm a mite busy right now fightin' a war, and I don't have it in me shoot ya and finish you off, but if your men don't find you, well, good luck."

"You got a powerful good memory there, Henry. Looks like your company found you."

Henry told Mason with a big smile, "Yes, Cap'm, and it's all because of you. What you ain't knowin' is that as I lay there, I saw a whole bunch of grey coats runnin' close, and was I scared. I was really hurtin'. You did a good job of hidin' me, so that's why I'm bein' here to be a thankin' you."

Mason limped slowly across the porch toward the steps. Henry hadn't known that Mason had been injured. Mason beckoned Henry to come up to him. Mason, with his warm countenance, reached out his hand. They shook, and Mason said, "Happy to see you made it out with your life and limb."

Henry managed a slight smile and answered, "Yes sir, and again, all my thanks be a-goin' to you. I guess it wasn't all true that they told us you Confederates were cut-throat villains, evil, dirty rotten, low down ...."

Mason laughingly interrupted, "That should about do it, Henry, we heard the same about you all."

Both had a hearty laugh. Mason yelled to Lydia, "We have a dinner guest." With that Henry was invited into the house, but Henry held back.

"I, ah, well you see, it ain't that I don't trust you, you savin' my life and all, but I—to be honest, sir, where I come from we just don't get invited into a white man's house— unless ...."

Henry lowered his head and continued, "Unless the masta has a chore for him to do."

By now Lydia was at the door and looked at Henry with her warm heart and loving soul, and of course she was confused. Mason told him, "Henry, I may be a Reb, but I never owned anybody, and I'm not gonna start now. I'm nobody's master, so best you put that out of your head."

Mason put his hand on Henry's arm and said, "It would seem to me that you might be a bit thirsty and hungry if you came all this way."

With that Lydia took Henry's other arm and helped pull Henry inside. Mason introduced Henry to Lydia.

No sooner had they sat down but Mark came through the door. Seeing Henry there, he asked, "You come lookin' for the job I posted in town?"

Henry looked at Mark a little bewildered and answered, "No, sir, I just came to tell Cap'm Caldwell something."

Mark answered, "Well, when you get done askin', I could sure use some help around here. If you're interested, I'll give you a try, and if you work out, I'll hire you."

Mason interrupted, "Mark, this here is Henry Bartholomew Hawkins. He and I were, well kind'a—well we served our country, so to speak."

Mark sat down, and Mason told the story of his relationship with Henry. Mark asked Henry, "Where ya headed? Got plans?"

Henry quietly said, "Well, I ain't gonna go back to my home. That place ain't changed that much since the war, and I couldn't git outta there fast enough. I ain't got no family. My pa was a slave to a harsh masta, and he ended up dyin' tryin' to escape. He was goin' to go away and find a way to get me and my ma to come later. Well, I run away and joined with the Yankees to git even with this man. Figured if we win the war, we be free, and I can get my ma. Trouble is, she got real sick while I was gone, and no one could help her. She died from the whoopin' cough, I think it was."

Henry stopped abruptly and with a stern voice said, "Why'm I tellin' you all this, I'm sure you ain't interested."

Mark answered, "Sure we are. If you've got nowhere to go and will work here, we'd like to know what kind a man we'd be hirin'. Of course he'd be of good character first, and then willin' to work hard. We got a lot of catchin' up to do since we're a bit behind in spring plantin'."

Henry wasn't expecting this, so he just sat quietly. Lydia finally said, "Mark, slow down, you need to let Henry here get his bearings. I know you mean well to offer him a job, but he may have plans that don't include ranching and farm work."

Henry told them, "I was headed west because I growed up 'round farm and horse country. I have experience in farmin' and horses. I hear the land in California is fertile and the soil is very rich, so I was thinkin' about headin' that way. Besides they grow a lot of cotton there from what I been a hearin'."

Mason asked, "What is all this California rush? Luke, you, the Jensens? What's wrong with this great land of Texas?"

Lydia and Mark smiled at each other, and of course Henry didn't get it. Mason told Henry, "If you like, you can spend the night in the bunkhouse, and we can discuss your moving on, wanting work, or whatever you think. Fair enough?"

The cold and wintery weather had pretty much passed, but it was not yet warm at night, and Henry was tired of sleeping under the stars and in the dampness. He welcomed some cover for the night not to mention a soft bunk. He replied, "Mighty kind of you, Cap'm Caldwell. Be mighty grateful to get a good night's sleep."

With that they set to eating the fine meal Lydia had prepared.

CHAPTER 32

Now that Luke had resolved his long period of indecision and asked Lela to marry him, he seemed to have developed a considerable degree of impatience. On the one hand, he almost couldn't wait to tie the knot. On the other hand, he was at a loss as how best to proceed from here. One morning at the breakfast table, Luke waited for Bo to finish and head for the barn, then he broached the topic to Lucas and Catherine.

"Uncle Lucas," he started, "I've gone and asked that beautiful scrappy woman to marry me. What am I to do now? We don't have no folks, 'sceptin' y'all and the Caldwells, of course. I jes' don't know the proper way to deal with these matters. They's more like women's matters. Once we marry, she'll be comin' here to live with me. This bein' your ranch, and all, I can't just take matters to myself with things like buildin' a cabin with a ramp for her chair or addin' on."

"Luke," started Uncle Lucas, "I want you to consider this ranch as much yours as mine. We understand that Lela has some special problems, and if you want to make the line shack larger, more permanent, add a ramp, even build another house—or any other change you feel is necessary—you feel free to do it. In fact, I 'spect Bo would be happy to help you some. He seems to be gettin' better every day, and while he may not be up to a full day's work yet, he can help some, and so can I."

Luke having thus opened the discussion, the three of them considered options that would accommodate Lela's special needs. After a long discussion, several ideas were proposed. Soon it was late morning, and the men felt guilty leaving chores to Bo, so they decided to take up the discussion somewhat later.

As luck would have it, there were things needed that entailed a trip to town. Luke volunteered to go because the trip would take him past the Caldwell farm. As much as he had grown to love Lucas, he still felt something of a father-son bond with Mason and wanted to seek his advice as well. Of course, there was also the fact that his soon-to-be wife was still living there.

Arriving at the Caldwells, he found Mason in a favorite spot on a bench in arbor.

"Captain," began Luke, "now I've gone and asked Lela to marry me. Honest, I don't know what comes next. We have no folks, so there's no one to ask for permission."

"That's something you would've done before speaking to her," countered Mason. "But as for the next step, have you talked to her about when and where? Once you two decide, I suspect most of the rest of your questions will fall into place. You'll need a place to live, so that's your first concern."

"Yes, I have the line shack, but that's no place for a woman to live, especially with Lela's needs," responded Luke. "But I spoke to Uncle Lucas just today. He's agreed to let me make whatever changes we need for her chair and such, even to buildin' a new house. Do you suppose Jonas would be willing to perform the weddin'?"

"Luke, how long have you two been with us now? Isn't it almost two years? Surely you know by now that we consider you —both of you—part of the family. You must do what your heart tells you, your heart and Lela's. Jonas is a man of God. He knows that if your hearts are true, God will bless this union as surely as he has blessed Uncle Lucas and Catherine and Jennie and Jonas themselves. As much as he has blessed my marriage to Lydia. Why should you two be any different?"

"Thank you, Captain. I guess I needed that. Now, where in tarnation is my scrappy bride-to-be? I think she and I have some plannin' to do."

"I think you'll find her in the sewing room with Lydia. Seems they've decided that Jonas' bare church can use some—what they call altar linens and some pretty pieces to hang."

With that, Luke entered the house. Finding the women just where Mason said, they made their plans.

It was a quiet affair just six weeks later. Luke wasn't all that well known in town, and while Lela had tended stores from time to time or sewed for some of the women, she too had not formed close relationships with anyone but the Caldwells and the Neiters.

With help from Lydia and Jennie, Lela sewed herself a new dress. It had to be simpler than the other brides, because of her wheelchair, but it was no less beautiful. A small party was planned to follow the ceremony.

Meanwhile, Luke had rounded up some helpers, and they built a small cabin on the ranch. It was only two rooms to start, but it was laid out so it could be added onto in time. Luke chose a spot in a clearing with some trees, just beyond a small ridge that was, as he described it to Lucas, "In shouting distance of the main house—or at least in range of a gunshot."

On a sunny day in June, the extended Caldwell and Neiter families met in the Caldwell living room. Jennie stood beside Lela as matron of honor, and Mason stood next to Luke as best man. Once again Pastor Jonas Coy performed one of his favorite duties and united the couple in marriage.

CHAPTER 33

Matthew and John reported back to the volunteers and to their commander. At headquarters they were instructed to meet McNelly at a small town some distance south of Dallas. Upon arriving, they found him in a very somber mood, conferring with the local sheriff.

John commented, "Captain McNelly, you seem to have somethin' mighty worrisome on your mind. If'n you like, we can come back later when you're feelin' a bit better."

McNelly replied, "No, boys, stick around, I'm waitin' for some more information. So far it's not good news. What's happenin' is that Barlow Jenkins is holed up at the bank he was robbin' and has a hostage."

John and Matthew look at each other puzzled as Matthew exclaimed, "How can that be? Barlow Jenkins is in prison ain't he?"

McNelly looked out the window and answered, "Was. And he didn't waste any time gettin' back to his old bad habits and trade soon's he was out."

John said, "Let's not waste time, let's git over to the bank and end this thing before he takes more people."

With a somber voice, McNelly answered, "The hostage is a little girl. He's already killed one person and another is bleedin' pretty bad. We know this because Sue got out of the bank on a run. He shot at her but missed."

The boys sat down, and the three started to analyze the problem. How to get this girl out safely was the question. They knew that Jenkins had no compassion and wouldn't hesitate to kill again, even a child. Matthew stood up, his face clouded in uncharacteristic anger, as he stated, "I'm not sure Jenkins will do this or not, but I'm going to go trade myself for the girl."

McNelly told him, "Bold move, Son, but he'll shoot you before you get to the door."

"Maybe not. I know he hates Asian people, and I have an idea the trade would suit him just fine."

John chimed in, "No, Matthew, if'n you even get inside and make the trade, he'll hog tie you before you can take him down."

Matthew told John, "Lot of confidence you have in me, Partner. At least we will see what he thinks he can do to escape. You see, it's when he thinks he's safe that he will shoot me. So, we'll have to figure a way to make him hold me 'til we—you, Captain McNelly, and I—can make a move on him."

With that the three moved to a location across the street from the bank. John and McNelly stepped off to one side, and Matthew called out, "Jenkins, hey Jenkins...."

Jenkins looked out the window and saw Matthew, who was now standing in the street without his gun or knife. He shouted back, "Looks like I got a target waitin' to have a hole put in it."

Matthew yelled, "That can wait 'til later. How about for now we make a trade—me for the girl? Only a coward would hold a little girl when he can have a man who can cause him harm. Or are you afraid of a little child?"

Jenkins barked, "You, a Chinaman and you call yourself a man and you're callin' me out? I can shoot ya right now."

Matthew didn't back down and called back, "Well I'm comin' up to the door. Let's see if you're the man you think you are, or a coward that hides behind a little girl."

John and McNelly were dumbfounded, and John was truly afraid for Matthew. With a sick feeling about what Matthew was doing, he felt he had to do something, so John started out from behind the wall where they had been observing, but McNelly stopped him saying, "It's too late, Son. If'n he's gonna kill Matthew, we couldn't stop him now."

Surprisingly the door of the bank opened just a sliver. All they could see was a gun, and it was pointed at Matthew. Then slowly, a little girl walked through the door.

Matthew reached for her, but Jenkins said, "Hands off her, Chinaman."

The girl, now free of the door, started to run. Her mother and father ran toward her in the street and, grabbing her, ran for cover. With that Jenkins motioned Matthew inside. Once inside, Jenkins had Matthew turn around and then knocked him to the floor. Jenkins didn't hit him hard enough to knock him out, just enough to immobilize Matthew for the moment. Jenkins kicked him once for good measure telling him, "The reason I traded was just so I could beat on you some."

With that he kicked Matthew again. This time he kicked Matthew in the arm, which paralyzed Matthew making it impossible to use his martial arts. Jenkins kicked him repeatedly in the same arm causing even more pain, then sat down to ponder his situation.

"I'm supposin' you have a plan to take me out somehow. Well that ain't gonna be happenin' 'cause I got a plan."

Matthew lay on the floor in pain. He had hoped it wouldn't go this way, but now he was useless as he heard Jenkins yell out the door, "You want to see your friend alive, then here is what you be doin' and doin' it pronto. Bring two horses here and put them up on the boardwalk in front of the door. Be sure they stand side by side. **Do it now**!"

John looked at McNelly unsure what to do. Being the wiser one, McNelly put his hand on John's shoulder and quietly told him, "We got no choice for now, Son. Let's just do it and see what Jenkins is up to."

With that they went to procure the horses. After the horses were at the door, Jenkins shouted to McNelly and John, "Now get across the street where I can see ya and drop your gun belts. **Do it now**, and make sure the sheriff is a-joinin' you."

McNelly and John did what they were told. Meanwhile, Matthew had recovered a bit and was able to move somewhat.

McNelly, John, and the sheriff were across the street stripped of their weapons, helpless as they looked on. Jenkins told Matthew to get on the horse farthest from the door. Jenkins stayed behind Matthew as Matthew struggled to mount. They slowly proceeded down the boardwalk. Jenkins, ever mindful of McNelly's tenacity, kept looking back at him and John. Soon they made it off the boardwalk and into the street.

Jenkins followed close behind as the two headed out of town, with Jenkins continuing to keep watch on John, McNelly, and the sheriff as they rode. Matthew realized they wouldn't get very far before Jenkins decided to kill him.

As they came to the edge of town, Matthew looked back at John and McNelly, then looked at the tree line at the end of town. He then looked back at John, and then again back to the tree line signaling that he had a plan. Matthew then bowed his head as a signal, hoping John or McNelly understood. As they reached the tree line, Jenkins began to relax. Big mistake on Jenkins' part.

Matthew took the chance that his comrades had understood his signals and kicked his horse. As he did so, he slumped forward, slid off the horse, and started running for the trees. John was faster than McNelly in grabbing the gun lying in front of him. Jenkins was confused and didn't know whom to shoot first.

As Matthew ran in a zig-zag line, Jenkins got off a round or two but missed. By now he realized he had become the target, kicked his horse into a gallop, and started to get out of there. What Jenkins did not know was how good a shot John was. Taking his time, John got a round off that knocked Jenkins from his horse. Matthew came out from the tree line as Jenkins was scrambling to find the gun that had fallen from his hand when John hit him. Matthew reached Jenkins before Jenkins reached his gun.

Matthew was still hurting but stepped on Jenkins' injured arm and said rather quietly, "I'm guessing there is a lot of pain. We sure have that in common right now, but I'll be healing soon. You will be doing your healing in prison. Bad enough to rob a bank, kill one man and wound another, and stupid to do it alone, but to take that little girl? Well let's see what your new acquaintances in prison think of your manhood when they find that out. You'll be looking forward to the day they hang you for murder."

It was midday when Luke stopped by the Caldwells' place on his way back from town to drop off some supplies he had picked up for Mason while doing his own shopping. Fortunately for both, the two spreads weren't that far apart, so it wasn't much out of the way. Mason and Mark greeted Luke, and they all headed to the barn to stow the supplies.

Out from the barn came Henry. Luke looked at him a bit inquisitively and waited for an introduction. Mason didn't hesitate and as he made the introductions, he was trying to guess what Luke was thinking. Luke looked intently at Henry. He saw a young man who seemed a little puny, maybe a bit small in stature to be out on his own, and obviously far from home.

He also noticed something else and inquired, "By the color of your skin, might it be you served with the Union army? I see you ain't got no gray on so maybe...."

Henry didn't miss a beat. "Well, Mr. Luke, the truth is I did serve with the Yankees, and proud of it."

Now that set Luke back a bit, and he asked, "What did you do? Water the horses? Shovel manure? You be a bit young, and I might add a bit scrawny to be carrying a rifle."

Mason frowned at Luke wondering if he was trying to be funny. Henry, however, was used to being picked on and went along with Luke, who truly was trying to be funny.

Henry put on a Deep South accent and told him, "Well now, y'all zee, Masta Luke, I'z a-not needin' a rifle. No sir-ree, Masta Luke. I jes' picked up one Reb with one arm, another Reb with dah uddah arm, and den I'z a-bashed dair heads togetha. Den I had da pleasure of throwin' dem more dan a hunnert feet, one by one, into da horse manure dat da other Reb prisoners raked up."

Mason, Luke, and Mark doubled over in laughter, and that pretty much cemented a new friendship.

CHAPTER 34

Christmas was now coming on, a season usually filled with joyful anticipation. But not so with Mason this year. Except for the time just before and after Jennie's wedding, Lydia had noticed that Mason seemed to have something weighing on him deeply. As the heart of this family, she felt the need to confront him.

"Dear Husband, it seems your heart is troubled. I don't see the joy in your eyes these days. I know you love the Christmas season as it brings to mind the birth of our Savior. All through the holidays this year, you have been preoccupied."

Sitting next to Mason and looking into his eyes, she continued, "How about telling your wife what troubles you so."

He never could hide his feeling from his precious woman. With a smile he took her hand and started to answer, "Do you remember when I was at war I sent you a letter about a young soldier who died in my arms?"

With furrowed brow, Lydia nodded her head as she replied, "Yes, I do remember. I felt your pain as I read it."

Mason continued to pour out his heart, "I haven't done what I promised to do and found that boy's family. I have papers that tell me where they live, so I must fulfill my promise. I could write these good folks, but my promise was to go to them though it may be a far piece I'd be traveling."

This "far piece" of which Mason spoke was a distance of 800 miles to the small town of Lewisburg, Tennessee. He had a strong mule to pull a wagon, but even with rest periods, it would mean at least forty days one way, and more than three months away from home for the round trip. Mason, however, was determined to fulfill his promise, and Lydia was in no way going to stop him. Although Mason had grown stronger over the previous three years, it would still be a challenge.

Mason was confident that Mark could handle the farm and take care of Lydia while he was gone, and Luke was just down the road to help if needed. Mason needed someone to go with him, however, which meant he had to leave Mark short-handed. Whom to take was the question. Taking Henry wasn't a great idea, as the South hadn't quite yet accepted the idea of colored people wandering around free. Besides, Henry had settled in with Mark and was too good a hand to take from Mark for this trip.

The best choice would be John, but he was now off with Matthew, enforcing the law wherever it required their services, and three months was too long for them to be away. So far, Bo was working for the Rocking Eagle Ranch. Luke would need his help, so Bo also was out of the question. There was one solution.

While at church one Sunday morning, Jonas had introduced Mason to Billy Lawell, a young man who was looking toward the ministry but as of yet didn't have the money to attend seminary. Remembering Billy, Mason had an idea. One day he had Henry hook up the team, and they headed for the Free Will Baptist Church, where they were greeted by Jonas.

Mason explained his plans to go to Lewisburg and asked if the young man was still around. Jonas called out, "Hey Billy, come on over here, there's someone here to see you."

A tall lanky young man in his early twenties appeared, dressed in coveralls and covered with dirt, clearly having been working hard.

"Billy, you remember my father-in-law, Mason Caldwell? He has a proposition for you. You might make a few dollars that can go for your seminary education. Want to hear what he has to say?"

Billy shook Mason's hand, and the boy's firm handshake seemed like a good start. Also, Billy had an energy that Mason could feel, something they sure would need on a journey this long.

"Howdy, Mr. Caldwell, pleasure to be a seein' you again. I've been lookin' for work around this here town, but seems it's just the wrong season."

Mason responded with, "Well, this may not be the season that I had in mind, but the sooner I get this done, the better I'll be feeling."

Mason told Billy that he needed someone to accompany him on a trip to Lewisburg, Tennessee. Winter was coming on. Not only would that entail snow and ice, but winter weather also played havoc with Mason's bones since being shot, and leaving before Christmas was out of the question. So this trip could not take place until spring.

Mason explained, "I know this will be a spell off, but I need to make plans now. This matter has been weighing heavily on my soul, and I can't rest until I know that I am going to take care of it."

Billy answered enthusiastically, "I'd like to help you Mr. Caldwell. Maybe I can get a job that would tide me over 'til spring."

Mason ventured, "I have already been giving this some thought, knowing you'll need some support, so I'd like to throw out an idea."

Billy and Jonas exchanged glances as Mason continued, "How about you help here around the church? I'll give you the money you need to eat and meet your needs. Jonas, this will be the Caldwells' contribution to the church. With Billy to help you, the work that needs doing will get done. As for you, Billy, it should leave time to study in the meantime. Besides keeping the church property itself neat and proper, the Glennwood Cemetery belongs to this church, and it requires upkeep as well."

Jonas had no objections and turned to Billy, who was overwhelmed that his dream of becoming a minister might be within his reach. Billy extended his hand to Mason and with a humble and sincere heart said, "Your kindness is overwhelming, Mr. Caldwell. I will be blessed and honored to take you up on your offer. Are you gonna be okay with this, Pastor Jonas?"

"Couldn't think of a better offer than that. You have my blessings, Billy."

With that Mason and Henry got into the wagon and headed for home. On the way, Henry said to Mason, "Sir, I'm a bit taken aback by the way you treat people. You surely are a generous man."

Never without a light heart and quick wit, Henry added, "If'n I borrowed a thousand dollars from you, headed for California, and never paid you back, I bet you would be just be forgettin' about it, and I'd be free to spend it on booze, women, and whatever gets my fancy. Yes siree, you are a soft touch."

Mason looked at Henry and could only shake his head and have a good hearty laugh, along with, "Don't be thinkin' on it, Henry."

CHAPTER 35

Ever since that fateful trip to town some weeks ago, Mark had seemed out of sorts. He had gone back to town more frequently than what was necessary to maintain the farm, especially during the winter months. He seemed to always come up with an excuse, however. Texas winters can be difficult, and with rain, sleet and sometimes snow, they can present obstacles that aren't easy to overcome with a wagon and a team of horses.

On one such day Mark was getting ready to head into town anyway. Lydia was concerned, as she still hadn't grasped the fact that her son had become a man, and tried to talk him into staying home.

"Listen to the wind out there, Mark. It's howling something fierce."

"Not to worry, Ma. I'll take care, and besides, it ain't but a few miles there regardless of the weather."

Mason took Lydia's hand and told her, "We've got to have those, aahhh, things for the barn, that's for sure."

Lydia, however, wasn't buying this. "What things for the barn? Surely they can wait at least 'til the weather lets up some. You won't be able to do the work until that happens anyway."

Mason's smile helped her to get the hint as he answered, "I'll bet a mule and barnyard chicken that Mark will get what he needs without having to spend too much time shopping. I'm sure that if he looks around a bit, he will find what he's looking for. I'm sure there are some ..." There was a pause as Mason looked deep into Lydia's eyes and continued, "... folks he may run into."

Lydia gave up as she realized that Mark could care less about "things" for the barn.

Mark made it town and none too soon. No sooner had he stashed the buckboard and team at the livery stable when down came the rain accompanied by relentless wind. He realized that the road would be pretty much washed out, so why take a chance going home? Wait a minute, was it possible that Mark had an ulterior motive? He took a room at the hotel run by Mr. and Mrs. DeWitt.

"I'll say this for you, Mark, you're using good judgment stayin' in town tonight. It may be wise to book a couple of nights as this storm ain't lookin' like it's wantin' to let up anytime soon."

That suited Mark just fine. He had "business" to attend to for sure. It was getting late in the afternoon, and Mark was ready for a good supper, so he stayed in the hotel to eat. It was way too messy out in the street anyway.

The next morning's weather didn't look much better. Mark started to wonder if he had made a mistake. *"She" won't be out in this mess nohow,* he thought to himself. What to do? *Guess I'll at least get over to the general store see if there are some things I may need anyway.*

On the way, he had to pass the livery stable so he stopped in to say hello to Mr. Teasley, the blacksmith. "I guess this weather isn't too good for business is it, Mr. Teasley? I'm on my way to...."

All of a sudden something caught his attention—the little figure of a certain guy he recognized immediately. "Samuel, what in blazes are you doing out in this awful weather?"

"Mum sent me here to wait for her, Mr. Caldwell. We have to leave, but I tried desperately to talk her into staying at home. I'm scared, Mr. Caldwell. I remember you from the candy store and you walked us home. May I prevail upon you to tell mum to stay home?"

Mark wasn't sure he wanted to experience another encounter with Emma by asking her to do something she might have made up her mind not to do. That hadn't gone too well the first time, and Mark was only too aware of her "seeming" independence.

"Where in tarnation is your, ah, mum in such an all-fired hurry to be off to? It must be some sort of emergency I'm a-guessin'."

Mark no sooner got the words out as Emma ran into the livery stable. Emma stopped short as she saw Mark, and when he looked really close, he thought he saw a flicker of a smile. Something, however, was pressing on her mind. "Good day, Mr. Caldwell. What brings you out in this weather?"

Mark was about to ask the same of her, but he wasn't about to tell her the real reason why he came to town, so he used the now worn-out excuse. "Aahhh, we needed some things for the barn," he blurted out.

"I hope you find what you're looking for, Mr. Caldwell. Samuel and I must be on our way without delay. I pray your day goes well."

With that Emma looked to Mr. Teasley and said, "I see the buckboard is ready, Mr. Teasley. We must be on our way."

Mr. Teasley started to plead with her, "Miss Emma, please reconsider leavin' right now. This looks to be as nasty a storm as I've seen in some time. If'n you get caught in a place where the water is overflowin', you can be in a mighty big heap of trouble."

Mark wasn't sure if he should get involved or not as she answered in her stalwart way, "I'm very much appreciative of your concern, sir, but you see, this is an emergency, and I need to be on my way."

Mark had finally had enough of her stubbornness and told her rather harshly, "Mrs. Livingston, please take Mr. Teasley's advice. He's been livin' in these parts a mighty long time, and he knows how the river can swell and swallow a man in no time. Also this is hilly country, and these hills can have a tendency to slide in a hard rain. Nothin' can be so important that you would put yourself and your son in danger."

"Please, gentlemen, you have no idea what is at stake. I thank you both for your concern, but please, please leave me alone."

With that she and Samuel climbed into the buckboard, put on the rain gear they had brought, and departed into the raging storm as if the barn were on fire. Mark was almost panic-stricken, incredulous that she would do such a crazy thing.

"Mr. Teasley, saddle me a strong horse if'n you would. I got a bad feelin' bout all this, and I can't let her go out there alone."

Mr. Teasley agreed and started to saddle one of the horses, actually the brother of the horse that was pulling Emma's buckboard. As he saddled the horse, he told Mark,

"Mrs. Livingston's horse and this here horse are two of the strongest animals I have, brothers comin' from the same stock."

As Mark mounted up, he said, "Thank you so much, Mr. Teasley. With this weather, I will need a stronger horse than my team."

By the time Mark left the livery stable, Emma was long gone. He knew she had headed toward the north, but with the rain, it was now impossible for him to track her. What he needed was some guidance from above. He shot up a short prayer.

Lord, this is miserable weather, and I'm a knowin' we need this rain, but can you give me a helpin' hand please? I just know this stubborn woman is goin' to git herself into a heap of trouble. Show me the way, Lord."

By the grace of God, the rain eased up to some degree as he came to a fork in the road. One road led to the town of Palestine. The other road only led to miles and miles of nothing but more miles and miles. Mark figured the town was his best bet. Palestine had little except a church, a school, courthouse, a general store and a saloon. Not much more than the temporary trading post that had preceded the town. What could Emma possibly want in Palestine that she couldn't get in Crockett?

The road led Emma and Samuel to a stream that could usually be forded but had become nothing short of a small river. Stepping cautiously into the water, her horse whinnied and snorted as she prodded him on. Sure enough, the water was too rapid to negotiate, and as she prodded the animal to go farther, he started to stumble. Emma realized she had made a serious mistake and was beginning to despair when suddenly Mark appeared beside her yelling, **"Pull back on the reins! Pull back hard!"**

Emma quickly reacted to Mark's command and as she did, the horse fortunately had enough footing to back up. It was just far enough that Mark was able to pull on the horse and get the carriage out of harm's way, preventing a disastrous ending for two terrified souls.

"What in tarnation is goin' on with you? You scared the livin' daylights outta me as well as this poor boy who is holding on for his dear life."

There was a short pause before Mark continued, but when he did, he had calmed down just a bit, and said, "There, you happy? You almost made me cuss, woman, and I hate cussin'. You can surely make the Devil come out in a man, and the Devil ain't one I like to relate to."

Emma sat with her head bowed unable to speak. Samuel was crying, and she was of no use in comforting him. Mark took the reins of the horse pulling the buckboard, and they headed for some trees. The trees weren't much shelter but better than the rain beating on them. It seemed as though God had answered Mark's prayer as the rain started to fall more and more gently. The water in the steam, however, hadn't subsided, and there would be no crossing for quite a while.

Mark told Emma, "There is no way to go forward, but we didn't git too far from town, so best we be headin' back. Besides, this storm is headin' in the direction that you seemed to want to go."

"I'm afraid I have caused you a terrible imposition. How do I repay the debt I owe you for saving our lives?"

Just looking at her had paid the debt as far as Mark was concerned, but he couldn't tell her that. His only reply was, "There is no debt to pay. I knowed you'd be needin' someone, and I was just thinkin' it might be me that, well, I knowed this rain would bring trouble, so I just followed. That's all there is to it."

Mark felt it best to say no more. He already had thoughts he knew he mustn't reveal. He was still unclear about Emma's marital status. Was she still married? Was her husband missing, or could he have recently died? Could that be the urgency that prompted this sudden ill-advised trip?

He looked at Emma and with a smile said, "It seems to me that Samuel could use a hug right about now."

Back in town, Mark prevailed upon Mrs. DeWitt to cook up some warm food and coffee. Mark wouldn't have minded a shot of whiskey right now, but he knew this was not the time. As Mark sat across from Emma, he couldn't keep his eyes off her. Samuel didn't let on that he saw a softness he hadn't seen in his mum's eyes in a long time either.

Maybe even a little peace? Children quite often have a sixth sense. At the same time, of course, he wolfed down his meal. Mark was careful not to ask questions, but he knew something was just plain wrong. Something that was bad enough to drive her out into a storm that could have ended in disaster.

Finally Emma broke the silence. "Mr. Caldwell, I'm sure you must …"

Mark interrupted, "It's Mark, ma'am, Mark, that's my first name. I'd be much obliged if you called me Mark."

"Well, Mark …" Emma smiled as she continued, "You must think I'm just a crazy woman going out into a storm like this. I do owe you an explanation. It's just that I really need to get to Palestine, and I wanted to be there by tonight. It is of grave importance. You see there is an appointment I want—I need to keep. It involves someone who isn't to be trifled with and …."

As Emma hesitated, Samuel jumped in. "It's my father, Mr. Caldwell, we have to see my father."

Children have neither secrets nor a sense of timing, so as the saying goes, out of the mouth of babes. Emma was becoming emotionally upset. There was part of her story she wanted to tell Mark, but not the whole story.

Mark, looking at Samuel, asked, "Is your pa, ah, I mean father okay?"

"We don't know, Mr. Caldwell, I think he may be having a legal issue."

"Enough, Samuel," Emma blurted out, "Our business is our own. We don't need to burden others with our affairs."

Mark now had his answer as to her still being married, but it only produced another question. How to proceed with this relationship, or should he do so at all? He was not one to become involved with someone else's wife. He was brought up to honor a marital union. He would very much like to have the kind of relationship that he saw in his father and mother. Love like theirs, commitment like that, had made its mark on him.

Emma now felt she must do some explaining. She addressed Mark with more formality, "Mr. Caldwell, my husband is a gambling man. I received a telegram from him this morning telling me to get to Palestine immediately no matter what. He said he was in dire straits."

With more understanding, Mark now told her, "I can see why you were wantin' to git out in such a hurry, sorry for bein' so obstinate about your leavin'. Just the weather and all, I was mighty concerned."

"You were right of course, Mr. Caldwell, that I should be thinking about Samuel instead of my husband, Richard. We have had to leave so many cities because of his cursed gambling problem. Indeed, we were asked to leave this good little city of Crockett. We had barely arrived, and he had already made some enemies with his gambling. He told us to stay, and he would find another place and send for us. I'm just …."

Emma caught herself, not wanting to expose the fact that this marriage had been nothing but a nightmare for her, but she was afraid to end it. As it was pretty clear by now, Richard was not a man of healthy emotions. His temper as well as his gambling problem gave her much cause for concern.

Emma finished, "Enough of my problem, Mr. Caldwell, we shall be on our …."

Mark interrupted, "Mark, my name is Mark. Let me be your friend."

Did I really say that? he thought to himself. *Should I be getting involved in a situation that has so many roads leadin' to trouble? This could be especially big trouble for me for sure. Besides, what could I do to help?* Mark and Samuel already had a close friendship to Mark's way of thinking, but maybe more than a friendship? He felt he wanted to take Samuel under his wing and protect him, take care of him. Mark thought to himself. *Wait! He is the child of someone else. You can't have a fatherly feeling for someone else's child. Get it out of your head, Mark.*

Mark waited until Samuel had eaten his fill of food and told Emma, "I bin thinkin'. Why don't I escort you and Samuel down to where you're stayin', and I'll be by in the mornin' about seven? Looks like the weather will be clearin' good enough to travel by then. I'll get you to Palestine. I know a short cut, sort of that is, and I'll get you there as quick as possible. Leavin' that early should get us to Palestine by nightfall."

"Mark, you've been more kind to us than anyone we have come to meet and to prevail on you any more than we have would be more than one could or should ask. I'm sure that we can make it there on our own."

In a resolute voice he replied, "I'll be here at seven in the morning, Mrs. Livingston. It won't be either a burden or a problem for me. I'm just a farmer waitin' for my land to heal from the harvest so I can get more seed in the ground come spring."

Emma was too tired to argue and just smiled wordlessly at Mark. With that they left and headed for Emma's boarding house.

Morning came and, as promised, Mark was at Emma's door. Samuel answered and with his usual enthusiasm pulled on Mark's arm. It was clear why Mark had an emotional attachment to Samuel. Poor boy seemed to have no father image, and Mark seemed more than willing to fill the gap. Emma quickly pulled Samuel away and apologized once again. Emma saw that Mark had the buckboard ready with his horse tied to the back. They loaded up and off they went. The shortcut was on the other side of the steam where Mark had rescued them the previous day. The swollen river could now be crossed, so getting to the shortcut would be no problem. Just as they were about to cross, they heard shouting coming from behind them.

"Mark, hey Mark! Where you bin? We bin lookin' for you. We were at the farm, and Pa said you were in town. Didn't see you there, so here we are a-lookin' for you."

"Hey Brother, hey Matthew! Y'all worried about your big brother?"

"I guess Pa thought you'd be home before this horrendous rain decided to wash half the county away."

On the other side of the stream they stopped as Mark made the introductions. "It ain't our business, Brother, but ain't you headed the wrong direction to git to the farm?"

"Well, John, I'm a-helpin' a lady to sort out a problem. No need explainin' it, but be assured that I have everything under control."

Samuel jumped in, "Yes, Mr. John, Mr. Mark has been a very big help to me and my mum. He even saved us …."

"That's enough, Samuel," Emma interrupted and turning to John, she added, "Mr. Caldwell is guiding us to the town of Palestine. I have business there. He was kind enough to offer since we are strangers here."

John and Matthew called to mind the conversation they'd had with Mason about a lady with an English accent and, having the same thought at the same time, just smiled at each other.

"Actually, Brother, we're headed in that direction too. We're to meet up with McNelly in Jacksonville and will be passin' through Palestine on our way."

"Good to have some company," came Mark's half-hearted reply.

This meant his time with Emma would not be as personal as he would like, but how do you say no to those you love? Besides most of what he wanted to say to Emma probably shouldn't be said at all—at least not at this time.

CHAPTER 36

Riding into Palestine they wondered how this small town with a population just over two hundred had any appeal to anyone. It was just a one-street town. When the Texas legislature established Anderson County in 1846, no community existed at the center of the county, so Palestine was established. A post office opened at the site the next year, and a contract was drawn up for construction of a courthouse that was built on the crest of a low hill.

As the group passed the courthouse, they saw a few people milling. The jail was just a few doors away, and folks were dispersing from there too. Farther down the street, they passed a saloon, an eatery, a small general store, a livery stable and finally a small hotel. Not much, but it had the makings of a solid little town.

Mark wanted to get Emma and Samuel settled in, but Emma pulled him aside from everyone including Samuel and told him, "My business with my husband must be taken care of first. I may already be too late."

Emma hesitated, then looking directly into Mark's eyes she continued. "Mark, I know I have imposed on you so very much, but I have one more favor to ask. You have been so very kind, and more than amiable. I do hate to ask but there is no one here I know, and trusting someone I don't know, would surely be a problem. Please, Mark, could you keep Samuel close to your side while I do what I have to do? I don't want him to see his father like this."

Mark had mixed emotions about her seeing her husband, but he knew he must do what is right. Being a follower of the Lord, his spirit felt her pain, and it was his Christian duty to help, but there was more. The thought of her seeing her husband didn't sit well in his soul. Mark, looking back into Emma's eyes and with a reassuring smile, answered, "Emma, I'm here for you. I only wish I could do more to ease the pain I sense comin' from your heart."

Emma knew that somewhere deep within her, there was not only a sense of trust but something more she sensed looking into his eyes that made her a little uncomfortable, even a little frightened. She was a married woman trying to fight emotions that shouldn't be there. Her thoughts should be only for her husband. She could only answer, "I am profoundly thankful to you, Mark. You're a wonderful blessing to Samuel and me."

Emma headed toward the jail, and Mark was uneasy about letting her go alone although he knew it was best he stay out of it —at least for now.

As Emma entered the jail, she saw Richard behind bars sitting on the edge of his cot. He looked forlorn and pitiful. The first emotion she felt was just a feeling of pity. Whatever love that was once shared between them had slowly been drained from Emma. Here she was only doing her duty as a wife and a mother, reaching out to this man who had managed to drain them of all their money, and as of now, emotion. She called out, "Richard!"

Recognizing her voice, he jumped up, and the first thing out of his mouth was, "Where have you been? I needed you here yesterday. Can you not do what is asked of you?"

His anger didn't help to foster a civil dialogue. With Richard, everything had to be *his* way and feed *his* ego.

"I was on my way last night, Richard, but got caught in this horrid rain storm. We almost lost our lives, but Mar ...." She cut herself off quickly and after just a slight pause continued, "Someone was able to turn us from a raging river."

"You still should have tried to come a different way. Do you not care that I am rotting away in this Godforsaken place of incarceration? I am not one to be trifled with. What do I have to do to make you more concerned about my intolerable situation rather than yours?"

Richard was now glaring at Emma as he continued, "Do you have the money?"

The true picture of this man's character thus became evident, leaving much to be desired and lending new meaning to the definition of someone self-centered. Emma was distraught enough without being so belittled and disparaged, especially by her husband.

"I have what money we have left. If I give it to you for bail money, I won't have any left to feed Samuel and myself."

She knew what his answer would be so she gave the money to the sheriff, keeping just enough for some food and a room for the night. As Emma started to walk out, she just couldn't let it go. This time his hard heart and selfishness had taken its toll. Emma had come to realize there was nothing she could ever say or do to cure this man of his self-serving arrogance.

Looking back at Richard, she told him, "I'll be leaving you, Richard. Don't come looking for me. I have nothing left. I am going to find a way to return to England. You have broken my heart for the last time. Your son will have to learn he has no father. Enjoy your gambling and whatever life you think will fulfill your dreams. My dreams may never come true, but at least I know in my heart that I can no longer live a life that will destroy not only me but my son as well."

With that she turned to walk out. As she did so, Richard, not to be out done, was determined to have the last word.

"Leave me? I don't think that will be the case. Know this, my dear Emma. I will find you, and my son will come to know me, as he should. Goodbye for now and good riddance."

Emma didn't turn around to look at him, but exiting the jail she leaned against the pillar at the end of the walkway. She buried her face in her hands and sobbed bitterly.

As this exchange between Emma and Richard was taking place, Mark, Matthew, John, and Samuel were sitting in the hotel eatery. Samuel's innocence freed the three men from the burdens and cares of the world at least for a while. Oh, how they wished the world were like this. John and Matthew knew they were off to possible danger. Mark had the farm to worry about, and now, Emma. Dear Emma. She was giving Mark fits unlike anything he had experienced before. He could control most things, but this?

"Mr. John, Mr. Matthew, I cannot see why men have to carry guns around. I see this no matter where my mum and I travel. It seems to me that men should get along. I see that Mr. Mark doesn't carry a gun, although he does have a rifle. I know that a rifle is for hunting. Food is an important part of life, and I like to eat."

The three had to chuckle as they wondered about the wisdom of this young man. Wouldn't it be a wonderful thing if all men's hearts were not so full of sin? The world wouldn't need sheriffs, Texas Rangers or any rangers, or any organization called law enforcement. How do you explain that to a child? How do you explain that to an adult? Of course, the real question was, how do you explain sin to those who don't believe in sin?

"You're sure full of wisdom for such a small tyke, Samuel. Someday maybe you'll understand, but I hope not too soon," said Matthew to Samuel.

"Tell us, Samuel, how long have you and your ma and pa, er, I mean your father and mother been in this country?"

"I don't know for certain, Mr. Mark. I know that my mother said she is very tired of traveling, but my father insists that we keep moving. I don't think he likes the towns we stop in. Mother says the towns we stop in don't seem to like him either. I hardly ever see my father. He is sometimes gone for days and days. My mother cries so very much, and I know that she very much hopes to go back to England."

That sent an arrow through Mark's heart. Go home to England? But what if …?

Don't even think it Mark, he said to himself. But he did think it nonetheless, and his body stiffened. John and Matthew noticed but just left him to his thoughts.

After a few minutes Matthew broke the silence and asked, "We'll be leaving at first light, Mark. Is there anything we can do for you to help you with, ah, any problems you might foresee?"

"No, none that I can see, my brothers. Just itchin' to get back to the farm and a life that ain't foreign to me. Seems this town is gettin' to me, and I ain't been here that long."

John and Matthew didn't press the issue. As they stood up, John told Mark, "We gotta set up camp, so we'll just mosey along. We'll be checkin' on you in the mornin' before we head out. Also, dear brother, we sent a telegram off to Crockett lettin' Pa know you're all right and should be comin' home in a few days."

Emma now returned from her heart-breaking meeting with Richard. She was drained and, approaching Mark, she told him, "I have to find a way to earn some income so Samuel and I can return to England. Again, I ask if I can impose upon you and your kindness. I—that is—Samuel and I, would be ever so grateful if you can take us back to Crockett where I can contact my relatives back home in England. I'm not sure they will be able to help us since we are a family of ordinary means, and our financial resources are limited. I should have listened to them and not left with Richard. I promise you two things. First, I promise I will find a way to repay you for your kindness and financial help with the hotel rooms, food and all. Second, this will be the last favor I will ask of you."

Emma's emotions were burned out now. She just appeared numb. Mark answered, "I'll be gettin' you both back to Crockett. We'll leave first thing after breakfast. I'll be gittin' no payment from you, Emma. I don't want to hear another word about money—please."

Emma was too drained to argue but only said, "I'm sure that after Richard pays his bail, he will head for another town so morning will be fine."

Turning to Samuel she quietly said, "Samuel, your father told me that he would find us someday, so I don't want you to worry about him." Trying not to sound too dismayed she finished, "He usually does what he says he is going to do."

"I'm not worried, Mum, I just don't want to see you cry anymore."

As Emma fought to hold back the tears, she bid Mark good night.

Morning came and, as promised, Mark, Emma, Samuel, John, and Matthew met at the hotel to have breakfast. There was little talking going on. Some things were probably best left unsaid at least for the time being. Of course this didn't hold true for a certain young man who didn't hold back anything that was on his mind.

"Mother, will it take long to get back to England? It's been such a journey getting here that I don't remember how long we have been gone."

"I can only tell you, Samuel, that it won't take near as long getting back as it did to get here."

"You know, Mother, I like it here."

Emma almost lost her English propriety and was speechless as she turned her attention to Samuel. Mark liked what he heard but remained silent. Matthew and John, not knowing that Emma had planned to go back to England, also had nothing to say.

"I don't remember much of our home in England, Mother. I don't remember father being with us much while we were there either. I remember grandfather and father arguing about us coming to the Americas."

Emma finally gathered her thoughts together and said, "We must go back, Samuel. We have no other means of taking care of ourselves. We have family there, and I sincerely hope they haven't forgotten us, as we've been gone so long."

Emma realized that she was talking to a child and any explanation about family and leaving wasn't likely to be understood as she would like. With that she looked at Mark and said, "When we finish with breakfast, can we leave immediately? It is a full day's journey back to Crockett, and I will need time to find a place to stay."

"Just as soon as Samuel is done," was Mark's answer.

John and Matthew were astride their horses as Mark helped Emma up onto the buckboard, which Emma called a carriage, with Samuel seated between them. They started to ride off, but as they reached the end of the street, Richard called after them in a very loud voice, "Didn't take you long, my dear Emma, to find some bloke to cling to."

Mark saw a man step off the boardwalk in front of the buckboard. He assumed this to be the infamous Richard.

Emma told Richard, "This is the man who saved the lives of your son and myself. He is taking us to where we can get transportation back to England as I told you."

Emma didn't want him to know that they were on their way to Crockett as she was afraid he would follow and be more trouble than she could handle.

"So you are planning on leaving your husband out in the cold, dear wife?"

"It seems you left your wife and your son. I might add, out in the cold."

Richard wasn't very happy with Emma's response and started to approach the side of the buckboard where Emma was seated.

"Not a good idea to be approachin' a lady with anger in your heart, mister."

"And you would be?"

"Mark Caldwell, if'n it's any of your business."

"My business is with my wife. It would be best if you stay out of it."

Mark was ready to jump off the buckboard, but Emma stopped him. "Richard, Mr. Caldwell just wants to help. He has been kind enough to help Samuel and me to find you."

"Kind? Is that what it is, dear wife? I have not found a good man this side of the pond."

During this conversation John and Matthew couldn't help but hear Richard's shouting and overbearing voice. They had only gone a few yards when they turned their horses around and headed back to Mark and Emma.

John said, "Hey, Brother, things gettin' a bit out of hand? Maybe its best if'n we stick around for a spell."

"Need help I see, Mr. Caldwell. Your brother needs to intercede for you?" That about did it for Mark. He was off the buckboard, but before he reached Richard, a cry came from Samuel.

"Mum. Please stop them! I don't want to see Father fighting again. Please, Father! Mr. Caldwell has been helping us, and I don't want to see him get hurt."

Emma intervened. "Richard, we will be in Crockett by nightfall and will stay there until you send for us or come to us. We will go back to England together. Right now, let us go. We haven't any money, so do what you need with the money you have left."

Emma knew he would more than likely lose it gambling because when he did win, he got greedy and gambled it all away again. Richard was silent, but his face said more than he would have liked the onlookers to know. He figured he could go to another town where he wasn't known and start gambling again. Besides, why give up gambling time just to take a trip back to a town where he really didn't want to be?

"You had better be in Crockett when I come to fetch you. If you are not there, there will be the devil to pay. I will rely on you to get a job, Emma, so we can have the money to go back."

Looking at Samuel he said, "You take good care of your mother, Samuel. I will expect to hear nothing but good news when I see you again."

He paused for a moment, then glaring at Emma he finished, "Soon."

Emma knew that his telling her to earn money only meant he would take it and gamble it away. Was it possible that she could earn enough for her to depart with Samuel before he came for her again? As Richard walked away, Mark couldn't help thinking, *What a poor excuse for a father and husband this man is. What kind of man would abandon his family, especially a beautiful wife and a child who can be so easily endeared to one's heart?*

Mark already had endeared both of them to his heart, and it pained him to think that he might have to try to forget them. He looked to John and Matthew as they shook their heads in agreement with Mark's unspoken thoughts. No wonder Samuel showed such emotion. Mark asked himself, *Is this what love is?*

John and Matthew stayed long enough for Mark and Emma to be on their way. There was no need to worry that Richard would pursue because this poor excuse for a husband had no horse on which to follow anyway. It was bad enough that Richard knew where Emma would be. Both young men figured it would be best to head back to Crockett as soon as their work with Captain McNelly was done.

When Mark and Emma arrived at the hotel in Crockett, Mason was there to meet them, accompanied by Henry, who, in his civilian clothing, attracted no notice by the town's people. At least no one said anything about Henry's color since he was with Mason.

Henry had by this time discarded any evidence of being a Yankee soldier. He was strong and willing to work and was a big help in lifting the materials needed to fix up the barn. After all, he assured them he could toss Johnny Reb into the manure pile. He still wasn't sure if he was on his way to California or not, so working for Mark and Mason in the meantime was a pretty good job that allowed him to earn some money for the trip west if it came about. He had taken a liking to these "kind folk" as he called them. He also knew he was in Rebel territory and kept a low profile.

In the previous year, Mason's embarrassment at his physical limitations had greatly diminished, especially as he met no pity from people in the town. As a result, he had begun to travel into town more frequently and engage again with his old friends, as he had done before the war.

Mason greeted Mark, "Been a long few days for you, Son. Are you okay? Are you okay, Miss Emma?"

"Mrs. Emma." Mark corrected Mason.

Trying not to look surprised, Mason replied, "Mrs. Emma. It would be Mrs. Emma Livingston, as I recall."

"Yes, Mr. Caldwell. But I prefer Emma."

Mark told Emma, "I'm gonna git you a room, and I suspect Samuel could do with some grub."

A wide-eyed Samuel answered, "Yes, oh yes, Mr. Mark, that would be jolly good. Grub, I like that better than food."

This lightened the heaviness that had prevailed for the past few hours. Mark's mind was in turmoil, and he wanted answers about Emma and Richard's relationship. He thought to himself, *How did I get involved in all this in the first place? She is like no one I've ever meet before, full of spunk, strong-willed, not asking for favors other than help in a time of real need, and oh, what a beauty!*

CHAPTER 37

Mark felt he had one last chore to accomplish; yet he felt he should know better. He wanted to find a way to keep Emma in Crockett. Mark had given Mason an account of what happened in Palestine.

Mason and Mark were at the stable as Mason had Henry prepare the wagon for the ride home. Always respecting his father's acumen, Mark inquired, "Pa, do you think you just might be knowin' someone here in town that could use some help, ya know a job that is suited for a lady?"

Though there was no doubt in his mind what Mark was up to, Mason wasn't ready to jump in with advice just yet. Question was, to what end would this lead?

"Well, Mark, I'm sure there are some who could use an intelligent woman to do some work. You could ask around, but I wonder Mark—and I'm guessing you refer to Mrs. Livingston, or Emma, as you prefer. Has she said she wants to stay in this town, let alone in this country?"

Mark wasn't going to lie, but he did fudge a bit.

"I know she talks about going back to England, Pa, but she doesn't have the money. I just thought that if she can earn some money, maybe she would at least feel somewhat settled in. Then she could make up her mind whether to go back—or maybe stay."

Mason already had the big picture, but as a father he had to pursue this.

"Mark, what's on your mind? If you'd level with me, I'll bet you have thoughts of her not leaving. Ask yourself, is she just trying to get rid of a gamblin' husband that she no longer wants to be with? Does she miss her family? Maybe she thinks it be best for Samuel to go back. Have you considered of all this? Also, if she's a Christian lady, is she willing to leave her husband? And Mark, have you given thought to what might be best for her?"

Mark started pacing while looking for some way to answer Mason. He started stroking a horse in one of the stalls as he pondered these questions. He wished he were as carefree as that horse, not having to make decisions. He knew however, these questions must be answered. He couldn't just come right out and ask her. That wouldn't be right.

"I sure miss the farm, Pa. I'll be gittin' back soon."

Mason and Henry were on their way home leaving Mark to make one last stop. Samuel was tucked in for the night, and as Mark entered the hotel, he saw Emma sitting alone at a table. Mark approached her and asked, "May I join you?"

"I'd be pleased if you would, Mr. Caldwell."

"Can't be joinin' ya 'til you get my name right. I know you're bent on good manners, but it's Mark."

With a sheepish grin she answered, "I'd be pleased if you would join me, Mark."

As Mark sat, he looked into Emma's eyes and saw what he would call distress.

"I know you're bein' polite, Emma, but if'n you need to be alone in your thoughts, I can mosey off. But there is somethin' I'd like to ask ya."

"No, Mark, please stay, I can use the company right now. I don't know what your question is, but I want you to know that you have always been a source of comfort. I mean, your kindness is most appreciated and welcomed. You have gone beyond what any gentleman would do to help someone in distress. My thanks could never be said with words.

"You will always be ..." She paused, knowing she must choose her words carefully. She managed a little smile and continued, "remembered—no matter what happens. I feel that I have been selfish in asking so much from you. It won't happen again. As soon as I raise enough money I've decided to go back to England. It would be best for Samuel..."

Looking down at the table as if it could help her to come up with an answer, Emma continued, "… and maybe best for me."

This cut Mark to the quick. He thought, *Well, I guess it's settled. God knows what's best, yet I ain't even asked him what I should do. I should know better, but now I do know what to do. Let go, Mark, let go. Give this—and her—to the Lord and search for your comfort in him. The farm is my life, I will go to the quiet of the fields and leave all these thoughts behind.*

Mark was on his feet headed for the door as he told Emma, "I'm thinkin' it's best I leave, but one last thing I'll do for ya Emma, then I'll be goin' back to my farm, and you and Samuel go your way. I know some folk here in town that may have some work for you. When you get enough money, you can leave."

He didn't wait for an answer but started toward the door as he concluded, "I'll be back tomorrow after I talk to some folk. See ya then."

Mark was out the door leaving Emma with more thoughts than she could handle for the moment. She went up to her room and lying across the bed, passed out from the emotional exhaustion. She was even too tired to cry herself to sleep.

Morning came and Mark, after a restless night's sleep in the dampness of the stable, cleaned himself up and started walking the boardwalk wondering whom he could ask to hire Emma. Stopping by each shop, he got the same answer, "Nothing here, Mark." Being an educated woman, Emma could probably do anything she put her mind to. A nice clean job would be best though. Seeing her scrubbing wasn't exactly what Mark had in mind.

After beating on a few more doors, he made it to the bank. He knew Mr. Henley pretty well. Here he might have a chance to get Emma a job. Upon entering, however, he got a big surprise.

"Howdy, Mr. Henley."

Looking off to his right he was taken by surprise as he saw Emma. "Ahh, howdy, Mrs. Livingston."

It seemed that Emma had beaten Mark to the bank that morning and already asked Mr. Henley for a job.

"I see you two know each other. Mrs. Livingston has asked me for a job, Mark. Since you know her, I wonder if you could give her a recommendation."

"You'd be doin' right good to hire her, Mr. Henley. She is a woman of good character and honesty."

"Mrs. Livingston has told me that she kept the family finances in order while she was still at home, and her background is in banking although she tells me that only men were allowed to handle the window and money transactions. She says she learned by watching and doing the necessary paperwork. Since Mrs. Livingston already knows some of the banking business and all, and Sidney is also from England, he will know where our ways are different from the English ways, so he can train her quickly. Otis is leaving next week, so the timing couldn't be better."

"Well, as I was sayin', Mr. Henley, Mrs. Livingston is a good choice. I'm guessin' you need not to be interviewin' other folk for the job."

Sticking his neck out again, Mark realized it wasn't his decision as to whom Mr. Henley hired. "Just sayin', sir,"

Laughingly Mr. Henley answered, "If you're so resolute, and I've known your family for many years, Mark, I guess you just might be right. Like I said, she certainly is more qualified than most I've been talkin' to. I'll give Mrs. Livingston a try."

As Mark started to leave, tipping his hat, he turned briefly toward Emma and said, "Best of luck, Mrs. Livingston. Give Samuel a goodbye for me. Maybe our trails will cross again someday."

She started to respond but Mark left quickly. At least for now she will be in town. *That's good, and that's bad*, Mark thought, *I best be gittin' back to the farm. Forget it all; no more stickin' your nose into others' business. Hope you done learnt your lesson. Now it's time to start forgettin' what might have been. Might have been? Never could be so anyhow. I'm a farmer and have my life cut out for me. I'll just forget her. That's it, I'll just forget her.* Mark left with a great pain in his heart knowing that forgetting her would be impossible.

CHAPTER 38

hristmas had come and gone, and it was now 1867. The Caldwells and their new extended family had enjoyed the Christmas season together, with joy and hope for the future in the hearts of all except for one. This year Mark hadn't come to the table of hope and joy that Christmas promises.

Mark had longed to have Emma and Samuel join his family for Christmas so their loneliness wouldn't be so painful, but how could he invite her knowing there was always a chance that Richard would show up in Crockett? It was not to be. As the weeks passed, Mark knew that sometime soon, with spring approaching, he would have to go into town to pick up seed for planting and "things for the barn."

One place he did not want to go was into the bank. He wasn't sure how he would handle his emotions if he were to see Emma. There were matters, however, that would require a visit to the bank, so what to do?

Mason was expected to leave in a few weeks for his trip to Tennessee with Billy Lawell. Mason's condition had improved more than originally expected, and no one doubted that God had had his hand in the healing. There was no doubt because there had been much prayer.

As for Billy Lawell, his studies had been going well. Jonas, having a mentor's heart, had Billy on the right theological road. Mason felt obligated to keep his promise to a dying soldier, and it had already been three years since he'd made that promise. Of course, his own injuries had prevented an earlier departure, but now that he had mostly mended, that promise weighed heavily on his heart.

Paying for Billy's room and board had worked out well for everyone, except for Mark at this time. He knew Mason had much to get ready for the trip, but Mark wouldn't have time to go with him to town, and of course to the bank. He had, however, temporarily solved the banking problem because Uncle Lucas was still on the bank account. He arranged for Uncle Lucas to go to town with him whenever banking needed to be done.

By late February, the time had come. Mason and Billy were ready to depart to Lewisville, Tennessee.

"Your journey will keep me in prayer from the time I wake 'til the time go to bed," Lydia told Mason as Billy and Mark helped him up onto the buckboard.

"I hope I didn't use up all my prayers when you went off to war or our trials with Culpepper and Pike. Of course I know that isn't true since our Lord tells us to come to him any and all the time. Be sure I will go to him, my dear husband. And the same goes for you, Billy. Please take care this man. He is ever so dear to me."

Turning to Mason she concluded, "I love you, Mason Caldwell."

"Not to worry, Mrs. Caldwell. We have plenty of supplies and everything we need. There are good towns along the way. I understand that since the war ended, many new towns have sprung up and a kind of peace is in the making. Being we won't be going north, well, I guess that will be a blessin' too."

As Mason looked down on his bride, he took her hand with such warmth that tears started flowing. Confidently he told her, "Nothing's going to happen to this ol' man. Don't be worrying your pretty head and heart for me. We'll for sure take all the praying you can send up though."

With that Mason gave Billy the signal, and they started to pull away. Mason looked back at Lydia as she did her best to smile and not to show all her emotions. She hadn't done too bad a job of hiding her emotions when he had left for war, but she had hoped she would never have to do it again. The rest of the family had given their goodbyes earlier and had gone their separate ways. Mark, however, rode along to the end of the road leading from their farm.

"Don't be a-worryin', Pa. I'll take care of Ma and get the plantin' done. By the time you get back, we'll have a fine crop on the way up."

"I know you will do fine. You make a father proud. You're the best farmer in these parts. That's why I'm not worried about leaving. I know for sure you will take care of your ma. Love you, Son."

Mason and Billy were now officially on their way.

CHAPTER 39

A few days later, on a Sunday morning, Jonas left the rectory and headed for the church. His service was due to start in an hour, but he needed to set up for communion, and that would take a bit of time.

Fortunately the church stood across the road just next to the graveyard. As he stepped off the rectory porch, a scruffy looking man with long, unkempt hair confronted him. He looked harmless enough to Jonas. He carried a rifle but not a holstered gun. This was very common, for men hunted for their food in order to survive, but also Jonas saw no horse. As the church was some small distance from town, Jonas knew this man hadn't walked here.

Jonas, politely asked, "What can I do for you mister?"

The stranger's reply, his bent posture, and his weary voice showed a man who was very weary as he answered, "Well, sir, I bin comin' from quite a ways, and I'm a bit hungry. I ain't been able to make camp or do much huntin' for ..."

He paused to choose his words cautiously, "... reasons, but I'm a mite hungry because I ain't had anything to eat but a few leftover rabbit and squirrel scraps."

Jonas was used to giving handouts to strangers, but this was not the usual beggar type. Jonas' love for mankind was a gift he had been given, and sizing up a person came easy to him. Not that he had always been right. He had been taken from time to time. This time, however, he sensed something more than just a down-and-out beggar. As Jonas contemplated what to do after feeding this man, a shout came from the church steps.

"Jonas, best you be hurryin' up. We haven't much time. I already have the bread and wine ready but need some help puttin' up the table."

"Well, stranger, I'll be happy to give you something to eat but I'm a bit rushed right now. How 'bout you come help me and after service we'll have a hot plate for you?"

The man looked anxiously around and told Jonas, "Well, I ain't much for churchin' and for church people so I guess I'll be movin' on."

"Wish you'd change your mind, mister, and if you're still here when the service is over, the offer stands."

With that, Jonas hurried off the church. Jonas felt uneasy but this was not the time to confront or try to help this poor soul.

After the service, Jonas as was his custom, stood at the church door shaking hands, bidding his flock goodbye and God's blessings. Once everyone had gone, Jennie came out holding the morning's collection in her hand. As she met him at the bottom of the steps, Jonas had his back to the road when a man rode up behind him and hit Jonas on the head with the butt of his rifle. Jonas slumped to the ground a daze. Jennie reached down to help Jonas as the man called out, "Give me the money bag, lady. Do it now or I will drop you."

Jennie looked up to the man and clutching the bag said, "This money is for the poor and for food on our table. Leave now and take your sin with you."

Jennie was brave to say the least, but the man pulled his gun and shot her in the arm, not ready yet to kill her.

"Next one goes through your head little la...."

He didn't finish his word as a shot rang out, and the man fell from his saddle. The horse, apparently not spooked, just stood there.

Jennie looked around but didn't see anyone. Reaching down to Jonas, she saw he was bleeding from a swollen gash in his head. She too was bleeding, but her concern was for her husband. Standing up she cried out, "Someone please help me. Please someone. My Jonas is hurt bad."

As she continued to call out, the stranger Jonas had confronted earlier came out from the bushes from in front of the house, approaching Jennie and Jonas slowly and cautiously. Seeing no one else around, he decided to help.

Reaching Jonas and Jennie, he lifted Jonas and carried him to the house leaving the dead would-be robber in the street. Jennie walked close behind and, reaching the top of the steps, opened the door to let the stranger and Jonas in.

The stranger laid Jonas on the table and started to leave. Jennie called out to him, "Please mister, we need a doctor but I couldn't go. My arm is mighty painful, and I won't be able to saddle up a horse."

"Sorry, ma'am, I didn't plan on stayin' this long, and I got to get on the road. I only stopped for a bite to eat. Didn't plan on all these goin's on."

"Please, mister, we need some help. You must have a kind and caring heart. You saved my life, and you wouldn't of done so if'n you didn't care about helpin' folk."

The stranger looked at Jennie for what seemed a long time. Propping his rifle against the chair, he grabbed the basin, filled it with water, and started to boil it.

As the water was getting hot, the stranger went back to the would-be robber and dragged his body behind the church. He also tied up the horse behind the house. Back in the house he cleaned and dressed Jennie's arm and tied a sling, telling her, "You are either a lucky or a blessed woman. The bullet passed through and didn't shatter any bones. You'll heal just fine but with a nasty scar. As for your man, I done all I can do for him. His wound is cleaned but by the way it looked, a stitch or two—or more—will be in order. Keep the wound clean, and I'll check on him in the mornin'. I'll hitch up the wagon for you then, so you can take him into town. By then you should be able to handle the reins."

He paused for just a moment and added, "I can still use some food, so if'n it's okay with you, I'll help myself."

"Of course you can. But you say you will check on us in the morning. Where will you stay and why are you comin' back?"

He walked out onto the porch and looked around to see if anyone was near. Turning back to Jennie he told her, "It's my way of payin' you back for the food."

With that he left the porch and headed for the woods, where he had left his horse so it would not be seen. Here he would stay the night.

Morning came, and as promised, the stranger knocked on the door. He wondered if anyone was up this early, but it was clear he was in a hurry to be on his way.

"Your wagon is hitched, so I'll help you load your man onto it."

As he started to come through the door, he was taken aback to see Jonas sitting up in the chair. Jonas even managed to crack a slight smile.

"Mister, you are without a doubt the kindest man I've run across in this here county. Please sit and tell us about yourself."

Jonas and Jennie could tell by the stranger's movements that he was anxious to be out of there.

"No, I best be on my way. No need to delay when there's so much ground to cover. Besides, you be lookin' pretty good for a man with a cut like that. No, I'll be goin' now."

Jonas had a way of putting a man at ease. Many in the community said that was one reason, besides his love of Jesus, his congregation was growing to fill their little church.

"Tell us your name. At least you can tell us that."

"Names ain't important. I ain't from these parts anyway, so no need to tell ya."

Jonas wasn't going to let this go and persisted.

"You saved the life of my wife, and that means more to me than anything. I want to thank you proper so please, what should we call you?"

Reluctantly, but feeling the peace in this house, he answered, "My name is Tom. Tom Richmond. Now I must go and no thanks are necessary. I feel that time is passin' by, and I really need to be travelin' on."

Tom started for the door, but Jonas in his best preacher's voice said, "Stop, Tom. You ain't gittin' away that easy. We owe you too much, and we aim to pay or help you for what you done for us in some way."

"Well if'n you want to help me, let me git goin' so the posse don't catch up with me."

Posse? This took Jonas by surprise. Whom did they have in their home, and whom had they trusted? Tom seemed too kind and caring to be chased by a posse. Tom was by then on the porch and headed down the few steps in front of him.

"We'll help you, Tom, we owe you that. Whatever we can do we will do. Come back in here, Tom, please, and tell us your part of the story. You must be tired of runnin', and maybe we can help you to stop."

Tom returned to the house and getting into Jonas's face asked him, "You gonna help me with a murder charge?"

This did seem to hit Jonas between the eyes, but he had offered and told Tom, "I swear we will be there for you if you explain what happened. That means you best not be lyin' or no help will come. If someone says you did a murder, there must be a reason you been called out on that. But we need to know what that reason was. Are you willing to at least have us try?"

Tom definitely wanted some support but was still not sure what he should do or say to Jonas.

"You got your preacher hat on now mister, or are you doin' this because you're feelin' obligated because I saved your lives? Either way, I don't see how this will get me out of this fix I'm in. I'm on my way to the hills and to the cold country in Utah. I'm hopin' they will give up chasin' me by then."

Jonas questioned Tom, "How long you been on the run? How far behind do you think this posse is?"

"Well, I know I got maybe one, maybe two days on them, I lost count. I do know I lost more time here than I would like to."

"Tell us what happened and why they're after you. If your story is true, there may be a way to get them off your trail."

Jonas bade Tom to sit down. Jennie, though she couldn't quite cook with her arm in a sling, brewed up some coffee and offered it to Tom and Jonas. Finally Tom started to tell his story.

"I'll make this quick. I had rode out to the ranch where my sister and her husband live. As I rode up to house, I could hear screamin' and yellin' coming out the window and door. There'd been times when I saw my sister with bruises on her face and arms, and when I asked her 'bout them, she'd say she fell. I didn't believe her, and I knowed her husband was a man with a temper. I was sure I knew what was going on. I jumped off my horse and ran as fast as I could into the house. What I saw scared me half to death. My sister was bleeding from her nose, head, arms. I just saw blood all over her. She looked half dead. I told her husband to leave her alone, and he just told me to get on my horse and git outta here afore he laid into me the same; it weren't any of my business.

"As I started for my sister, he tried to stop me. We got into a fight, and he pulled his gun on me. I don't carry a gun, or I would have shot him on the spot when I saw my sister. As we struggled, I was lucky enough to turn the gun away from me, and as I did, it fired. It struck him clean through his heart. I knew I had to run."

Jonas and Jennie were gripped by the heartbreak they saw and heard from Tom. Jonas collected his thoughts and told Tom, "You got a sure case of self-defense and maybe a charge against him for attempted killing of your sister. No judge will find you guilty—especially after they see your sister's condition."

Tom, with a cynical grin across his face, looked at Jonas and responded, "They saw my sister, but when you kill the mayor's son, it don't make a lick of difference if you're innocent or not."

Jonas sat back in his chair and tried to wrap his head around the politics of all this. Surely justice should prevail in a case like this. In the meantime, he knew he needed to have his head looked after.

"I think I have a plan if you trust me. Will you trust me to get you out of this? If you do, you'll be free from anyone who would do you harm."

Tom was tired of running, his horse was tired, and he wanted to—no, needed to—put an end to all this. "What is your plan, preacher?"

Jonas smiled and looking at Jennie told her, "Get your coat, and let's be off to see Doc Thompson. Here's what I need for you to do while we're gone, Tom."

With that Jonas gave instructions to Tom, and he and Jennie went out to the porch, down the steps, and left for Doc Thompson's.

It took most of the day, but as they returned to the house, they saw that Tom had not left. That meant he had fulfilled the first part of Jonas' plan. Day turned to night; night turned into a new day. Jonas had started to work on his next sermon, which just might have had "trust" in its title.

Dark clouds crept over a sun that was getting low in the sky as a group of men came riding up. It was quite plain to see they were a posse. Jonas stepped out onto the porch as they pulled up. He told Jennie to stay in the house. As the men rode closer, Jonas saw the sheriff's badge plainly.

The sheriff started the conversation, "Howdy there, Mister. Hey, that looks like a pretty bad hit you took in the head? That's a whole lot of bandage."

Jonas answered, "Yeah, it is, Sheriff. Was helpin' a neighbor fix his roof when a piece of lumber come flyin' off and hit me pretty hard. I still get a mite dizzy, but I'm guessin' I'll be fine. Can I help you gentlemen with somethin'?"

Jennie cringed as she heard her dear husband tell a lie for the first time. She never quite expected that. As the sheriff gazed to and fro over the landscape, it was clear he was looking for Tom, but all he saw was a bald man tending the graveyard, digging, hoeing, and in general just fixing up around a freshly dug grave.

"I'm the sheriff from Alexandria, Louisiana, and we bin chasin' a man that's wanted for murder there. I'm a-wonderin' if'n you may have seen a man runnin' through here?"

"Sure have."

Jonas was back on the honest trail as he continued, "At least a stranger came through here a day or so ago. Looked kind of haggard and like someone on the run, but he was a stranger to me. Being the parson around here, I know pretty much everyone here 'bouts."

That had the sheriff's attention as he asked, "Are you knowin' which way he headed, and can you describe him?"

"Sure, Sheriff. Well, first off he begged some food from me and said he was headed for the hills. Utah, I believe he said."

Jonas then described Tom to a tee. So far Jonas had been totally honest.

The sheriff sat up in his saddle as he said, "That's Tom all right."

He then turned his attention to his posse and said, "Jehosephat! We bin chasin' this man for over 200 miles. I'm tired of chasin' him and have a mind to call this off. I'd of killed that no good woman beater m'self if'n he had beat my sister like that, even if he was the mayor's son. I ain't too fond of the mayor anyway. Maybe I'll get his job after all this."

That was music to Jonas' ears. Now he knew for sure Tom had been telling the truth, so Jonas continued with his plan. "If you mean that, Sheriff, maybe I can help you out a bit."

The sheriff looked interested, and asked Jonas to explain. Jonas was happy to oblige. "Well you see that man over there at the graveyard?"

"You mean that bald-headed man?"

"Yes, Sheriff, he just got done buryin' a man that has no name. He was a thief caught trying to steal the church's money. Well one of my parishioners shot him dead because he wouldn't surrender his gun when asked to. Instead of surrendering, he drawed his gun. Guess he wasn't as fast as he should have been."

The sheriff was wondering where Jonas was going with all this. The same Jonas who always told the truth. The sheriff asked, "What does that have to do with me and my men?"

Jonas was glad he asked. "You see, Sheriff, I believe this Tom, as you call him, ain't ever comin' back this way again, so maybe we can get you home and, if you and your men can keep a secret, here's what I suggest."

Jonas paused for a moment, looking back and forth among the men in the posse and the sheriff as he wondered if he could get away with what he was about to suggest. Finally, he decided to give it a try.

"We don't know who this man is that tried to steal the money bag, 'cause he was also a stranger. My man over there just buried him, and because we don't know his name, why don't you let me carve a headstone with your Tom's name on it. I can make up some date close to when he was born, and we know what date he died in case someone comes a-lookin' for him. We can put Tom's name on the headstone, and no one will be the wiser."

Jonas smiled at the sheriff and added, 'You know, Sheriff, I guess you must have shot him dead."

The sheriff looked at his men who were smiling at him. To a man, they too just wanted to get home to warm beds and their women. They were looking a bit weary too.

The sheriff asked Jonas to back off while he talked with his men. The sheriff had the men gather around him and quietly told them, "Look, I'm tired and wantin' to get home, and this plan seems okay to me. Ya know, it feels kinda like a blessin' comin' from a preacher, so it must be okay, and it ain't like we're doin' somethin' wrong and sneaky. The preacher must have a kind heart to worry 'bout our pushin' on. Besides, I ain't itchin' to ride all the way to Utah but, if'n we do this, we are all sworn to secrecy. So what do you think? Tom didn't do nothin' any of us wouldn't have done."

There was no argument from the men as they murmured their approval. They were just as happy to be heading home.

"Well, preacher man, Tom's name is Richmond. Give him a good burial," said the sheriff and with a smirk added, "If'n ya know what I mean."

The sheriff laughed as he and his men turned their horses and headed down the road and out of sight. Jennie came out and told Jonas, "Preacher man, you should be ashamed of yourself lyin' to those men! What the Lord ought to do is wash your mouth out. Best you go into that church and confess your sin."

Jonas just loved this woman and holding her tight said, "I didn't lie. He did say he was going to the hills and on to Utah."

"Well, that may be true, but you are pushing it a bit, Jonas Coy."

As Jonas and Jennie walked over to the graveyard, the bald man turned to greet them. Jonas said, "Well, Tom, you can put your hat on now. The sheriff and his posse are gone. Sorry you had to shave your head, but better a bald one than a dead one. Besides, it'll grow back. Now you can get your horse from out the woods and do as you please. You're a free man."

Tom looked intently at Jonas and told him, "Both our debts are paid, Preacher. Maybe when I get to my new home, I'll find a preacher man like you."

Tom tipped his hat to Jennie and went to get his horse. Maybe, just so as not to make Jonas a liar, Tom headed over the hills, and off to Utah, or at least points west. It may be they would never hear from Tom again, or maybe, just maybe, they might.

In the meantime, Jonas and Jennie prayed that Tom would find that preacher man.

CHAPTER 40

With spring finally coming in all its glory, the time had come for planting. Rains would come to feed the soon-to-be-planted seed that would grow into a fine crop to sustain the Caldwells and provide some income. The warmth of the spring sun would nurture the crops as well.

This, of course, meant getting the seed; getting the seed meant a trip into town, and a chance meeting with Emma. Mark was sure, or at least hoping, she hadn't made enough money to transport herself and Samuel off to England as yet. So he would use the ace he had up his sleeve to do the banking. That would be Uncle Lucas.

Mason was still away and, as promised, Uncle Lucas went into town with Mark. He did his own banking at the same time, so it really wasn't a burden on him.

Luke was well on his way to being a good rancher so the Rocking Eagle Ranch was in good hands, and besides, Luke had his new wife to keep him in line, something Lela was good at.

Mark left to pick up Uncle Lucas. As he rode, he kept telling himself he didn't want to see Emma, but did he really believe that? As Mark and Uncle Lucas rode into town, the conversation was about planting, mending fences, and all that goes with farming, ranching, and herding cattle. Mark really didn't want to hang around in town too long to avoid any chance meeting with Emma, but not wanting to reveal his feelings about this, he told Uncle Lucas, "I don't want to keep you too long, Uncle Lucas. We can leave soon as we're done with our business."

"Mark, I ain't in no hurry. Jes' thinkin' I would like to see some old friends if'n you got a few extra minutes. Want to catch up. I heard the Wardles are gonna have another little one, and Catherine is wantin' to make a little something for the child."

Not wanting to hurt Uncle Lucas' feelings, Mark replied, "Well, I guess time ain't much of a factor. As long as I git you home before dark."

Uncle Lucas laughed at this knowing that it was so early in the morning they would be home by sunset anyway.

"When you're ready to be gittin' back, Mark, you jes' let me know, and I'll be ready."

Mark felt he had slighted Uncle Lucas and told him, "Hey, maybe a stopover to the saloon for a bit will help us to unwind before we head home. Besides, I'm sure we can find a bunch of ol' friends in there if'n they're still able to stand up."

This got a laugh out of both of them.

Arriving in town, he and Uncle Lucas made their usual stop at the livery stable. The horses needed water and feed. From there they headed out in separate directions to do the necessary shopping and, of course, banking. The streets had pretty much dried from the previous rain, but there were still some mud puddles to negotiate.

As Mark entered Mr. Harris' store, the first thing to catch his eye was the candy in the window. Memories start with the smallest of things, and Mark's were especially poignant.

"Howdy, Mr. Harris. Bin a while since I was here last. Anythin' new to catch me up on?"

"Howdy, Mark, good to see you again. Want a piece of candy? It's on the house today. Mr. Harris started to chuckle as he continued, "I recall your little friend tuggin' at your arm. I remember your kindness to him. He's turning into a good boy, I hear."

Mark just smiled so as not to be rude. He really didn't want to recall too much of that day. Mark politely answered but changed the subject quickly, "No thanks, Mr. Harris. I just need some supplies, and then I'll be gittin' on my way. Mr. Neiter is with me, and I have to get him back real soon."

What a lame excuse! Uncle Lucas was happy to be enjoying some time away and hoping to see some old friends. Mark gathered the supplies they needed and had them ready near the door to load in the wagon. He peered out the doorway to see Uncle Lucas come out of the bank. Mark didn't go to meet him but instead waited just inside the door of the store.

There was no way he wanted Emma to see him should she come out of the bank. Besides, Uncle Lucas mentioned he needed some supplies too. Uncle Lucas entered the store and greeted Mr. Harris. Lucas pulled out the shopping list that Catherine had given him and gathered his purchases on the counter.

"These womenfolk, they sure have a hankerin' for the funniest things. I don't know what she is going to do with this new fancy gadget. She saw it in a catalogue and said we needed it. I guess you can mix with this here rotary egg beater better than with a spoon. Are we spoilin' these womenfolk, Mark? I jes don't know any more."

Lucas chuckled. Anyone who knew him knew how much he enjoyed spoiling Catherine. As the two headed for the saloon, Mark kept his head down. As they entered the saloon, Mark was stunned to see Richard and thought, *When did he get to town? How long has been here? What does he want?* Mark's mind went wild. *None of my business, stay out of it, just let Lucas have his fun, and I'll just go sit where no one can see me.*

Too late. Richard walked over to him, "I say, ol' chap, I guess I got here just in ruddy time. Just arrived this morning, and look! Whom do I run across? I see you haven't let go of Emma's hem as of yet."

Mark was ready to get up and do some business here and now but instead came to his senses in time and just answered, "Ain't been to town for months, friend. Just arrived here myself. Don't want no trouble."

"Of course I would like to believe you, but you see, Emma has been ignoring my telegrams, and now I see why."

"Uncle Lucas," Mark called out, "hate to cut our visit short, but best we be leavin' a-fore there's a problem."

Uncle Lucas stopped short with the conversation he had just started with his friend. Not aware of the situation with Richard, he told Mark, "If'n there's a problem, Mark, maybe there's somethin' I can to do help?"

"No, Uncle Lucas, I doubt anyone can help when someone ain't willin' to listen."

Mark started for the door, but Richard followed. Lucas could see that this stranger was the problem. Knowing Mark, he didn't expect what happened next. Mark, unable to contain himself any longer did something most uncharacteristic—turned and slammed Richard a hard one to the jaw. Richard went down and out.

"Let's git our supplies and git out o' here, Uncle Lucas. This could get ugly if'n I let it."

They headed for the store, and as they did, Emma came out of the bank. It was closing time, and Mark hadn't thought of that. Mark spotted her and was in even more of a hurry to leave, but just then Richard came up from behind Mark and hit him in the head with his fist. Mark reeled around and stopped another blow. A horrified Emma saw all this and started to yell, "Richard, Mark! Stop! Please stop!"

At the same time, Mark pushed Richard into the street. He wanted to go after him but seeing Emma, he stopped. Uncle Lucas grabbed Mark's arm and tried to persuade him, "I don't know the situation, Mark, but this ain't goin' nowhere good, I'm sure of that."

Then it happened. Samuel came from around the corner but hadn't seen any of this. Both Mark and Richard saw him and ended the melee. Samuel saw his father and ran up to him.

"Father, you're here. We thought you wouldn't be coming for us."

This told Mark that Richard had been telling the truth and that he had just arrived.

Emma crossed the street and stood between Richard and Mark. Samuel was still at his father's side. Emma was the first to speak, "Samuel doesn't need to see any fisticuffs. Let's all be on our way and sort this out at another time."

Mark was totally out of his element with this. He was used to a simple life, and all he wanted was peace. Then again, maybe it should come to a head. Emma had said one thing about leaving this gambling man and going back to England, and now she was defending him? Samuel must be her first concern, however, and Mark realized that.

"I'll be goin'. No need to hang out here anyway," Mark irritably told them.

He and Uncle Lucas headed for the livery stable, loaded up their wagon, and headed out. Richard, Emma, and Samuel had disappeared, and Mark was once again feeling heartache. He thought to himself, *Oh Emma, if only you could leave my memories and thoughts. Why did I have to see you again, especially under these circumstances?* It was a quiet trip back to the Rocking Eagle Ranch. Uncle Lucas asked no questions. He ached for Mark, but he wouldn't interfere with Mark's thoughts.

CHAPTER 41

Weeks passed. Then one day, as Mark returned from the barn having unhitched the team and put the buckboard away, he saw another buckboard coming down the road to the house. What he saw was not something he ever expected. It was Emma. He wondered what she could possibly want that Mark might have to offer her now. He dared not get his hopes up that Richard had done him a favor and up and died. That would not be an answer to prayer—or would it? *Stop it, Mark* came out of his mouth. *I'll just see what she has to say and send her on her way.*

As Emma arrived at the hitching post in front of the house, Lydia came out onto the porch to greet her. Mason was still away, so Lydia stayed very aware of anyone (or anything) that came down the road, especially when Mark was in the field.

"Good day," came the English accent from the carriage. "I hope I am not troubling you by coming to your home on a Sunday."

"Not at all, young lady, and who might you be?" Lydia asked, as if she didn't know.

"My name is Emma Livingston and I'm a ..." There was a slight pause, then she continued, "a friend of Mr. Caldwell, that is, Mr. Mark Caldwell."

"Welcome, Mrs. Livingston. Mark has mentioned your name. Please come in. May I get you something to drink? I'm sure you're thirsty after your trip from town. We just got home from church and something cool sounds good to me too."

Emma climbed down from the carriage as Mark came up to her. It was too late assist her down, but he took her arm and escorted her up the steps onto the porch. As they entered the house, Emma told Lydia, "I met your lovely husband and must say that he is a kind and amicable soul. He was able to stop a verbal argument before it got out of hand."

Mark looked at Lydia with a straight non-committal face.

"I wasn't aware of a situation as you describe it, Mrs. Livingston. Was there someone I know involved in this?"

Mark was quick to jump into the conversation, "Ma, this is the lady I mentioned to you who had us a bit worried on her trip to Palestine. She's probably here to see how farmin' people live. She works at the bank and needs to know if'n loanin' money to us farm folk is a wise idea or not. You know, how the crops grow and such."

Where did this come from? What gave me that idea? Mr. Henley does all that investigating for farm loans. Lydia could see Mark stumbling over himself and tried to help him.

"Did you forget to make a deposit or make a mistake in your figures, Mark? Mr. Henley has been doing our banking far too long to worry about our work ethics."

Caught. Mark had his foot in his mouth and thought it best to keep quiet, but Emma spoke up, "No, Mrs. Caldwell, all the banking transactions are fine. I do need to have a word with Mr. Caldwell," she said turning toward Mark. "That is, Mark, if it isn't an imposition. There seems to be a mistake in another area that needs some clarification."

Lydia smiled at Emma and told her, "We will be having our noon meal shortly. It would be our pleasure if you would join us."

"Your kindness is so appreciated, Mrs. Caldwell, but I do have to get back very soon because I have Samuel to gather from his little friend's house. May I say something, Mrs. Caldwell?"

Emma looked like a lost soul seeking relief from a pain coming from the very depths of her being.

"There is such a peace here. I only wish I could stay for a …" Emma caught herself but then finished, "much longer time than this."

Lydia, sensing her struggle to keep it together, replied, "Just know that you're welcome in this house any time you desire to come here. Why don't the two of you go out on the porch? It's such a beautiful day. No rain that I can see coming, so you two visit while I go prepare our meal and get us something to drink."

Mark led Emma to the bench in the arbor that Mason and Lydia enjoyed so much. Emma looked at Mark and told him, "I came to apologize to you, Mark. You have been avoiding me, I can tell, and I want you to know that I do so very much want to be your friend. Dare I say that I miss your—cheerful—spirit? I don't see much of that anymore."

"And what of Richard? To be seen jes' talkin' with you would lead to a fight."

"Richard, yes Richard. He has already gambled away all the money I have saved for our journey back to England. But Mark, that's not why I'm here. I have no one to talk to, and I feel so alone."

Emma wasn't telling the whole truth. After all this time living in Crockett she must have made enough friends to have someone to talk to. Was she going beyond the limits of decorum for a married woman? Had absence made her heart grow fonder? Mark got off the bench and looked out over his beloved fields. What could he say to someone he realized he was truly in love with? In his heart he knew she could never be his. If not Richard, it would be off to England. But how could he say no to her? He could tell her how much he loved her and gamble she would both leave Richard and not go back to England. Leaving Richard would most likely lead to another confrontation that would result in someone getting hurt, badly hurt. It could even go beyond that.

Mustering up as much courage as he could, he told Emma, "I'll be comin' to town next week. I'm sure Richard will be gamblin' and maybe we can have a little time together, maybe a dinner. I'll try to be a friendly face you can find some peace in. Ain't a face much to look at, but this is as good as it gets."

They both managed a halfhearted laugh as Emma told him, "It's a handsome face, dear Mark, and thank you for your continued kindness."

Mark took her hand as she stood and said, "Also remember that the invitation to come here is always open."

Emma called out to say goodbye to Lydia, and with that Mark helped her onto the buckboard. He watched her as she headed down the road. A friend, that's all she needed. That was asking much of him—but *I'll do my best* Mark told himself.

Mark went to town the following week and stopped in at the bank. He figured he might just as well start dealing with his emotions and maybe, just maybe, he would find her to be just what she has asked him to be, a friend. He quietly told her that he would be at the hotel when she got off work.

After the bank closed, Emma joined Mark at the hotel. Looking around Mark asked, "Do you know where Richard is now, Emma?"

"Richard has gone to visit some gambling friends at someone's farm a few miles outside of town. I'm sure he won't be coming back for quite some time if he comes home tonight at all, and Samuel is at his new friend's house where he has been wanting to go for some time now. I told him I would come to retrieve him before dark."

After putting Mark's mind at ease, she continued, "I realize that I'm putting you in an awkward position, Mark, by being so selfish. Maybe this is not such a good idea, but I am going to make the best of this time we are together. I do want to tell you that your mother is a complete delight. Of course, I would have never thought otherwise. You are a reflection of her sweet spirit. I have been trying to think of ways to repay you for saving my life and Samuel's, and the only thing I could come up with is …."

Emma reached into a bag and pulled out a vest made of leather with all the trimmings of a rich rancher. She bowed her head and blushed as she said, "I know it's not considered proper for a lady to be giving gifts to a gentleman, especially— but my dear Mark, you saved my life and Samuel's, and even with all the grief I've brought to you, you've remained my friend. Please do not read more into this, but accept it with my gratitude."

He looked at her smiling and shaking his head in disbelief.

"Ain't never seen anything like this before; it's a mite dressy for a farmer," was Mark's observation. Then with a somber look and concern in his voice, he continued, "I know you bin savin' your money, and this looks like a gift that took more than some extra earnin's to come up with. I can't accept it because I know you bin strugglin'. Especially with Richard's gamblin' and all."

Placing her hand on Mark's arm she said, "Mr. Harris got this vest in the order he sent to his supplier. He said he didn't order this particular vest, but when he notified them, they told him to just keep it as it would be too much trouble and cost too much to send back. He said selling this vest in these parts might be a problem, so when he saw I had an interest in it, he gave me a price that was just too hard to pass up. He also told me that with all the help I've been to him with his banking needs, it would be his honor to sell it to me at such a wonderful savings. *Please*, Mark, accept this as it comes from my ..." She paused, and looking up into Mark's face, continued, "... my most humble thanks for saving our lives. And—it comes from my heart."

Mark was speechless. He thought to himself, *It would not be honorable to refuse this gift. I can't let my pride get in the way. Besides, she said it was from her heart, didn't she? Well, that makes it even more special.*

He quietly replied to Emma, "I thank you, Emma. It's more than a man could ask for." Then, trying to lighten the mood, he finished, "Guess I'll hafta wear it to the next barn dance. We ain't got much in this little town to git all gussied up for. I thank you kindly, Emma. I'll wear it no matter where I go. Except in the field of course. Ain't wantin' to get it all muddied up and all."

The rest of the evening was given to small talk about banking and farming except for one thing.

"How is Samuel doin', Emma? I'm sure he's a mite happy about his pa bein' here."

Emma hung her head and answered, "His—pa, as you call him, isn't much of a father. He is unfit to be a father to Samuel, and, as you might guess, he is not here most of the time, and when he is, his silence is overwhelming. He doesn't say much to Samuel, only to tell him to do his homework and grow up to be something. He keeps telling Samuel he is going to take us back to England, but that isn't going to happen I'm afraid.

"Richard spends all the money I make at the bank on his own whims and gambling. Of course he buys Samuel little gifts, especially candy, to show some sort of love. Samuel does love his father, and that puts him in an awkward position. Samuel sees me holding back the tears as his father belittles me while giving him things. One day he asked Richard why mum cries so much. Richard just told him to keep quiet. I know that at one time Samuel didn't want Richard around because he saw the heartbreak I go through, but how do you separate a father and a son? Samuel is too young to understand. I just have to tolerate it as long as I have Samuel to love and to be loved by him in return."

"I'm sorry, Emma. I know in my heart that someday this will all go away. I pray, that is, my family and I pray for you and Samuel every day. We also pray for Richard. Please don't give up hope. The Lord knows your heart, and he answers prayer."

This was the first time Mark had broached the subject of religion, God, or any spiritual things. He didn't know where Emma stood on this. It could be that she didn't believe prayer could accomplish anything in a situation as desperate as this was for her.

"I deeply appreciate your prayers dear Mark. I treasure our friendship and I—Mark, there is so much I want to say to you. My feelings are ...."

Emma stopped short of what she really wanted to say but finished with, "Thank you, Mark, for being here."

Mark wanted to hear more about how she felt, but again and again that still small voice spoke. *Stop Mark there is no place to go with this.*

They stood up simultaneously. Mark laid money on the table, and they left.

As they exited the door, they were met by a sight they weren't prepared for. There in front of the bank stood Richard, home unexpectedly—or maybe not. He must have lost all his money in the first few hands. Richard spotted Emma and Mark and was quick to anger.

"Well, well, dear Emma. When I saw you were not at home I came to see if you might be working late. I see you are working late. This is the last of it, Emma. This man will have to be put in his place."

Richard reached for a gun he had hidden in his belt behind his long-tailed coat. Mark didn't carry a handgun, as was his custom, but he didn't have his rifle either. Emma stepped in front of Mark, and that stopped Richard for but a moment. Mark pushed her aside and started a dash for some cover.

By now Richard was in the street trying to hunt Mark down. Just then a rumbling sound from down the street signaled that a wagon had gotten loose from the hitching post and the horses were in a dead run. At the same time Samuel came from the corner of a building, and seeing his father, ran toward him oblivious of the wagon.

Emma screamed, "No, Samuel, no! Stop! Richard, the wagon is headed for Samuel!" Mark jumped out from behind his cover and started for Samuel. But before Mark could react, Richard, seeing Samuel, ran to him and pushed him away from the runaway horses and wagon, an action that cost him dearly. Losing his balance, he was unable to move away in time as the horses trampled him. Emma screamed as Mark grabbed Samuel and took him to his mother. Mark then went over to Richard, who was still alive though barely.

Mark called to a few men standing nearby and told them, "Let's lift him gently. We need to git him to Doc Thompson. Easy, easy. He's bleedin' bad, and it looks like he has some broken bones."

They carried Richard to the doctor's office and laid him on the examining table. Doc looked at Mark shaking his head. Richard would not live but for a few more minutes. Mark looked out the window to see Emma and Samuel coming that way. Leaving Richard to the doctor, Mark stepped outside to stop Emma.

"Don't be takin' Samuel in there. Please, Emma, leave him with me. Go and say what needs sayin'."

She knew by his tone how serious the situation was. Going into Doc's office, she saw a broken man, maybe more than just physically.

Richard took her hand and said something she could never have dreamt he could say, "Forgive me, Emma. Forgive me please. I don't deserve your forgiveness, but it's all I have left to wish for. I should have been man enough to know that I was just hurting those I love. I do love you, Emma, please believe me. Please tell Samuel that I love him.

Tell him to grow up to be a man I would be proud of and not to waste his life on selfishness."

Emma, overcome by her emotions, broke down in tears.

"I love you also, Richard. I forgive you. I forgive you."

By now, Richard had pretty much bled out and was losing consciousness. Finally, Doc Thompson pronounced Richard dead. Emma sat there numb for a moment pondering all the thoughts one has when someone close dies. Finally, she went back outside to find Mark holding Samuel close.

"Samuel, I don't know how to tell you, your father has ...."

There was a pause as she was having a hard time saying the words, but Samuel with his wonderful childlike perception told her, "I know, Mum; Father has passed away. Please, Mum, don't be afraid. I will take care of you. But, Mum, I will miss him terribly."

Samuel started to cry, and Emma held him tight. They needed no words between them. After a moment, Mark knelt beside Samuel and turned him so they were face to face. With a compassionate voice, Mark told Samuel, "There's somethin' you need to be knowin', Samuel. Your father was a hero. He gave his life to save you, and this is how you must always remember him. He loved you, I'm sure of that, Samuel."

Emma reassured Samuel, "Your father did love you, you never have to doubt that. He told me; he told me he loved us both."

The three of them walked off as night started to set in. Mark would stay through the night to reassure Emma that anything she or Samuel might need would be taken care of.

CHAPTER 42

Mason had been back from his journey to Tennessee for a while and was happy to be home with his loving wife.

When he had first returned, his heart had been heavy as he told her of his meeting with the family of the fallen young soldier.

"I guess I never mentioned the young soldier's name before, Lydia, but he was Private Benjamin Montgomery. When Billy and I arrived at the Montgomery home, I was struck by the humble homestead. These are folk like you and me, scratching out a living tilling the land. I told them of the bravery of their son and his final request. I told them of his love for them. Told them he forgave them and wanted forgiveness for the fight they'd had before he left for war. There were tears of sadness and of joy as we all shared his love for the Lord. My pain was also lifted off me from waiting so long to keep my promise to go see these loving folk."

Mason's relief was complete as Lydia put her loving, understanding arms around him.

oc Thompson was a loving man as well as the town doctor. That had been evident in his care of John when he was shot. As Jennie and Jonas waited nervously in his office, the doctor went about checking his tests and records.

When they'd arrived, Jonas had explained worriedly, "You see, Doc, Jennie hasn't been feelin' very good, and we are concerned that it might be something serious. I'll take care and do whatever you tell me to do to make her well. Just give me the word."

Finally, Doc Thompson returned and announced sternly, "Jonas, as I stand here before you and Jennie, all I can say is you better not let her do anything strenuous. At some point you will have to git the household cleanin' done yourself, do all the liftin' for her, carry the water bucket, and all those things."

Jonas looked horrified as he searched for words of reassurance from Doc Thompson.

"Tell me, Doc. What is it, what's wrong with my Jennie?"

Doc looked at Jennie with a twinkle in his eye and said in an exuberant voice, "You're gonna have a baby!"

Jonas was at a loss for words—but not Jennie.

"Oh, Doc, what wonderful news! The miracle of having a child; to be a co-creator with God himself. What a privilege and joy."

Jonas looked at her, both of them with tears in their eyes as they felt a oneness they had never felt before.

"Now, Jonas, you take good care of Jennie. I've been taking care of her since she was a little tyke, so you see to it she isn't over-worked, or you'll have me to answer to."

"Doc, you can bet your life on that!"

As they left Doc Thompson's office, Jonas was already kowtowing, gently guiding her, and all but carrying her to the buckboard. Now another journey would begin.

"Jonas," pleaded Jennie as they got underway, "could we swing by my folks' farm on our way? Please? I can't wait to share the news."

L uke was herding cattle, happy not to have gone to California. Lela, of course, no longer worried about her wheelchair getting stuck in the mud because Luke would be there to pull her out.

Lucas and Catherine had quickly settled into their new home together, and were enjoying their love for each other. Their extended family now included Luke and Lela, and for Lucas, it was like having a second chance at raising a son. For Catherine, whose only son was away so much of the time, it partly filled her void, and for both it was as if they had been given a daughter.

Jonas and Jennie were busy with a growing church, getting to know their congregation, and looking forward to their new life as parents.

John was away with Matthew serving with their good friend and mentor, Captain McNelly, as guardians and peacekeepers of the great state of Texas. This meant more travel and less time at home for them, but it also gave them a rich sense of fulfillment to serve their country in this manner.

Bo was still undecided what he should do or where he should go. He was just happy to have found a warm peaceful home until he could make up his mind about his future and who he really was.

Henry? Well, Henry couldn't have been more content. He had found a home where he was accepted for who he was. He loved them for who they were and knew that in their way they loved him too. Considering their respective backgrounds, Bo and Henry couldn't ask for more than that.

Only Mark was left with a troubled spirit, and this he took out in work on the farm that he loved as his solace and his support.

Planting was finished and summer was approaching. All were living life as it should be under God's grace, protection, and will.

As Mason and Lydia stood on their porch holding hands, they admired the beautiful sunset that only a loving God can paint and thoughtfully contemplated their journey from Mason's time in the war until now.

Almost as a sigh, Lydia told Mason, "We have come a long way, my dear husband. The day you left for war and the months you were gone from me were some of the most painful days I have ever had to endure. I know I leaned on God so much I'm sure he is still leanin' over. But by his many blessings, and by his abundant grace, I found my strength. Who would have imagined that the trials we were going to face would be so hard."

"We never questioned God's will in our lives, Lydia. I believe that he honored that by giving us more than we deserve. We see a beauty in this land that he has given us and a family strong in faith held together by his almighty love, mercy, and grace. And you, my dearest one, have also been my strength. A blessed man I am. I've said it before, and I'll say it 'til my dyin' day."

Mason finished, "Let's go to the throne of grace and give him the praise he deserves." With that, they turned and entered the house arms entwined with such a love that it could only be from above.

But what of Mark? What of Emma? Were his questions answered?

Emma had taken the Caldwells up on their open invitation and found time to come to the farm with Samuel once in a while. Samuel loved these visits to the Caldwells, and why not? They had a tendency to spoil him. He was actually becoming a good rider and learning to hitch up a wagon.

Emma was still working, but was she saving to go back home to England? Will Mark let her go if she decides to leave? Will Samuel have a say in his and his mother's fate? Who can know? Only with time would these questions be resolved.

THE END

Or—just the beginning

ENDNOTES

Chapter 8:

[1] "Lee Surrendered: April 9, 1865," *America's Story*, website operated by the Library of Congress (accessed June 18, 2015) *http://www.americaslibrary.gov/jb/civil/jb_civil_surrender_1.html*

Chapter 11:

[2] Isaiah 41:18, NKJV, Thomas Nelson

Chapter 14:

[3] James B. Ronan II, "Battle of Chickamauga: Union Regulars Desperate Stand," *America's Civil War* magazine, originally published July 1999 and on line June 12, 2006, *HistoryNet, http://www.historynet. com/battle-of-chickamauga-union-regulars-desperate-stand.htm* (accessed June 20, 2015).

Chapter 30:

[4] Ephesians 2:8-9, NKJV, Thomas Nelson
[5] John 3:16, ibid.

HISTORICAL NOTES

Wherever this story incorporates actual historical personalities into an otherwise fictional story, every effort has been made to portray them as accurately as historical research allows. Thus, their ranks, titles, units, and other details reflect their actual lives.

Two of those personages are David Crockett and Leander McNelly.

While David Crockett (Chapters 2, 20) is known to all today largely from the Disney TV series as King of the Wild Frontier, he was a true hero of American history. Despite less than one year of formal education and not learning to read and write until age eighteen, Crockett was possessed of genuine integrity and such drive as to justify the hero status bestowed upon him. One thing that he did *not* appreciate, however, was the appellation "Davy," and deferring to his preference, this work does not use it.

Lack of formal education clearly did not hold him back, as Colonel Crockett, in his fifty years, held several local elective public offices as well as serving in both the Legislature of Tennessee and the U.S. House of Representatives. In addition, he held several military positions in both Tennessee and Texas before meeting his unfortunate destiny at the Alamo.

Of course, the events at the Alamo predate our story by almost thirty years, so David Crockett does not appear in the story as a character, but the setting is the city named for him, the legend about his fondness for pecans has a ring of truth as eastern Texas is "pecan country," and his name is mentioned by a major character.

Leander McNelly (Chapters 11, 14, and throughout) was an actual officer serving in the early Texas Rangers who, like many of his fellow Rangers, enlisted in the Confederate Army when hostilities broke out. He actually served as a captain with the Texas Mounted Volunteers, part of Company F, Fifth Regiment. This regiment was one of the last to disband at the end of the war and was in fact tasked with rounding up deserters. Later, he served in a unit called the Special Force that was organized in 1874, a subunit of the reorganized Texas Rangers.

Captain McNelly died from tuberculosis at the age of thirty-three but still managed to accomplish enough in his short life to be inducted into the Texas Rangers Hall of Fame. Although this story fictionalizes his activities, we hope the way we have imagined him is in keeping with the man he really was.

Everyone has heard of the Texas Rangers, if only through its most famous, albeit fictional, member, the "Lone Ranger." The somewhat on-again, off-again organization was originally founded in 1823 when Stephen Austin employed ten men to protect several hundred families newly settled in the territory following the Mexican War for Independence. More formally organized in 1835, they grew to a force of more than 300. The Rangers were largely disbanded in 1848. Restarted in 1857, the organization fought Indians and protected settlers briefly and were yet again dissolved.

When Texas seceded in 1861, many former Rangers left to enlist in the Confederate Army, and after the war, they were for a time replaced by a Union-controlled organization called the Texas State Police. It was not until 1873 that they were again recommissioned and have remained organized since that time. Our story takes place during the years when the Texas Rangers were mostly disbanded. Thus, when Captain McNelly speaks of his desire to reorganize the Rangers, the words we have given him reflect the actual circumstances of the time.

Non-Hispanic whites who were not settlers of Spanish or Mexican heritage (known as Tejanos) but who settled in Texas when it was still part of Mexico came to be known as Texians (Chapter 9) or by several other variants, such as Texasians, Texilingans, Texicans, and Texonian. The term "Texian" was used briefly after annexation by the United States in 1845, but residents eventually came to be known as Texans, as they are called today. (*https://en.wikipedia.org/wiki/Texians*, citing Herbert Fletcher, *Texian*. *Handbook of Texas Online* [Texas State Historical Association] retrieved January 9, 2015.)

Many actual locales are mentioned in our story, especially in the chapters where John and Matthew take their adventurous odyssey.

The story is primarily set in the city of Crockett, location of the Caldwell farm and home to most of the other characters. Located in east-central Texas in a hilly area close to the center of Houston County (but far north of the city named Houston), it serves as county seat. One of the major industries in the mid-1800s was lumber, including pine and pecan trees. During the Civil War, Crockett served as a training center for Confederate soldiers.

In Chapter 28, Jonas sends to Nacagdoches for his pastor friend. Situated in East Texas just a bit more than fifty miles from the Louisiana border and about the same distance northeast of Crockett, Nacagdoches would have been a relatively easy ride by stage line, by which it was then linked to Crockett. The city's convention and visitors' bureau touts Nacagdoches as the oldest city in Texas, with evidence of settlement there dating back nearly 10,000 years. With a population around 32,000 today, the city has a varied history that includes the first oil well in Texas, being the site where debris from the Space Shuttle Columbia fell in 2003, and home to numerous celebrities. It is also the site of Stephen F. Austin State University.

In Chapter 35, Emma must follow her husband to Palestine (pronounced by locals as PAL-es-teen), then just a hamlet about thirty miles northwest of Crockett. Today it is more than twice the population of Crockett. Like Nacagdoches, it also received debris from the ill-fated Columbia.

Houston, Galveston, and San Antonio are still there, of course, having undergone enormous growth and modernization. So are Victoria and Del Rio. The battle at the Alamo is necessarily condensed to a few paragraphs, but the shrine still stands today in downtown San Antonio, dwarfed by that city's skyscrapers. The famous River Walk along the San Antonio River is a more recent development, but the river itself has been there from antiquity. Who is to say that early locals did not use its banks for picnics, walks, and even wedding festivities?

Although the far southwestern parts of the state are still sparsely settled, Fort Stockton exists, as does Menardville. Only today the latter's name is Menard, having been shortened to accommodate the request of sign painters when the railroad came through.

Brady Creek and Brady Lake exist, now expanded into a large reservoir and recreation area. Today they are enhanced by the city of Brady, which took its name from the creek and is the county seat of the same McCulloch County that appears on the "wanted" poster. Named after the creek, the city did not come into being until some years after our heroes turned in the three wanted deserters. Incidentally, today's city of Brady is just fifteen miles southwest of the geographic center of the state of Texas and is situated at the intersection of several major highways.

McCulloch County is named for Benjamin McCulloch, who had been a neighbor of David Crockett in Tennessee. When Crockett set out for Texas, McCulloch accompanied him but contracted measles shortly after arriving in Texas. Bedridden for weeks, he was prevented from traveling to the Alamo until after the decisive battle, thus saving his life. He would later serve as a Confederate general, in the Texas Rangers, and be elected to the Texas Legislature.

The area that today comprises Big Bend National Park surrounds the crater of an extinct volcano, which gives the region the dramatic character described in Chapter 11. The valley where our two adventurers spent nights in the open and practiced their martial arts today has motels, eateries, and other accouterments of a national park, including horses and guides to some more remote parts of the park.

Many battles were fought during the Civil War, though the largest number and fiercest were mostly in the eastern states. In particular, two battles were fought in the town of Manassas, Virginia, along the creek known as Bull Run, the first on July 21, 1861, and the second on August 28-30, 1862. The North referred to these as Bull Run while the South spoke of Manassas.

Of the other battles named in Chapters 13 and 14, perhaps the most historically well-known is Antietam, the bloodiest single-day battle in U.S. history, with a total of more than 22,000 casualties. The Battle of Chickamauga was named for the creek that runs through the northwest corner of Georgia into Tennessee.

Towns named Wilderness and Spotsylvania (originally spelled Spotssylvania), still exist in Virginia about forty miles south and slightly west of Manassas, not far from present-day Fredericksburg. Part of the battle that lasted for several days involved the Courthouse at Spotssylvania, so this long battle is variously referred to as the Wilderness Battle, the Battle of Spotssylvania, or of the Spotssylvania Courthouse.

Only in the last 150 years or so have weddings in the United States been performed in churches. Earlier, they were most likely performed in the family home, in a parlor or living room, especially in the wilder parts of the youthful nation. This story takes place when changing customs seemed to converge; hence, each wedding has been tailored to be most appropriate to the circumstances of the couple. For example, because Lucas has lived in the region for much of his life, he was widely known, so it was reasonable for his wedding to Catherine to take place in the church where a number of townspeople could attend. The other two weddings were quite properly performed at home.

Until the twentieth century, a woman generally wore her dressiest dress, irrespective of color, to be married (Chapter 26). The economics of the Wild West were such that having a dress for just one occasion to be packed away for a later generation was not practical for most families. The dress a woman wore for her nuptials was generally intended to be worn for many other occasions until it was shabby or threadbare.

The oft-given explanation that a white gown and veil are symbols of chastity and virginity is a tradition that seems to have sprung up after the fact. Today, when a woman marries for the second time, she often chooses a pastel color such as pink or pale blue in deference to the virginity tradition. In earlier times, wedding dresses were of dark colors such as deep green or brown, even black, because darker colors were considered more practical.

The white dress, though not original with the British Queen Victoria, was given major impetus by her wedding in 1840 in the same way that we see knock-offs of gowns worn by celebrities a few days after "red carpet" events. White was one of her favorite colors, and she chose it for her nuptial gown. Nor were such gowns pure white as usually seen today but more likely soft cream or ivory, which shades were considered more flattering to the complexion.

The floral headdress also follows Victoria's custom, using orange blossoms (a symbol of fertility) where available, fragrant myrtle or other flowers when orange blossoms were not available.

What? A wedding gown in muslin? Today's gowns are made from the richest of fabrics woven from the finest natural or synthetic fibers. For European royalty and the East Coast affluence of yesteryear, this meant lavish silks, satins and laces. To today's bride, the idea of being married in muslin (Chapters 10, 25) would seem absurd. In earlier centuries, however, muslin was a far finer fabric than the sturdy utilitarian cloth used today for sewing inexpensive fitting garments, straining jelly, or as painted theatrical backdrops.

Muslin originated in India as far back as Roman times, and some of the finest was woven in what is now Bangladesh. It is believed to have originated in the city of Maisolos, from which the name muslin is derived. Made of cotton fibers, muslin came in a much wider range of weights than we see now, from delicate sheers with a soft drape to coarse sheeting such as the utility fabric of today. There is even a famous 1783 portrait of Marie Antoinette in a softly draped sheer muslin gown known as the "muslin portrait." Thus, for our fictional western family, who probably had neither access nor funds to purchase lavish silks and satins, sheer muslin would be an entirely appropriate choice for a wedding gown.

In our story, the wedding of Jonas and Jennie is recorded in what will become their family Bible (Chapter 29). Most marriages in early U.S. history were recorded in the family Bible or the records of the local church.

Although a few eastern colonies issued licenses for marriage from an early time, it was not a widespread practice. Once the Emancipation Proclamation freed the dark-skinned slaves, however, there arose concern about intermarriage between the whites and other races. This gave rise to laws in many states prohibiting miscegenation (the mixing of races). Legally defined, a license is permission by some authority that makes legal what would be illegal without the license. But since when has marriage been illegal? Its origins are as old as recorded history. Thus it was not the act of marriage itself that prompted the license but the mixing of races.

Of course, getting any license entails a fee, and once bureaucrats saw a rich future in fees, the practice of insisting upon a license for an otherwise totally legal act grew by leaps and bounds. There are those today, however, who believe the State should not be a party to a contract between two people and their God.

In Chapter 28, the ladies have decided to use leftover fabric from Alice's grandmother's tattered ball gown to make "paraments" for Jonas' church. Later, in Chapter 32, Mason tells Luke that the ladies have decided the church needs some "altar linens and pretty pieces to hang." Readers who have not served on a church Altar Guild may be unfamiliar with the term "parament," from the Late Latin *parare* meaning to adorn. While the term once applied to decorations in a room of state, its meaning has more recently been narrowed to describe the liturgical hangings on and around an altar, including the cloths hanging from the pulpit or lectern. It may also be applied to ecclesiastical vestments.

There really is a plant called strawberry cactus (Chapter 11), whose botanical name is *Mammillaria dioica* and whose fruits reportedly taste like a mixture of strawberry and kiwi. Found in the southwestern desert and dry slopes from elevations of 100 to 4,000 feet, it is also referred to as fishhook cactus. The fruits are eaten raw. The item one might find today in a specialty or Hispanic grocery most likely to resemble the fruits of strawberry cactus would be the fruits of the prickly pear cactus known as tunas. Some tunas come with red skins and are quite tasty, as the author can attest. We look forward to tasting the real strawberry cactus for comparison at some time.

Catherine tells Lucas in Chapter 18 that her father worked for a publication called *The Prairie Farmer*. This paper, first published in 1841 in Chicago and weekly thereafter, is still in existence today. Likewise, when she describes her missionary work in Ningbo, China, the events cited are as historically accurate as possible. The treaties cited are real, as is the Church of England Missionary Society.

Oriental, and specifically Chinese, martial arts (Chapters 7, 11) have existed for centuries. Some forms can be traced back as far as 4,000 years and include many different styles and schools. Kung Fu, the term known in the western world today, is a loan word of fairly modern coinage. In the original Chinese, its meaning is not restricted to martial arts but translates more closely to "work" or "skill." Thus, it can also refer to areas as diverse as cooking or calligraphy. Furthermore, it has come into English largely in the twentieth century, which places it later than our story. Cai

Li Fo (as it is called in Mandarin, Chuy Li Fut in Cantonese) is a school of martial arts founded in 1836 by Chan Heung and, as described in our story, is particularly effective when the practitioner is faced with multiple attackers.

ABOUT THE AUTHOR

DENNIS L. RICOTTA is a native of Southern California where he had a varied occupational history before finding his calling as a music editor in the motion picture industry. As a private pilot, he promotes the Christian lifestyle as a member of Pilots for Christ. He also partakes in several Bible study groups, sometimes as student and sometimes as facilitator.

Dennis has two sons and three grandchildren. He lives with his wife, Janice, in La Quinta, California.

Made in the USA
San Bernardino, CA
16 May 2016